J

THE FALLEN

THE FALLEN
Glasgow Southside Crime Series
Book 4

MAUREEN MYANT

This edition produced in Great Britain in 2024

by Hobeck Books Limited, 24 Brookside Business Park, Stone, Staffordshire ST15 0RZ

www.hobeck.net

Copyright © Maureen Myant 2024

This book is entirely a work of fiction. The names, characters and incidents portrayed in this novel are the work of the author's imagination. Any resemblance to actual persons (living or dead), events or localities is entirely coincidental.

Maureen Myant has asserted her right under the Copyright, Design and Patents Act 1988 to be identified as the author of this work.

All rights reserved. No parts of this book may be used or reproduced by any means, graphic, electronic, or mechanical, including photocopying, recording, taping or by any information storage retrieval system without the written permission of the copyright holder.

A CIP catalogue for this book is available from the British Library.

ISBN 978-1-915-817-87-7 (pbk)

ISBN 978-1-915-817-8-0 (ebook)

Cover design by Jayne Mapp Design

Printed and bound in Great Britain

Are you a thriller seeker?

Hobeck Books is an independent publisher of crime, thrillers and suspense fiction and we have one aim – to bring you the books you want to read.

For more details about our books, our authors and our plans, plus the chance to download free novellas, sign up for our newsletter at **www.hobeck.net**.

You can also find us on Twitter **@hobeckbooks** or on Facebook **www.facebook.com/hobeckbooks10**.

Chapter One

SHIT! He'd forgotten to set his alarm. Quarter to eight and he was due in at work in fifteen minutes. Alex Scrimgeour stumbled out of bed and made his way to the bathroom, cursing as he stubbed his toe on one of the numerous boxes of tiles blocking his hallway. The builders were coming in a couple of weeks to remodel his bathroom, and all the materials were stored there. He half-hopped the rest of the way and tried to make up for lost time by rushing through his ablutions. What was it they said? More hurry, less speed. Too fucking true. A nasty cut on his chin meant he wasted several more minutes trying to get the damn thing to stop bleeding. By the time he left, it was well after eight. If he'd been less distracted when he came out of the tenement close, he might have taken more notice of the man lingering across the road not far away.

It was a beautiful morning. Perfect. Alex stopped at the bottom of the steps for a moment to take in his surroundings. April was his favourite month, well, maybe it was May. Spring, definitely. Sparrows chitchatted their business, both to those prepared to listen and to those who were oblivious.

A blackbird sang from a nearby branch and several goldfinches were lined up on the telephone line. Alex had the good fortune to live opposite a tiny patch of green filled with shrubs and trees. The rowans, birches and horse chestnut trees were all coming into leaf, and although the daffodils were all but finished, tulips poked their heads above ground. The leaves on the trees were a soft velvet green, as yet unmarred by pollution from the ubiquitous cars, and although he knew it was unlikely, the air tasted fresher and cleaner now than it had done last week. He took a deep breath and immediately went into a spasm of coughing. So much for the fresh air.

Out of the corner of his eye, he spotted an empty crisp packet on the pavement in front of him and bent down to pick it up before one of his neighbours saw it and bombarded the local Facebook forums with complaints. As he did so, there was a loud bang, and he jumped, startled. His first thought, which he dismissed immediately, was that it was a gunshot. A second later, he reconsidered as he saw a man running towards nearby Queen's Park. There was something in his right hand that looked like a... no, surely not? What the...? He turned, ran back up the stairs and fumbled to open the door to his close. Once inside, he slammed it shut and leaned against it, panting as though he'd been running up Ben Nevis instead of a few steps. Had someone just shot at him? Fuck. He was going to be sick. Deep breaths, that's what he needed to do. What was it again? Take two shallow breaths and exhale slowly. He tried, but it wasn't working. Oh God, he was going to have a panic attack. No, he had to stay calm. The sound of a door opening brought him to his senses. It was Alice, one of his neighbours. He could hear her talking on the phone as she came down the stairs.

The Fallen

'Yes, definitely a gunshot. No, no one is harmed. Please come quickly.' She put the phone away and ran over to him. 'Alex, are you alright?'

He'd only met her once before, on the day she moved in, a few weeks ago.

'Oh God, you're bleeding.'

She gawped at him, her mouth half open.

Alex's heart gave an uncomfortable thump. Had he been shot? He didn't feel any pain. Then he remembered his shaving cut. He touched his face and looked at his fingers. Blood. It must have been deeper than he realised.

'It's fine,' he said, hoping his voice didn't show his fear. 'I did it myself while shaving.'

'Christ, Alex. What were you using? A machete? Time to buy yourself one of those electric shavers. Can't have you going around looking like an escapee from a chainsaw massacre.' She placed a comforting hand on his arm and gave a shaky laugh. 'Let's go upstairs to my flat. What if he comes back?'

God, what was going on with his heart, why wasn't it settling down?

'You're right, yes, we should get inside. You've phoned the police?' Fuck, there was a tremor in his voice.

'Yes, I phoned them and they're on their way.' Alice's voice grew serious. 'It *was* a gunshot, wasn't it? I didn't think so at first but when I saw that man haring it down the street, I called the police. He'd been there for a while. I spotted him earlier.'

'Had he?' Alex felt a twinge of apprehension as he considered the possibilities. Had he or someone else been the target or had it been a random weirdo having a pot shot at squirrels? Alex didn't have to search long for the answer.

3

Glasgow had its share of nutters, but they generally didn't have guns and those who did, on the whole, kept them for their enemies. No point in wasting good ammunition on animals. He ushered her forward. 'Shall we go into your flat?'

'Of course.'

Before they could move, though, they heard a buzz of excited talk from outside. More people from neighbouring closes had appeared. He had to get out there and ensure they were safe. He ran downstairs to the entrance.

'All of you. Get inside now. Go back to your flats and lock your doors. That was a gunshot you heard, not a car backfiring. I repeat, get inside now.' He waited until they were all away before going back upstairs. Alice handed him a coffee. It was the last thing he needed, something else to make his heart beat faster. Nevertheless, he took a sip.

'He was there earlier. I saw him.'

'What time was that?'

'Seven-thirty. I looked at my watch.'

'Really?'

'Yes, really.' A wave of pink passed over her face, so faint he thought he might be imagining it. But she didn't meet his eye. Why was she blushing? Surely she hadn't been watching for him? He was usually very punctual in leaving the flat at that exact time. No, who was he kidding? It was chance, nothing more.

'Did you notice anything unusual about him?'

'I watched him for a couple of minutes. He was staring at the door of our close. I'd say he was jittery. He kept looking at his watch as if he was waiting for someone. Then I looked again later. That would have been a few minutes before I heard the gunshot. He was on the phone. It looked to me as though he was arguing with someone.'

'Anything else? Description?'

She shook her head. 'Hard to say from this distance, but I'd guess he was in his early twenties, perhaps on drugs. He had an underfed, skinny look. To be honest, I was worried about what he was doing here, and I thought about calling the police at that point. But what could I say? It isn't against the law to stand in the street.'

'No,' said Alex. 'It isn't.' He was disappointed. It sounded as though there wasn't much to go on. 'You didn't see the gun, then?'

'Sorry, no, not clearly. Enough to be sure it was a gun but that's all. Not my area of expertise, I'm afraid. What about you?'

'I didn't get a good view of it either,' said Alex.

'It looked to me as though he was trying to shoot at you. You're a police officer, aren't you? He was close to you. Don't you have to shoot handguns from up close?'

Alex ignored the first question. 'The majority of handguns have an effective range of forty-five metres. He was much nearer than that.' He didn't want to say more so he changed the subject. 'Right. I'd better call my work and tell them where I am and what's happened. You don't have to go anywhere, do you? They'll want to interview you as a witness.'

'I'm on a late shift today.'

'Well, I'd best get upstairs. I expect the police will be here soon. Thanks for the coffee.'

As he left the flat, more neighbours appeared, faces white with worry. They gathered round him, desperate for information. He reassured them as best he could, telling them to stay inside until the police advised otherwise and set off upstairs, waiting until he was inside his flat before phoning his office.

He kept an eye on the street outside in case the gunman reappeared.

Moments later, uniformed officers arrived to secure the scene followed by the rest of the team, SOCOS, forensics and a couple of detectives unknown to him. They told him there was an armed response team out looking for the gunman as well as a helicopter. He heard it whirring overhead. Not an unusual sound in the area as Alex lived a mile or so from the national football stadium at Hampden Park.

'This must be strange for you, to be on the other side of an interview,' said the DC, a young woman in her thirties called Deirdre.

'It is,' he admitted. 'I feel nervous.'

'Don't be,' she said. 'I'll be gentle.' She flashed him a disarming grin. Once she'd taken basic details from him like his name and age, she asked him to recall exactly what he'd seen.

'Nothing much,' he said. 'I was coming down the steps outside the close and I'd stopped to pick up an empty crisp packet. I hate litter. One of my neighbours said he'd been there for a while—'

'I'll stop you there. Please keep to what you actually saw or heard. We'll interview your neighbours separately.'

'Of course,' he said, inwardly cursing himself. Reported evidence isn't worth the paper it's written on, and he ought to have remembered that. He carried on. 'When I was picking up the litter, I heard a loud bang. My first thought was that it was a gunshot, but I dismissed that until I looked up and saw him.'

'What did you see? Take your time.'

'I'd already spotted him when I came out of the close. He was standing right over there against the railings, but I didn't think anything of it. The only thing I noticed was that he looked grubby. I was too busy enjoying the sunlight and the sounds of the birds to pay proper attention.' His laugh was embarrassed. 'A second after the bang, I caught sight of the same man running away and that made me suspicious. As I said, I was ready to dismiss the possibility of a gunshot, but he had something dark in his right hand and the shape of it and the way he was carrying it made me think it was a gun. He ran towards Queen's Park.'

'Did you see him enter the park?'

'No, you can't see the entrance from where I was standing, because of the curve of the street.'

'Right. Did you notice anything about him other than his grubbiness? Height, age? Anything you can think of.'

Alex closed his eyes and thought back. His legs were shaking. The shock was catching up with him.

'He was wearing dark clothing, a black or dark grey jacket, definitely, and blue denim jeans. He was wearing a baseball cap, so his hair wasn't visible.'

'Anything else? What age?'

'I'd say he was young, from the way he moved. And by that, I mean under thirty, possibly younger. I can't be more specific, I'm sorry. He was pretty fast.'

'Height? Build?'

'Wiry, definitely, but as to height... He looked small, under one hundred and seventy centimetres I'd say, but I was too far away to be more accurate than that.'

'Perhaps there was something in the street to compare him with?'

Of course, he should have thought of that earlier.

'Yes, he was standing near that blue car over there. The Skoda Kodiak. I'd say he was a couple of centimetres smaller.'

She made a note and asked one of the uniforms to go and check.

'How close did he get to you?'

'I'm not sure. No more than fifteen metres I'd say.'

'Was there anyone else in the street?'

Alex closed his eyes and thought for a second before replying. 'There was a man in the distance, nearer the end of the street. He was getting into his car.'

'Do you know him?'

'I didn't recognise him or the car, no. It was a Range Rover, I think. Dark grey. Parking is so bad round here he might not live in the street.'

'Nonetheless, that's very helpful. Where was he when the gun was fired?'

'He'd gone by then.'

'Is there anything else you can think of?'

'No. My neighbour downstairs was looking out of her window and spotted him earlier. I'm sure she'll be able to give a better description.'

The DC made a note.

'We'll interview all your neighbours of course.' She looked at him, her bright blue eyes piercing. 'I want you to think carefully. Is there anyone who might bear you a grudge?'

'Not one that merits me being shot. I daresay, one or two of my colleagues find me difficult at times but not enough to kill me.' Alex grimaced. 'I doubt that I was the target. More likely it was someone taking a potshot at a squirrel. We're plagued by them round here.'

She saw through his false bravado. 'Mm. I doubt it. I'm afraid we can't rule out you being the target. What cases have you been working on lately? Anyone you might have upset?'

'Look, I'm a detective. I've upset people, of course I have. You know the score. But trying to kill me? That's a whole different ball game.'

'What about the bloke who tried to murder your mother a couple of years back? Don't you have history with him?'

'Jamie Taylor?' His voice rose. 'You know about him?'

Her cheeks turned pink. 'It was all over Police Scotland, well, Glasgow police, anyway. You know what gossips we are. And, you have to admit, it was a pretty amazing story. Your long-lost daughter coming home, Taylor thinking she was his sister. You should write a book!'

Shit. Was this what his life had become? A 'pretty amazing story' for people to gossip about. He'd had no idea the police service had been talking about him, but when he thought about it, of course they would. He kept his face neutral. 'Aye, but Taylor's safely inside now.'

'He'll have pals though. Could he have paid one of them to get you?'

'No, I mean, aye, he'll have pals, but his beef with me is personal. It's not as if I broke up a drugs gang or anything.' A thought struck him, and he tailed off. 'There is one thing. That recent case, the drugs gang that got busted. Know the one I mean? It was all over the news.'

'Was that you?'

'I was involved but only in a supervisory role and only at the beginning of the case. No, I don't think they'd be after me. Not sure they even knew my name. I was very much behind the scenes, and then of course, Organised Crime took over the case.'

'It's worth thinking about, though. Is there any way they could have mistaken you for someone else?'

'In Organised Crime? No.'

'What about in your team?'

Alex thought for a few seconds before answering. 'DS Nicholson started the ball rolling. He was the initial lead in the investigation into what looked like manslaughter but turned out to be so much more. The suspect appeared to be innocent of anything other than being in the wrong place at the wrong time. He'd been in a fight outside a pub and a punch had killed his opponent. When Mark looked into it, though, he found a connection between the suspect and the victim's girlfriend. They'd worked together to get rid of the victim and take over his drug dealing business. In the end, the case was transferred to the Serious Organised Crime Division, but Mark had to give evidence in the trial three weeks ago. He was staying with me at the time, had been for a while since his relationship broke up. But he got his own place last month and moved in two weeks ago.'

The DC pursed her lips. 'Mm, I'm not convinced you aren't the target, but this is worth thinking about, too. Give me his name again, and we'll look into it. Although, surely they'd have gone after him before the trial?'

'You're right. That's more likely. Anyway, his name is Mark Nicholson and he's based in my team.

Mark's name was duly noted.

'Thanks, we'll be sure to interview him, too. What about your neighbours? No drug dealers or criminals living up your close?' She raised her eyebrows.

Alex shook his head. 'Well, you never know, but I'd be surprised. As far as I know, they're all professionals. Couple of teachers, a civil servant, that sort of thing. I don't know them well. My downstairs neighbour, Alice...' he stopped unable to remember her second name. But the officer already knew. 'Alice Tremaine, yes. She's being interviewed at the moment. She dialled 999 when she heard the shot. What about her?'

'Nothing important. I don't know what she does, that's all.'

The DC looked at her notes. 'Psychiatrist, works for CAMHS.' She looked at Alex seriously. 'It might be best if you left the flat for the time being. For your safety. Do you have relatives or friends you can stay with?'

Three years earlier, Alex would have struggled with this question. He'd have put a brave face on it and muttered that he'd stay where he was, thanks very much. But not now. He had been reunited with his daughter, whom he'd believed to be dead, two years ago. Even better, she now lived in Glasgow with her partner, Conor.

'Yes, I'll go to my daughter's for a few days.' He gave the woman Kate's address.

'Good. Well, no doubt you'll hear how the investigation's going, but we'll keep you informed anyway. At the moment, we have a team from the Armed Response Unit out in Queen's Park, though if that's where he went, he'll be gone by now. It doesn't take long to walk through it, but we're hopeful we'll at least get a decent description, and who knows, he might have decided to try to hide in the bushes. We'll also interview your colleague, Mark Nicholson. Perhaps he's had direct threats that he didn't mention to you.'

Mark would have told him, but Alex didn't say anything. He was glad she was taking the possibility that Mark was the target seriously. Too often, police officers stuck with the obvious hypothesis.

He watched from the window for some minutes after the officers had left his flat. Two cordons had been set up. The first was around the entrance to the flat. Forensics were searching there for the bullet or any other evidence. It would be great if they found it because they weren't going to catch the bloke now. Although the police had arrived quickly, it wasn't soon enough to guarantee he'd still be hanging around. There were several exits to the park, mainly to busy main roads. Victoria Road to the north and Pollokshaws Road to the west were generally mobbed at this time of day, so he'd soon be lost in the crowds of people heading into work. The entrances to the east and to the south were quieter, but the nearest entrance to here was in Langside Avenue, and Alex thought it was more likely that the gunman would go west towards the bustle of Pollokshaws Road. There would surely be an appeal for witnesses, and as there were plenty of buses in the area, someone might have seen something from the top of one of them.

The other cordon was around the garden area where the man had been standing. Alice was there pointing out the exact spot, and it looked as though they'd got a footprint and were making a cast of it. There might be other clues there, too. A cigarette butt would be a good find.

One of the forensic team at the tenement entrance had found something. He spotted Alex watching and gave him a thumbs up. Alex decided to go down and have a word with them.

It was the bullet.

'Confirms what your neighbour said,' said the forensic scientist. 'This might give us good evidence if it turns out the gun is linked to any other crime.'

Alex nodded. Handguns weren't smooth inside the barrel like shotguns but had what was called rifling. This left unique patterns on any bullet that passed through it. 'Have you found anything else useful?'

'We've worked out where he was waiting, thanks to your neighbour,' he gestured towards where Alice was standing. 'And there's a few promising footprints in the earth in that wee garden place across the road, as well as a few fag ends. If we're lucky we'll get DNA from them.'

'Sounds good,' said Alex and walked over to where Alice was standing chatting to one of the team. She spotted him and came over.

'What are you going to do now? Do you want another coffee? You didn't finish your last one.'

'Thanks, but I'd best get on. I'm going into work now after I've dropped my stuff at my daughter's place. I'll be staying with her for a few days.'

'Well, take care and stay safe. Once you get back you should come down for a drink. It'll do us both good.' She winked at him.

Was she flirting with him? He couldn't tell, he was so out of practice with women. It was years since he'd had any sort of relationship. The last woman he'd seen for any length of time had given up on him. He was 'commitment phobic' according to her. Alex swallowed and gave Alice an awkward smile. 'Yes, that would be good.' Time to make an exit.

Alex went back upstairs to pack the essentials and to get in touch with Kate. He FaceTimed her on his phone, and she answered immediately.

'This is an early call for you, Dad. Is everything all right?'

The thrill of being called dad hadn't worn off. He'd thought he was doomed to be Alex to her forever, but that changed after a silly row they'd had.

'Yes and no,' he answered. 'I'm fine, unhurt, but someone took a potshot at me on my way to work this morning.'

'What! With a gun? Have they caught him? Are you sure

you're not hurt? Who's behind it?' The avalanche of questions spilled down the phone.

'Yes, with a gun, but I'm not hurt, no.' For a moment he thought of telling her how different it might have been if he hadn't spotted that piece of litter and bent down to pick it up. No, best leave her in ignorance. He carried on. 'They've not caught him, or at least they hadn't five minutes ago, but there's a manhunt going on as we speak, and no, we haven't a clue who it is. They've got some forensics to work on, so with any luck they'll get info from that. I'm not convinced it was me that they were after though. Who'd want to kill me?'

'Well, Jamie Taylor for one?'

'He's in prison, Kate, and he's small beer. There's no way for him to get at me.'

'You don't know that for sure. Doesn't he have contacts?'

'He's inside, his assets have been seized. There's no way it was him, I'm sure.' He paused when he saw the scepticism on Kate's face. 'Ok. I suppose there's always a slight possibility, but believe me, although he likes to play the big man, he's small beer in the criminal world, and he definitely wouldn't have the money to pay for a hitman. Anyway, I have a theory it's Mark they're after. If it wasn't a random nutter, that is.'

'Mark? You're not serious?'

Alex repeated what he'd told the detective. He finished by saying, 'The thing is, because they're not sure exactly what's going on, it's been suggested I should move out in case I'm in danger.'

Kate didn't hesitate. 'You must come to us. I'm not going to accept no for an answer, so get your bag packed and get on over here. I'm working from home today, so no excuses.'

'I'm already packed,' he said. 'Fifteen minutes and I should be there.'

Chapter Two

ALEX WASN'T GOING to be caught out a second time. He scanned the street as he left the building. It was unlikely anyone would be back so soon, but you never knew. Forensics were still busy looking for evidence, and there were also the uniformed cops who had the thankless task of informing the residents what had happened. Alex's neighbours wouldn't be happy. Theirs was a quiet neighbourhood where a piece of litter, a bin left out or an uncut hedge raised eyebrows. Alex would never look at litter in the same way again. After all, it had saved his life. He chatted to the uniforms outside his close for a few seconds and then left them to it before getting into his car for the short drive to Mount Florida. This was where Kate and Conor had bought a flat in a tenement situated above Prospecthill Road. With any luck, he'd find a parking place not too far away. He loved their flat – the views over the city to the Campsie Hills and beyond were amazing – but the parking was terrible, worse than where he lived, and that was saying something.

Kate buzzed him in and was waiting for him at her door.

'Quick, get inside before they have another go.' She was laughing but her eyes showed concern. He didn't want her to be worried, but fuck, it was good to have someone who cared.

Although there were only two bedrooms, the flat was large and spacious with the high ceilings so typical of tenements. Kate showed him through to the spare bedroom which was not unlike his own spare room in size. The similarity ended there, however. Where his guest room was somewhat stark, Kate's was welcoming and homely. He unpacked, putting his things away in the upcycled chest of drawers that had been painted sage green and looked fresh against the white walls. Once he was settled, he went through to the kitchen where Kate was working, and apologised.

'I'm sorry, Kate, but I'll have to get into work now. I'm the latest I've ever been, and I have a report due today.'

'No time for coffee?'

'Is it instant? I can't stand that ground stuff. Way too strong for me.'

'I bought it especially for you, you peasant. Fancy not liking real coffee.'

Alex laughed. 'It was Mark who put me off it. He drank it by the gallon. I swear it was so thick you could stand up in it. Terrible stuff. OK, if it's instant, I'll take one, but I'll need to be gone in ten minutes.'

They chatted while Kate made the coffee.

'How's work?' asked Alex.

'I was about to ask you the same thing. You go first. Are you sure there's nothing behind this attempted shooting? It's really worrying.'

'Can't think of anything. Things were quieter for a bit during the pandemic, though it's got worse again recently. To be honest, the only explanation I can think of, other than a random attack, was that it was someone going after Mark. I'm not in the front line any more so...'

'My money's on his ex, or that other woman, Susan, is it?'

'Her name is Suzanne as you're well aware. No, I can't see her being behind it. She's unstable but that would be taking it too far.'

Kate grinned in reply. She couldn't help herself when it came to Suzanne. She was always having little digs at her. It was clear how much she despised her. 'Unstable is too kind a way to describe her. How dare she leave that gorgeous wee boy?'

'She might be dying,' said Alex. 'And Mark's a great dad. What would any of us do in that scenario? She wasn't acting rationally.'

Kate twisted her mouth. 'Has she been in touch at all?'

'Well, she's alive for sure, because every so often, an envelope containing wads of cash comes through my letterbox addressed to him. There's always a note with it, but she's never let on where she is, or how she is. Once she asked Mark to leave some photos of Angus in the flat for her. He's tried to find her, but she's elusive. Mind you, I think she'd have a custody battle on her hands if she did turn up out of the blue. He's crazy about the boy.'

Kate smiled. 'Aren't we all? Gus is a born charmer.' She sounded bright, but her eyes were sad, and Alex knew she was thinking about the miscarriage she'd had the year before. It had been early on in the pregnancy, but she'd been inconsolable. He changed the subject. Best stay away from the topic of children. 'What about your work? Anything interesting?'

Kate had worked as a lecturer in journalism before moving up to Glasgow, and unable to get a similar job here, decided to go freelance. It was hard for her, and she bemoaned the fact that she didn't have a regular income. Fortunately, Conor had a good job, and she had her adoptive mother's inheritance.

Kate brightened at the chance to talk about her work. 'I'm thinking about doing a story about this spate of teenage suicides,' she said. 'I'm sure you've heard about them.'

Alex had. More than he wanted to. Over the past five weeks, four teenagers in Glasgow had killed themselves. They were similar in that they'd all been from falls. Two had been killed on the subway, one had fallen in front of a bus, and the other from a bridge. One set of parents had been a constant thorn in the side of the Procurator Fiscal, adamant their son would never commit suicide.

'Yes, I have. But why write about them?'

'One of the parents contacted me. She'd read the article I wrote for *The Herald*, the one about the increase in mental health problems in young people. I made a passing reference to the recent suicides, and she wants to "set the record straight about her son". She's a psychiatrist herself, and while she agreed that there's a terrible increase in mental health problems, she's adamant her son was not one of them.'

'Be careful, Kate. I know of at least one set of parents who have been plaguing the PF about their son.'

'Yes, my first instinct was to say no, but I've been researching this and something's not right here. That number of suicides involving teenagers over such a short period of time is unlikely to be a coincidence.'

'Is it?'

'I've researched it. A recent report looked into teenage suicides across the whole of Scotland over a period of approximately ten years. There were eight hundred and twenty deaths in the five to twenty-four age group attributed to suicide. It averaged out at seven a month.'

'There you are, then. Doesn't sound unusual to me. It's been what? Four suicides in five weeks? Where's the problem?'

'That's across the whole of Scotland. Glasgow has around eleven percent of Scotland's population, so that would mean fewer than one death a month would be due to suicide in that age group.'

Alex drained his coffee. His head was buzzing with a surfeit of figures. 'I'm not convinced. Coincidences do happen. It could be a run of bad luck, copycat suicides, or a statistical anomaly.'

Kate sighed. 'Two things strike me. The age range of these four deaths is between fifteen and eighteen, not five to twenty-four like in the report. But also, what are the chances that they would all choose jumping as a suicide method as opposed to what is the most common method, strangulation or hanging? It doesn't add up, Dad.'

Alex frowned. Perhaps Kate was right to think there was a story in this. 'So, what's your angle going to be?'

'I'll see once I've spoken to the parents, but there's a lot of speculation on social media that might be worth following up.'

'Really? Isn't it a lot of crap posted on there? I thought you despised social media, said it was mostly rubbish.'

'Well, yes. But sometimes it's worth tackling the wilder issues head-on. A couple of theories are reasonable. One theory is that they are accidents and not suicides at all. Another is that they're murders dressed up to look like suicide, but that's very rare. There are others, but they're crazy.'

Alex intervened before she spouted more figures to confuse him. 'Tell me about these.'

'Oh, they're ridiculous. One theory is that there's a coven of female witches in Glasgow secondary schools who've put a spell on teenage boys to make them want to kill themselves.' She stopped when she saw Alex's face. 'I know, right! Bonkers. The fact that one of the teenagers was a girl hasn't stopped the conspiracy theorists who see this as proof that the witches are cunning as well as evil. There was also one particularly nasty one suggesting Muslim gangs are behind it. Again, the facts don't seem to bother these people. One of the boys was a Muslim. It's abhorrent that people post this sort of thing when family and friends are grieving.'

'Yes, it's horrible. So, what are you going to do?'

'See what this woman and her husband say and take it from there.'

'And they're happy to speak to you?' Alex remembered how he was hounded by the press when his wife had taken her own life after Kate had been stolen from her pram when she was little over a year old. He hoped Kate wasn't intruding on their grief.

'I know the woman is because she contacted me. I assume her husband is, too. I'm meeting them later this week.'

Alex didn't have the time to discuss it now. He hoped Kate was fully aware of what she was getting into.

'Hmm. Well, be careful.' He glanced at his watch. 'Shit, is that the time? I'd better go. I'll see you later, OK? I'll be back about seven, with any luck.' Alex finished his coffee, rinsed his cup out, and left it on the draining board. He'd better get in to work.

The Fallen

By the time Alex got there, Mark was out on a case. Damn. He'd wanted to discuss the attempted shooting with him, to see what he thought about it possibly being aimed at him. Alex had a number of questions for him. Had anything stood out when he was giving evidence? Had there been any indication that the accused were more pissed off with the police than normal? The case had been a big one, and Mark had been one of the main players, at least to begin with. Was that enough to make him a target? The more Alex thought about it, he was certain he wasn't the target here. There was nothing to suggest he'd pissed off any criminals. His was a hands-off role. No, it had to be Mark. The drugs gang had been discovered last year when one of the gang members had been killed in what appeared to be a drunken altercation outside a pub. At first, Mark had been taken in by the apparent remorse of the perpetrator. However, he soon discovered that it hadn't been an accident but a deliberate targeting in order to get inroads into the gang. There had been an outbreak of murders after that, and one of the biggest drugs gangs had been ripped apart. Not that it meant much. There was always another scrote in the wings waiting to step into the role of 'big man'. The case had finally come to court and several gang members, both men and women, had been put away. Surely it wasn't a coincidence that the attack happened a short time later?

Within minutes, he was surrounded by well-wishers asking how he was. A couple of officers stayed clear. Alex knew he wasn't liked by everyone – who was, after all – but, honestly? Not to say anything? He watched as Chloe Gray studiously avoided looking at him, head down, seemingly engaged in her work. Well, that made a change. She was known for opting out as much as possible, her attendance record wasn't great. As for Shane McGowan? The man set his teeth on edge. What was it he'd said? 'Probably one of your neighbours took a shot at you because of that old jalopy you drive. That affects house prices, you know.' What sort of a comment was that? Wanker drove a Range Rover. Alex hadn't been quick enough to think of a smart reply and had come out with, 'Better that than the gas guzzler you use.' McGowan had sniggered and responded with, 'If you know, you know,' and tapped the side of his nose. Tosser.

It was hard to settle to work with this on his mind, but he did his best, and by four o'clock, he'd finished the report his DCI had requested. It was a few hours late, but given what he'd been through, he didn't anticipate any problems.

As he stood in front of DCI Pamela Ferguson, he reflected that he had got it wrong again. She was as sour-faced as he'd ever seen her.

'Ah, DI Scrimgeour, thank you for this. Better late than never, I suppose.'

Alex stared at her. Had she not heard about his ordeal this morning? He decided to chance it.

'Are you aware a gunman took a potshot at me this morning?'

Her lips moved into what you might call a smile. 'Yes, I'd heard.' Was there a hint of irritation in her voice? Alex was never sure why he annoyed her so much, but she did little to hide her dislike.

He waited for her to sympathise with him, but she didn't.

'Will that be all?' he asked.

She dismissed him with a wave of her hand. Jeez, she was a piece of work. He didn't close the door behind him. Petty, but there it was.

When Mark came back into the office, Alex grabbed him. 'Did you hear what happened to me this morning?'

'No, I've been out all day. Haven't heard anything.'

'Right. Come through to my office.'

When they were seated, Alex told him what had happened.

'Fuck,' said Mark when he'd finished. 'I heard on the radio that there'd been an incident near Queen's Park, but I didn't think for a minute it was you. Are you OK? You're not going to stay there, are you? Why don't you come and stay with me and Gus. We owe you.'

Alex ignored the offer. He had more pressing things to discuss. 'Listen, Mark, I'm not at all sure it's me they're after. Why would I be a target? I'm not in the front line.'

Mark grimaced. 'So, what was it then? A random attack? A man out with a gun who happens to hit on you?'

'It could be.' Alex paused to think how to put this. Best spit it out. 'Or maybe it's you they were after.'

'Haha, very funny.'

Alex said nothing.

Mark paled. 'You're fucking kidding me.'

'No. Think about it for a second before you dismiss it. That drugs case you were on that got a big result last week? You helped take down that gang. And they lost, what? Over two million pounds worth of cocaine and heroin.'

'But why would they pick on me? I was only part of it. No, it doesn't make sense. Apart from anything, why wait until now?'

'I don't know. But can you think of any other reason? Other than a random attack? I mean, I realise I get on people's tits, but enough for them to take a pot shot at me? My gut's saying it's gang related.'

Mark was silent, his handsome face brooding.

'No way would they have mistaken you for me, though. I mean, there's twenty years at least between us.'

Alex tried his best not to be insulted. He'd got close to Mark when they'd shared a flat and often forgot the age difference between them. In any case, it was only seventeen years.

'Yes, I know, but we're the same height, and now I've lost weight, it's possible someone who'd only been given a description might make a mistake.'

Mark raised an eyebrow. 'You think?'

It was obvious he didn't.

'Maybe. He was standing several metres away.'

'Hmm. Anyway, where are you going to stay? With Kate? It would be daft to come to mine. What should I do, do you think? I won't risk anything happening to Gus.'

'Yes, I'm staying with Kate for a few days until this has blown over. And you, too, you should get away from your flat. Is there anywhere you could go?'

'First person I'd turn to would be you. But that's not possible. No, there's nowhere.'

'Book into a hotel, then. Police Scotland will cover the cost.'

'Do you really think it's necessary?'

'Yes, at least until we've got a better idea of what's going on.'

Mark started to pace the floor. 'But hardly anyone knows where I live.'

'Who does know?'

'You, Karen of course, oh, and the nursery. I had to tell

them.' He stopped pacing. 'Moving out would be an overreaction. I'll be OK to stay at home.'

'I don't know, Mark. People talk in nurseries. It doesn't take much. Another parent spots you on Paisley Road West and mentions it to their pal, and two minutes later, the whole nursery knows where you live. It's too risky.'

Mark sat down again.

'You're right. I'll get us booked in now.' He paused. 'You don't think they'll go after Karen and the children, do you?'

'You've been separated for well over a year now. I doubt they know of their existence.'

'Right, well, if you're sure? Looks as though we're going to have to be on the ball for the next little while.' Mark sounded much more cheerful than he looked. He left Alex behind, pondering what to do next.

It wasn't long before news came in of a development in the case. A woman out jogging later that morning had been caught short and had gone into bushes near the rose garden in the park for a pee. There, she had spotted a gun and immediately called the police who came to pick it up. Alex shuddered to think what might have happened if it had fallen into the wrong hands. It went straight to Forensics to see if they could find anything on it. Alex prayed they would. He was desperate for the case to be solved so he and Mark could stop worrying, but he had to accept they wouldn't get anything that would allow him to go home tonight. With a sigh, Alex packed up and set off to dinner at his daughter's flat.

Chapter Three

KATE HUMMED to herself as she got the ingredients together to make the sauce for the pasta dish they were having for dinner: Pasta Puttanesca with extra anchovies, her father's favourite. Well, for a few days, anyway. He changed his mind every week. It had been paella the week before last, and he hadn't been able to get enough of risotto at the beginning of the year. One of their favourite pastimes these days was for her to teach him to cook easy dishes. For too long he'd existed on junk food or high-calorie ready meals. Before Mark had moved in, Alex had lived alone and had got into bad habits. Now at least, he had a staple of dishes from which to choose. She smiled to herself as she chopped a small onion. It would be good to have him stay for a few nights, though she wished the circumstances were better. She prayed Alex was right and he wasn't the target, though the alternative of Mark being at risk was abhorrent, too. It would be awful if he were harmed.

Over the past year and a half, she'd been living in Glasgow, she'd grown close to Alex, or 'Dad', as she now called

The Fallen

him. When her adoptive mother had died, she'd thought she'd never be truly happy again, that she wouldn't have anyone who unconditionally loved her. Yet, here he was. The father she thought didn't exist. And she had Conor, too. It was perfect, save for the miscarriages. She'd had three. The first time she'd fallen pregnant, her joy had been immeasurable. She'd taken the pregnancy test on a Tuesday morning and told Conor in the evening. Together in bed that night, they'd planned out their child's life.

'I hope he has eyes like yours,' said Kate.

'No, no. *She* has to have blue eyes like yours.'

'Do you mind what sex it is? I don't, all I want is for him or her to be healthy,' said Kate.

'...and able to look after all the brothers and sisters they'll have,' said Conor. 'Only kidding, two will be enough,' he added when he saw the look on Kate's face.

'Let's compromise with three? I always wanted brothers and sisters.'

They'd talked for hours, forgetting the old saying that 'man plans and God laughs'. The next morning, Kate had woken to blood-soaked sheets. She'd been pregnant for such a short time that she made Conor promise not to tell anyone. 'After all, we'll get pregnant again soon enough.'

That had been last summer. The baby would have been born by now. Kate hated going out and seeing mothers and fathers with tiny babies strapped to their chests. In her irrational state, she imagined them to be pleased with themselves, smugly looking down on those who are without children. Deep down, she knew the expression on their faces was down to exhaustion, but it didn't help. It was worse when she had the second miscarriage. She'd been right; it didn't take them long to get pregnant again. That pregnancy lasted longer. Thirteen weeks; they'd thought they were safely past the dangerous first trimester. They'd told both families. Kate's grandmother, in a nursing home and with Alzheimer's, didn't take it in. At times she thought Kate was Alex's dead wife and didn't understand why they were having another baby 'at their age', but Alex was thrilled, and Conor's large family were already making plans for the inevitable celebrations. Telling them it was over had been the worst thing ever. Nobody knew about the third miscarriage. She'd kept it to herself.

She was sure she was pregnant again. Her breasts were tender, and she was starving all the time. She felt nauseous, too, though, so far, she'd managed not to be sick. No, best keep it to herself. She'd only tell Conor when she had to. It would be unbearable to live through everyone's disappointment again. So far, she hadn't taken a test, but it was probably time to.

It was good her father was coming to stay for a while. Having him here would stop her being morose about her losses, and with any luck, It would take her mind off her worries about this possible pregnancy.

The key turned in the door and Conor came in. Kate went to greet hm.

'We have a guest,' she said. 'Dad's come to stay for a few days. Someone tried to kill him this morning.'

One of the qualities she loved in Conor was his sangfroid. There was no fussing, just a quiet nod. Others would flap about asking questions. These would come later no doubt, but it was in his nature to think about what he was going to say first. For the moment, all he did was to ask if her dad was OK and whether everything was made up in the spare room. Kate thought of her former lover, Jack, and how he never once offered to help, never put so much as a cup in the dishwater. Lazy sod. He turned out to be married as well. The contrast was stark.

Not long after, Alex arrived. He rang the doorbell, although he had a key. He looked tired. Older. A shock did that to you, she reckoned.

'I'm ravenous,' he said as he came in. 'What are we having for dinner? It smells delicious.'

'Pasta Puttanesca. It'll be ready in ten minutes. Time enough for you to unpack. By the way, use your key. I know you want to give us privacy, but as long as you're actually staying here, you should use it.' She didn't miss the smile of delight that passed over his face.

At the dinner table, they steered clear from talking about the attack. By the end, though, Kate had had enough. She was desperate to find out if there were any developments. Alex told her about the discovery in the park that afternoon.

'We should find out tomorrow if there's anything on it. Forensics are hoping to get some evidence, maybe fingerprints. If there are fingerprints, let's hope they're in the system. There's also the possibility it's been used in another crime. They found the bullet yesterday, and the rifling marks on it will be compared with others we have in the system. But that's it, so far. Oh, apart from cigarette butts, but we don't know yet if they're from the gunman.'

The rest of the evening passed pleasantly. Alex was good company when he was in the mood, and Kate smiled as she remembered how much she'd disliked him when they'd first met, and her dismay when he had revealed he was her father. Now she was happy they'd found each other before it was too late. At half past ten, she stood up.

'I need to get to bed, now. Heavy day in front of me tomorrow.'

The truth was, she was utterly exhausted. Another sign of pregnancy. How long would she be able to keep it hidden?

The next morning came all too soon. When she awoke, Kate felt as though she'd had no sleep. She was nauseous, too, but managed to keep her breakfast down. A quick shower and she felt much better.

Today she was meeting the parents she had mentioned to her father, Mr Peterson and Ms Carr. Ms Carr was a consultant psychiatrist but hadn't mentioned what her husband did. She suggested Kate come to their flat in the west end. A quick google suggested taking a bus into town, and then the subway from Buchanan Street, but she chose instead to go to Bridge Street subway. Two of the suicides, including Ms Carr's son, Callum Peterson, had taken place at the station, and she wanted to get a feel for the layout there and what might have happened. On the bus to Bridge Street, she read through her notes about what she'd discovered so far concerning Callum. It wasn't much.

Callum had been seventeen and in his sixth year at Westfield Academy. He'd been an only child. His mother had told Kate that he'd been a gifted young man with everything to live for and this was reiterated in every piece written about him. He'd had a place at Edinburgh University to study medicine, due to start later this year. Most of his friends supported his parents' claim that he had not been suicidal, however, one newspaper article quoted two of his friends as saying he *had* been suicidal.

The Fallen

Kate underlined this last sentence. She had to bring it up with his parents, though it was bound to be painful. To tell the truth, she was dreading the meeting. The phone call she'd taken from Callum's mother showed she was a formidable force, and utterly convinced her son had not killed himself. Kate looked again at her notes. Callum had got off at Bridge Street with another young man who wasn't named. According to witnesses, they both appeared distressed, and Callum looked drunk. The other boy had been trying to calm him down and was heard shouting, 'Please, don't Callum,' before Callum jumped or fell from the platform. She sighed, wishing she hadn't agreed to this interview. It was getting near her stop, so she put her notes away so she could get off the bus. She crossed the road to the subway station, one of only fifteen in the city. When she'd arrived in Glasgow, she was thrilled to find out the locals called it the Clockwork Orange. There were two reasons for this. The carriages of the trains were currently painted a bright orange, although they were going to be replaced soon with white carriages. But the other reason remained and always would. The Glasgow subway didn't have a network of lines like those in other cities. It was a roughly oval route covering part of the west end and the city centre. It had two lines, the inner circle, which ran counter clockwise, and the outer circle, which ran clockwise. Of the fifteen stations, eight were north of the river and seven to the south. To someone like Kate, used to the extensive underground networks in London, it was like a toy train set. The locals would no doubt come up with a new nickname – the ghost train, maybe – once the new rolling stock was introduced, but it would always be the Clockwork Orange to her.

Outside the station there was a pop-up coffee stall doing

good business. Kate checked the time on her phone. Plenty of time to get herself a coffee. She hadn't wanted one this morning and was missing the caffeine hit. A flat white would liven her up. She joined the queue and bought one when she reached the front of the queue, but as she raised it to her lips to take the first sip, the aroma of coffee hit her, and a wave of nausea swept over her. No doubt about it, she *was* pregnant. Her previous pregnancies, short-lived as they were, saw her forswear coffee.

She ought to be happy, but instead she was apprehensive and dreaded going through another loss. She recalled a friend telling her about a cousin who'd had seven miscarriages, one of them at twenty-two weeks. How had she been able to bear it? Kate thought it might destroy her if she lost another baby, and yet it happened all the time. And the women survived. She drew her shoulders back. *She* would survive. Later on today, she'd buy a test.

As she looked around for a bin to dump the coffee, she spotted a homeless man near the entrance to the station, and offered it to him, instead, assuring him she hadn't touched it. He accepted with a grin and a cheeky, 'Got a bacon roll to go with it?' Kate smiled an apology and went into the station and ran down the stairs. A train was drawing out as she got there, but it didn't matter as she wanted time to get a feeling for the place.

She'd only used the subway a handful of times, and it never failed to amaze her how small it was. There was only one platform to serve the two lines, and it was approximately forty-metres long, she guessed. Her research hadn't told her where Callum had jumped, but she thought it had to be at the entrance to one of the tunnels, with the train coming into the station. The report on Callum's death said he was thought to be already dead when the train arrived as he received an electric shock from the conductor rail. Once again, Kate asked herself if it was right to intrude on the grief of his parents, even if they had approached her? She didn't have an answer.

A bunch of students got on the train at the same time. They served to remind her how much she missed her previous job as a lecturer in journalism. So far, her tentative approaches to local institutions had met with apologetic refusals or offers of tutorials at a paltry hourly rate that she would have been foolish to take. It would effectively mean working for the minimum wage or less when you accounted for the time needed to prepare properly. The lack of decent offers didn't bother her, though she was sorry for those who had to take on such work in the hope of a permanent contract in academia. Her first love was writing, but she missed the to-and-fro banter with the students. Three young men opposite were talking about shows they liked. *Married at First Sight* was their favourite. She noted it down in her notebook. Perhaps she'd do a feature, interview a few students about their favourite TV programmes. They always had bizarre tastes. *Bargain Hunt* came to mind. Shit! She'd gone into a dream and hadn't noticed she was at her stop. She hadn't imagined it would be so quick. She squeezed past the people swarming onto the train and managed to get through the doors before they shut. She made her way up the escalator to Byres Road, opened Google Maps and typed in the address she'd been given. It was a ten-minute walk. When she reached the tenement where Callum's parents lived, she pressed the buzzer at the close door. It was answered immediately.

'Second floor, we'll be at the door,' said a disembodied voice.

The close was beautifully kept with a border of art nouveau tiles in the 'Glasgow style'. She paused to examine them. She'd seen them before of course; there were postcards available all over the city of the stylised lilies. They were more beautiful in real life. Stunning. Locals called them 'wally' closes, she guessed it was a compliment. She climbed the stairs to the Peterson's flat where Callum's parents were waiting. They shook her hand and ushered her inside.

The hall was bigger than most people's living rooms.

'What a lovely flat,' exclaimed Kate. Dear God, what was she saying; this wasn't a social call, but she was nervous and the rooms with their high ceilings and original cornicing *were* outstanding, even for a city that had more than its fair share of amazing architecture. The doors were all stripped wood, as was the fashion in lots of old houses and flats. She'd done the same in her own flat but where hers were made of pine, these were oak with beautifully carved surrounds of inter-twined ivy leaves. The fireplace was exceptional, too. It was also oak and had what looked like original tiles round an open fire. It was sad that the trend towards minimalism had led to these types of features being torn out of the Victorian buildings.

'Come and sit down,' said Mr Peterson. 'Would you like a coffee? The kettle's on.'

Kate asked for tea, hoping the smell of their coffee wouldn't make her feel sick again. Once they had their drinks, Kate took out her notebook. 'Do you mind if I take notes while we're talking? Thank you for offering to meet with me. If it gets too much at any time, ask me to stop.'

'Not at all,' said Mrs Peterson. 'We're pleased to be listened to at last. We're blue in the face trying to get help.'

The Fallen

'Ms Carr, I understand this is going to be very difficult for you, and I apologise in advance for anything I might say to upset you, but if we're going to get a clear picture of what's gone on, I need to be robust in my questioning.'

'I understand and please, call me Alison, and this is Bill.'

'Thank you, I'm Kate,' Kate took a sip of her tea. 'Why don't you tell me about Callum. What was he like as a person?'

Alison rose and went over to the mantelpiece. She took down a framed photograph and handed it to Kate. It showed a good-looking teenage boy, fair wavy hair flopping over his forehead. He was smiling, showing even, white teeth. Kate saw at once why everyone thought he had the world at his feet.

'He was a good-looking boy,' said Kate.

'Yes, he was,' said Bill. His eyes welled up and he wiped them with a tissue. 'I'm sorry.' He took a deep breath. 'Callum was one of life's leaders. He had dozens of friends. The flat was always full of teenagers hanging out. Many of his friends were those he'd had since nursery. We were very proud of that. This is a mixed area. It's not all beautiful flats like these and some of his friends lead much less privileged lives but Callum stuck by them no matter what. He was head boy of his school and Dux last year.'

'Dux?' queried Kate.

'It's the pupil who gets highest grades in fifth year after they've done their Highers. Lots of schools in Scotland have them. I suppose it's like valedictorian in the USA.'

'Oh,' said Kate, she'd never heard either term before.

Alison went on. 'He wasn't perfect, he had moods like any teenager does but he was fantastic. All you want in a son. A happy-go-lucky boy who was desperate to go to university and study medicine. When he heard back from UCAS, he had offers from everywhere he'd applied to. He chose Edinburgh University. Far enough away to give him some independence but near enough to his family and friends. This suggestion that he killed himself is ludicrous, but no-one listens to us.'

'Tell me more,' said Kate.

'My speciality is in psychiatry is suicide ideation.'

'Forgive me, I'm not sure exactly what suicide ideation is.'

'It's having thoughts of suicide. I helped develop a questionnaire for just such a thing, to help professionals determine whether their client or patient was likely to kill themselves.'

'What are the signs?'

There is a link between suicide and mental disorder especially depression and alcohol abuse. Callum had no such problems. Warning signs include giving away possessions, withdrawing from school or work, from family and friends, loss of interest in hobbies, misuse of alcohol or drugs, recklessness, behaviour changes, self-harm, impulsiveness. They also show no signs of interest in their appearance, disturbed sleep, loss of appetite. They have feelings of worthlessness, sadness, anger, loneliness. I could go on and on. Callum had none of these.' Alison sat back in her seat and closed her eyes as though exhausted.

She certainly put forward a convincing case.

'I read somewhere that it can be as a reaction to a time of great stress. Could this be a possibility? There was something stressful going on and he impulsively decided to end it all?' Kate paused. 'Wasn't he under the influence of alcohol?'

'Yes, and we don't understand why. Callum didn't drink

or take drugs. He was a health freak. Kate, this was a boy who had a high sense of self-worth. He was popular, loved by his friends and family. Above all, he wanted to help people. I know it's a cliché but that was Callum. He couldn't wait to start his medical degree.'

Kate chose her words with care. 'I read in one of the tabloids that he wanted to study music not medicine.'

Bill pursed his lips and looked thoughtful.

Alison shook her head. 'Callum was good at music, as he was at everything he did, but he'd wanted to be a doctor, ever since he was a small child. I don't know where the idea that he wanted to study music came from.'

'I believe it was one or more of his friends,' said Kate. She picked up her bag and rifled through it until she found the newspaper article she was looking for. She skimmed through it until she found the relevant paragraph.

'Yes, here it is.' She read it out. "Callum was a gifted musician and wanted to go to the Conservatoire according to two of his friends, Ailie Brand and Sean Gibson. Ailie said, 'I'm not disrespecting his parents, but it was their dream he was following, not his own.' Sean, who had said nothing up until then, added that Callum was dreading all the work and study ahead of him.'"

'Let me see that,' said Bill. He took the paper from Kate and studied it with intense concentration. 'I've never heard of either of those kids, have you, Alison?'

'No, I don't recognise those names at all.' Alison looked tearful. 'Was he keeping secrets from us? I can't believe he would have said that. He was a fiend for hard work, and saying that medicine was our dream, not his? We never pressurised him into medicine. If anything, we tried to dissuade him. We know what it's like, after all.'

'I don't believe this was said by a friend of Callum's at all,' said Bill. 'He knew all his friends were welcome here, and I've never heard these names until now.'

Kate wished she'd never raised this. They were clearly shocked by it, and especially the suggestion it was their dream he was following, not his own.

'Have you spoken to any of his friends?' she asked. 'Perhaps if they put you in touch with these two, you'd find out more from them.'

Alison and Bill looked shattered. It was a few seconds before Bill had gathered himself together enough to speak. 'If this pair actually exist. We've met up with several of his friends since the... the incident. They've not mentioned this to us and Callum never suggested to us that he wanted to go to the Conservatoire. If he did, he would have said. He knew we'd support him no matter what he wanted to do.'

Alison took up where he left off. 'We've heard nothing about this until now,' she said. 'When he died, we didn't read much about it in the press, and we kept away from social media. It was all too raw. Now I'm beginning to think we should have been more proactive.'

'I don't know how to say this without causing you pain,' said Kate, 'but are you aware of conspiracy theories surrounding the deaths of these teenagers?'

'What?' The colour left Alison's face. 'Conspiracy theories?'

Kate hated to contaminate them with the dirty world of conspiracy. 'I'm afraid so. I don't know whether you're aware or not but there have been four deaths over the past few weeks. The press reports have focused on suicide pacts and possible copycat suicides. The police looked into this in detail and found no links between the young people. They didn't live near to each other, go to the same school, hang out in the same places. Nothing links them.'

'Hang on, we know this already. But it's hardly a conspiracy theory, is it?'

Kate put her cup down on the side table. 'I'm coming to that. Social media is where the conspiracy theorists are to be found. They've come up with several lunatic ideas. One is that it's terrorist related. That an Islamic group are influencing young people through subliminal messages in the music they listen to and suggesting they kill themselves.'

'That's ridiculous,' said Bill.

'Yes. And there's more. The most prominent theory is that Glasgow schoolchildren are being targeted by a coven of witches based in schools, and they have cast a spell to make them suicidal.'

Alison gave a derisory laugh. 'What else?'

'They involve aliens, as is so often the case, the after effects of the Covid vaccine and the "deep state". That's a favourite of theirs. Each one as bad as the other.' Kate knew she had to be very careful with what she was now going to say. 'Do you have any theories about what might have happened? It's odd for there to be so many similar deaths in such a short time. Not just odd, a statistical anomaly.'

'I'm ashamed to say that I haven't given the others much thought,' said Alison. 'From what I've read, it looked as though they were suicidal. But Callum definitely wasn't. I'm sorry, but Callum has always been my main focus. I'd say he was murdered. Does that put me in the conspiracy theory camp?'

'You've never said that before,' said her husband. He was staring at her in what Kate could only describe as disbelief.

'You never asked,' snapped Alison. 'Over and over you

say your boy, not our boy, mind, your boy would never have killed himself, but you never come up with any other explanation. If he wasn't murdered, he must have been under huge pressure to do something like that. And in my eyes, that's murder. But I don't believe he killed himself willingly.'

The interaction left Kate puzzled. This was a couple who knew their child's friends well, who were hospitable and welcoming to them. So why didn't they recognise the names of these two who claimed to be close friends of Callum's? Why would they tell lies about Callum? She had to follow it up. She, herself, didn't see how he could have been murdered if, as the witnesses claimed, he'd jumped straight on to the tracks. But if it wasn't suicide and didn't look like an accident, what other explanation was there? Extreme bullying? It might be, but he wasn't the type to be bullied. A natural born leader, a boy who was popular and well-liked. He didn't sound like a good target for a bully. She'd keep the possibility in mind, though.

She left not long after with the phone numbers of three of Callum's friends, and a promise from Bill and Alison that they'd approach them and suggest they speak to Kate. Kate wasn't sure what was going on, but she didn't like the sound of these two so-called friends, Ailie Brand and Sean Gibson. She'd get in touch with the newspaper that had printed the story tomorrow and see what she could find out

Chapter Four

FORENSICS HAD DRAWN A BLANK. 'What? Not even a partial fingerprint?' said Alex. 'No DNA? Nothing?' He'd been convinced they'd find something on the handgun. 'What about the fag ends? And the bullet, what there?'

The DC who'd given him the news, shrugged. 'Sorry, boss. There was DNA and fingerprints from the woman who found the handgun. And we got DNA from the cigarette ends, but it was from a female. Not on the system anywhere. We reckon it's from one of the neighbours who doesn't want to pollute her flat. The bullet definitely came from the gun found in the park, but it's not linked to any other crime.' He winked at Alex. 'Don't shoot the messenger.'

Alex turned his back on him, not wanting to show how shaken he was and how irritated he was by the DC's nonchalant attitude. He'd been so sure this case would be wrapped up quickly. In his mind, fingerprints linked the gun to the drugs gang, and with any luck, it would also be linked to a previous crime. But now there was nothing.

'Has CCTV been checked? Area checked for doorbell

cameras? Neighbours asked if they have dashcam footage? For fuck's sake! Everywhere you turn these days someone's taking your fucking photie.'

The DC reddened. 'I'm sorry, sir. I wasn't in yesterday and I haven't been brought up to speed yet. I was told to tell you about the forensic report.'

'Anything from the public? Surely someone was out running. You can't move for them ordinarily. Where are they when you need them?'

'I'll go and check.'

'Fuck's sake, man. That should have been done already.' Alex found it hard to rein in his frustration. Only then did he realise how frightened he was. Had he done the right thing by moving to Kate's? He'd never forgive himself if he brought trouble to her door. He'd book a hotel right now.

He googled a hotel booking site and chose a city centre hotel. He was on the point of paying for it when he had second thoughts – perhaps it would be better to stay with Kate and Conor, in case he had made them a target. Shit, he didn't know what to do. Better leave it for the moment; he wasn't thinking clearly. The lack of progress had rattled him.

Later in the morning, he called together the small team who were working on the case.

'What do we have so far?' he asked.

Megan Webster was first to answer. As he listened to her summary, Alex gave himself a mental pat on the back for taking her on last year. She was even smarter than he'd thought.

'We've interviewed everyone in your street; from your

block of flats down to the one nearest the park. We'll do the upper half today, but it's questionable whether anyone saw anything there. Several people we spoke to remembered seeing a man hanging around. One said he was sure he'd seen him before, and he got a good look at his face, so we've asked him to come in later to see if he's able to identify him from a rogue's gallery.' She looked down at her notes. 'All of them gave similar, though not identical descriptions, which is what you'd expect, but there was a consensus that he was smallish – five foot six or thereabouts – with dark hair. Age estimated to be between twenty and forty-five.'

A groan escaped from the listeners and Megan laughed.

'I know, I know, but given there was only one person who said forty-five and she was an elderly woman with poor eyesight, we can go with the seven who said he was between twenty and thirty.' She carried on. 'He was wearing a black jacket and blue denim jeans. No one saw him actually fire the gun, but two people saw him enter the park at the Langside Avenue entrance nearest the monument. The gun was found in bushes near the rose garden. It takes four or five minutes to walk there – less, if he ran – and there are a couple of paths he could have followed.'

Alex interrupted her. 'Did anyone see him in the park?'

'I'm coming to that. Let me finish with the witnesses from your street first. One of your neighbours, who lives in the block nearest the park, bumped into him as she was getting into her car. It must have been right after he fired the shot because this woman remembers hearing what she thought was a car backfiring. She says he was agitated, sweat running down his face and he smelled strongly of alcohol. Apparently, she got a good look at him.'

'Description?' said Alex.

'Much better. She's an artist. She promised to sketch him, and she handed it in this morning.' Megan held up an A4 sheet of paper with a detailed drawing on it.

'Brilliant,' said Alex. His spirits rose immeasurably with this revelation. 'Make sure copies go to all community police across the whole of Glasgow.'

'Already done, sir.'

'And in the park? Did anyone see him there?'

'A teenager out walking the family dog saw a man fitting that description running towards the entrance near the five-a-side football pitch on Pollokshaws Road. But he wasn't able to give a detailed description. Said he noticed him because he was running fast but wasn't wearing running gear.'

'Good to know, thanks.'

Mark was next to report. He had responsibility for trying to trace the suspect's progress after he left the park.

'Here's what we've got. There's not a great deal of CCTV cameras around the park. A couple on Pollokshaws Road, which is probably the way he left. Next step is to collect the footage and go through it.'

'I would have thought Victoria Road was as likely to be a destination as Pollokshaws Road, so why not look there?' said Shane McGowan who was always asking questions. He must have been told once it was a good thing to do. Shame they were never intelligent ones.

Mark's response was curt. 'Three reasons. We have to start somewhere and there's been a sighting of "a distressed man in a hurry" running towards the Pollokshaws Road exit. He entered the park on Langside Avenue and was making his way down the park towards one of the more westerly exits. He left his shotgun in the bushes that are west of where he went into the park. Finally, there's a possibility he's part of the drugs gang that was put away recently. That would certainly give him a motive. If that is the case, he's likely to live in the south west of Glasgow so that's the obvious exit to use. Any other questions?' He looked round the room.

There were none, so he carried on with the briefing. 'PC Gray is going to take the artist's impression to show to shopkeepers along Pollokshaws Road in case anyone else saw him. We're also asking bus drivers who were in the area at the time. So far, no one's got back to us.'

'Thanks Mark,' said Alex. 'The priority now is to get the picture out there, so we'll get on to Comms and see if they can arrange for a press conference before this evening. I won't be allowed to head it up as I'm too involved, but I'm sure the DCI will be happy to step in.'

In truth, he wasn't at all sure Pamela would be up for it, but that wasn't something he was going to share with his team. How would it look to admit he didn't have her confidence? Her attitude yesterday baffled him. She'd sounded as though she was sorry he hadn't been shot. A year or two ago, she'd hinted at him retiring, but she'd not mentioned it for a while, and he didn't think he had annoyed her recently. Not intentionally, anyway. He was self-aware enough to know he did more than irritate a number of people, though he liked to tell himself they were getting fewer and fewer. He hadn't been the easiest person to like in the past. A lost baby and dead wife tended to sour your outlook, but his demeanour had improved since Kate came back into his life. He looked over at Mark.

'Mark, if you get on to Comms, I'll speak to the DCI as soon as the press conference is arranged. Or better still, I'll check with her now.'

Upstairs, he hesitated before knocking her door. One of the things he disliked about Pamela was how she blew hot and cold. You never knew what you were going to get. On a good day, she'd welcome him in. Tea would be offered, and she had ample time to listen to him. On bad days, and to be honest, these were increasing in number, she'd be brusque and rude, much as she was yesterday. He braced himself.

'Come in.'

It was impossible to deduce anything from her tone. He pushed open the door and went in.

'DI Scrimgeour, what can I do for you?'

Did she realise how nervous she made him, and if so, was it deliberate?

'You asked to be kept updated, ma'am. On the attempt on my life.'

She rolled her eyes. 'Not a particularly successful one, I have to say.'

Was she joking? He wanted to ask if it bothered her but refrained.

After outlining briefly what he'd learned from his team, he said. 'So, will you be free to take the press conference this afternoon? The sooner we get his likeness out there the better.'

She tapped her fingernails on her desk. They were talon-like, painted a washed-out shade of peach. Her hands betrayed her age, and the whole effect was one of a vulture, waiting for its prey to die.

'What time?'

'I was thinking three o'clock?'

'That's fine. Get a set of briefing notes to me by two p.m.'

The Fallen

She went back to her computer. 'Is that all?' she asked when he didn't move. Her tone was snippy as if his continuing presence annoyed her.

Alex couldn't stop himself. 'I'm fine, thank you for asking. I've moved in with my daughter for the time being, and as I think Mark Nicholson is also in danger, I've instructed him to take a room in a hotel.' He turned and left the room, but not before he saw her jaw drop in surprise. No doubt he'd get a snarky email later.

Downstairs he regretted saying anything. It wouldn't do any good and it might make her dislike him all the more. Tough. He settled back down to work.

The press conference went well. STV and BBC were there as well as representatives from local and Scotland-wide newspapers. Shootings were rare in Scotland, especially those directed at serving police officers. Despite his ambivalence towards the DCI, he admired the way she handled the press. She never became flustered or annoyed by the more stupid comments, and she easily deflected any questions aimed at finding out the identity of the targeted police officer. Alex slipped out of the room before she caught sight of him.

He spotted Mark in the corridor.

'Mark,' he called after him. 'What you doing tonight? Fancy a drink? A chance to catch up.'

'Sure, where were you thinking?'

'Well, as you have a young child to look after, I'm assuming it'll be your hotel room.'

'Oh, aye, right enough. I forgot my responsibilities there,' he laughed. 'Come round about eight, Angus should be asleep by then, but don't, whatever you do, let them phone up to my room. I'll have my mobile on. You sure it's safe?'

'Och, I'll be fine. Nine lives, me.'

Mark threw him a sceptical look. 'Well, if you're sure.'

Kate wasn't happy he was going out, but he'd made up his mind and nothing would stop him. He was determined to give her and Conor privacy whenever possible.

Once at the hotel, he rang Mark's phone before going in to announce himself at reception. It was the same hotel where Kate had been attacked the day she'd found out he was her father, and the receptionist recognised him.

'You're that bloke—'

'Ssh, keep it down.' The last thing Alex wanted was to advertise his presence. He noted a couple whose stillness betrayed their interest in the interaction.

The receptionist held up his hands in surrender.

'Here on a job?' he whispered.

'No, to see a friend. Room 316. Don't phone up, I told him I'm coming and he's trying to get his toddler to sleep.'

'No problem, on you go. Good to see you again.'

Despite the age difference, he now thought of Mark as his closest friend. He missed having him around the flat and he missed Angus, too. It was a shame the wee man was asleep, but it did give them a chance to talk. For an hour they chewed over the shooting before deciding to give it a rest.

'We're going over the same ground again and again,' said

Mark. 'We have to hope something comes of the press conference this afternoon. I take it you haven't heard anything?'

'No. Anyway forget about that. How are things with you? Settled into the new flat all right?'

Mark had bought a flat in Paisley Road West not far from what had been the family home where his ex-partner, Karen, still lived. It made things easier all round for seeing his other children, and he was now much more involved in their care than he had been.

'It's brilliant. I miss your flat, though. All that space. But my new place isn't bad. There's work needs to be done. A new kitchen and bathroom are the priority. And everywhere needs a coat of paint. I'll be looking for your help with that.'

'Christ, you won't want me to help you there. Not unless you like brush strokes everywhere with a side order of splashes on the carpet. What do the kids think of it?'

'They love it. There's three bedrooms, so the girls share one when they stay over and Oscar goes into Angus's room. I got a joiner in to build Oscar a cabin bed. The great thing about tenement flats is their high ceilings. The bed's high up and there's space underneath for a desk and a wee chair. He loves it.'

'And what about Karen? Any progress there?' This was a difficult topic. They'd separated for the second time when she found out about Angus. They had been on the point of reconciliation when Suzanne had dumped Angus on his doorstep saying she couldn't cope with both him and her illness. Karen had found it too hard to be faced with the possibility of taking Angus on full time.

'Nope. She's friendly enough but she's got a new bloke now, so...' Mark drained his drink. 'Fancy another?' It was an obvious get out. Alex got up. 'It's past eleven. I'd better get back.'

On his way home in the taxi Alex thought about Mark. There were times when he blamed himself for Mark's breakup with Karen. Alex had always had a soft spot for her and didn't understand why Mark had got involved with Suzanne who was a 'piece of work' as his old mum would say. He had tried to get Mark to tell Karen about the baby before she found out for herself. But Mark had chickened out. Perhaps it would have made no difference in the long run as it was the prospect of looking after another woman's child that finished their relationship in the end, but he couldn't help feeling he should have done more to impress upon Mark the need for honesty. Ah well, there was nothing to be done about it now.

Chapter Five

WHEN ALEX GOT into work the next day, it was alive with activity. There had been a stabbing the night before. A young lad had been knifed on his way home from the cinema with his pals. His parents claimed he had no links to any gangs and had been a hardworking boy with an apprenticeship in joinery, which he loved. Alex was put in overall charge of the case with Mark as operational head. He sent him and Megan off to start the investigation and settled himself in front of his computer.

As usual, his inbox was swollen with emails. He skimmed the headings to see if any were important. Shit, there was one from Pamela. Dare he ignore it? It had no subject line. Damn it, he'd have to read it.

He opened it warily, cursing himself for his impetuousness in challenging her yesterday. He should have kept his mouth shut, not poked the bear.

DI Scrimgeour,
I would be grateful if you would come to a meeting in my

room at 10.30 this morning. A representative from HR will also attend.

No sign off, nothing to say what it was about. Fuck, fuck, fuck. Should he get a representative from the Police Federation to attend with him? No, he was over-reacting. It could only be about what he'd said on leaving the room. But it hadn't been that bad, had it? For fuck's sake. He might have been killed, and she hadn't asked how he was. He looked at his watch, an expensive piece of kit Kate had bought him for Christmas in an attempt to inspire him to take more exercise. It wasn't ten o'clock yet. More than thirty minutes to go. How could he concentrate on work in these circumstances?

The time passed slowly but at ten twenty-five he got a notebook and pen out to take upstairs with him. He was going to make sure he took his own record of the meeting.

He waited until the half hour exactly before knocking on Pamela's door. The HR person was already there, a young woman who was fiddling with her scarf and didn't acknowledge him as he went into the room.

Pamela stood up. She was all smiles. So, it was going to be one of those days, was it?

'Come in and sit down, Alex. This is Beth Simpson from HR. I'm hoping she can be of help.'

Alex sat down without saying a word. He had already decided to say as little as possible. He nodded at Beth without smiling.

The only person in the room who was at ease was Pamela. She might have been at a cocktail party she was so relaxed. 'Beth,' she said without further preliminaries, 'you know of course that DI Scrimgeour was shot at on his way to work two days ago.'

The Fallen

Was it only two days? Felt more like a lifetime. Alex braced himself for what was surely coming next. Something about how that didn't excuse his rudeness to her yesterday no doubt. He prepared himself for a lecture from Ms Simpson about boundaries.

'I need your help to determine what support is available in such circumstances. Perhaps DI Scrimgeour should stay at home for a few days.'

He hadn't been expecting that. "No, thank you,' he said at once. 'I'm better at work.'

'I'm not sure we can protect you at work.' There was a sly smile on Pamela's face. She was up to something.

'We can put several measures in place,' said Beth, earning a look of disdain from the DCI. 'To be honest, I'm surprised this hasn't already been arranged. Based on the information you passed to me earlier, Pamela, I've done a risk assessment. It's good that DS Scrimgeour has already moved to his daughter's. It's not safe for him to stay in his own flat at present. We'll send an unmarked car to pick him up and take him home again. The assessment suggests DI Scrimgeour will be safe at work. No one's going to get near him while he's actually in the building, although of course he can work from home if necessary.'

Ha! Stick that in your pipe and smoke it, thought Alex. Pamela's face was priceless. What did she expect? HR was never going to say, *Oh there's nothing we can do so best stay at home until it all boils over*. 'I'll be fine,' he said to Pamela. 'Thank you very much for your concern.' He got up from his seat.

'Wait,' said Pamela. 'This is serious, you could be killed.'

What was this? There was none of her usual edge to her voice. She sounded like she cared. Not her style at all. 'I'll take the risk. But remember, I told you I'm not the likeliest target. That's DS Nicholson who's currently hiding out in a hotel, so perhaps redirect your concern there. Have we finished? I have a lot of work to do.'

'No,' said Beth. 'We've not finished. You've been through a very traumatic experience, so I can arrange for you to see a psychologist.'

'Not necessary. I've talked it all through with my daughter and with friends. And as I keep saying, I'm not the target here.'

Pamela tutted. 'Alex, we have no real evidence they were after DS Nicholson. The only real clue we have to their target is that he tried to shoot you. You have to be our priority for the time being.'

With an effort, Alex controlled himself. He had to stay calm. Mark's life might depend on what he said next. 'Why would anyone be out to get me? I barely set eyes on any of that gang. But Mark, on the other hand, there is a motive there all right. Let's take a second to go through the facts. One, In the last fortnight, members of a major drug gang were found guilty and sent to prison for many years. Two, DS Nicholson played a very large part in their downfall. Three, one of the prisoners shouted, "Watch your back, Nicholson. We know where you live," from the dock.' Pamela made a move as if to protest but he carried on. 'Yes, I know that's commonplace, but given what's happened, it can't be ignored. Four, Mark was living with me until very recently. They probably didn't check before they took a pot shot.' He gave his boss a quizzical look. 'What does that suggest to you?'

Pamela pushed a lock of hair behind her ear.

'You were in overall charge of the investigation, Alex.'

She had a point. Perhaps he was in danger. Was he denying it simply because he didn't want it to be true? 'I'm going to continue to come in to work regardless. Maybe I am in their sights, but if I am, then it's doubly true for DS Nicholson. And he ought to have protection, too.'

Pamela put down the pen she'd been toying with and stood up.

'Well, if you're sure... I'm not happy, though, Alex. If you get killed on my watch...'

Ah, so that was it. She was scared of a lawsuit, of being held to account.

'Honestly, I'm better at work.'

'At least let me arrange for an unmarked car to pick you up and drop you.'

He shook his head. 'There's no need. I'm staying at Kate's. Her surname isn't Scrimgeour, so if anyone's after me, they're unlikely to find out where she lives.'

'I hope you're right, Alex. I hope you're right.'

He got up to go before she asked him to sign something absolving the department of all responsibility. But no, she was way ahead of him. 'Beth will send us minutes of this meeting outlining what you were offered and what you refused.' He didn't acknowledge her.

Later that morning, he called Mark into his room and told him what had happened. 'What do you think?'

'She was trying to help? She's signed off on my hotel bill for the next few days to give us a chance to work out what's going on. And I get picked up and dropped off in an unmarked car.'

Fuck, he'd got it wrong. His paranoia had scuppered him, not for the first time. Perhaps he should have accepted her offer. What was he going to do now?

He didn't have long to ponder because ten minutes later he got the news that the witness who'd been invited in to go through photographs, had identified the shooter as a Kai Anderson: a young man from Corkerhill who'd not long been released from prison. At the same time, he got an email to say that the stabbed boy from the night before looked similar to the artist's impression of the man who'd shot at him. He grabbed a copy and called to Mark. 'Come on, we've got a dead body to look at.'

At the morgue, they stood over the corpse. There was a resemblance, especially around the lower part of his face, but his mother said he was a quiet lad who lived for woodwork. He was also younger than the witnesses had identified, only seventeen. More importantly, his name was Dylan McNeill not Kai Anderson. What was going on? Was it a coincidence? Or was there something more sinister going on? Time to get back to work and see what he could find out about Kai Anderson.

The photo the witness had pointed to was of a twenty-four-year-old male who'd been picked up several times on drugs' offences. He wasn't long out of Barlinnie, having served two years of a four-year sentence for drug dealing. That was his second offence. If he was caught and found guilty a third time, he'd get a minimum sentence of seven years. Time to bring him in. A little digging around and a DC came up with the news that he had a meeting with his probation officer in an hour's time.

'They've arranged to meet in the social work office. If we go now, we'll be in time to grab him as he comes out. He won't have a weapon on him when he goes to meet his probation officer. Though it would be good if he did because that would be him straight back to jail. But I think on the whole it's safest if we nab him there instead of his house. He's probably already on his way anyway.'

Two uniforms were going to wait outside for him to come out. Two DCs were also sent to watch his house in case he was missed leaving the office. One way or another, they'd get him, and once nicked, they'd set up an identity parade and bring in the witness to see if he picked him out.

Two hours later, they heard Anderson had missed his appointment with his probation officer. The uniforms had checked, and he was a no show. He hadn't come out of his house. Immediately Alex applied for a search warrant. He was in luck, and it was granted within the hour. But when officers went round with it, only his mother was in. PC Gray reported back to Alex.

'Mrs Anderson said she hadn't seen Kai for three days. She thought he was with his girlfriend but doesn't have her address. I asked her to phone him, but she said he hadn't got round to getting a phone.'

'Was she telling the truth do you think?'

'About the phone? No way, but it's hard to say about the rest. She was plausible enough, and she didn't put up any resistance to the search of the house. Said she was used to it. I think she was resigned to having a useless lump of a son who did nothing but bring trouble to her door. She said as much.'

Alex took a sip of water. His throat was scratchy, was he coming down with a cold?

'Anything interesting turn up in the search?'

'Afraid not. A small amount of cannabis, no more than for personal use.'

'Hmm, that's suspicious in itself. Had he got wind of the fact we were on to him?'

'Don't see how. If he was ordered to shoot someone and missed, he'll have decided to lie low before and after the shooting.'

Alex sighed. 'Right, well that's disappointing. I was hoping we'd have that all tied up today.'

PC Gray left, and Alex thought about what to do next. He called Mark through to his office.

'Are you free for the rest of the day? I'd like you to interview the friends of Dylan McNeill. They were with him when he died. They gave statements at the time, but they were in shock and they're a bit garbled. Anyway, one of them says he's remembered more about what happened. They've been asked to come here later today. While they're in, get them to have a look at some photos, OK? See if any of the faces look familiar. I'll observe.'

'Not a problem. I'll look through all the evidence we have first and I'll ask Megan to assist with the interview.'

'Great, she's shaping up all right, isn't she? Seems smart.'

Mark avoided eye contact as he answered, 'What? Oh yeah, right. Aye, she's doing fine.' He left the room.

What the fuck was that about? Alex frowned. There'd been the tell-tale hint of a blush when he'd mentioned Megan. Surely nothing was going on there? Mark was pushing forty and Megan was in her twenties. Alex wasn't sure exactly what age she was, but she hadn't been that long in the job as far as he remembered. She wasn't any more than twenty-five or twenty-six. Ah well, it was none of his business what Mark did, but it worried him, nonetheless.

Alex settled down to observe the interview. He must be getting old. He'd swear the two boys in the interview room were no more than fifteen. Since he'd turned fifty a few years ago, it had become more and more difficult to tell people's ages. Most people under fifty looked young to him, those under twenty-five looked like children. But apparently, they were both eighteen. No need for a responsible adult to sit in on the interviews, then. He leaned closer to the viewing glass. They looked shattered. One of the boys must have been crying all night. His eyes were red and swollen.

'Thank you for coming to see us today,' said Mark. 'I'm sorry for your loss.' He paused for a second or two. 'Can I have your names and dates of birth, please.'

'Sajeed Anwar, 20th February 2004.'

'And I'm Sam O'Donnell, 14th July 2003.'

'I understand you have remembered more about the incident and wish to add to the statement you made last night. Before we go on to that would you mind telling me again everything that happened?'

Sajeed spoke first. 'We'd been at the cinema to see *The Batman.*'

'Which one?' asked Megan.

'It was Cineworld at Silverburn.'

'And what time?'

'It was done by ten thirty. By the time we got to the bus, stop the bus had gone. It was half an hour until the next one, so we decided to walk home.' Sam's voice trembled. 'If we hadn't, Dylan wouldn't be dead.'

Megan pushed the box of tissues towards him. 'It's not your fault what happened. That's down to the guy with the knife, no one else.'

'So my mum keeps saying, but it was me who suggested walking home.' He blew his nose noisily and put the tissue in his pocket.

'We all agreed, though,' said Sam. 'Like you said, it was half an hour until the next bus. And half the time it doesn't turn up.'

'You all live in Cardonald, right?' said Mark.

'Yes,' said Sam. 'In the same street. We went to nursery together and have been friends since then.' There was a tremor in his voice.

'So, what happened? Take your time.'

Sajeed closed his eyes. 'We were walking up Corkerhill Road. It was about quarter to eleven and this guy appeared out of nowhere. It was near the train station. He had a knife and a horrible smile on his face. He walked right up to Dylan and stuck the knife in his chest. He pulled it out right away, twisting it as he did so.' His voice was getting shakier and shakier. A tear ran down his cheek. He was about to break down.

'It's all right, Sajeed. Take your time. You're doing really well.' Megan's voice was soothing.

Sajeed closed his eyes again. 'It all happened so quickly. The guy ran off. We were helpless. The blood was everywhere. I took off my jacket and bundled it up and pressed it against the wound but I... I think Dylan was already dead when I did it.' The tears came freely now.

Alex's heart went out to the two kids. No one should have to witness their friend being killed. It would scar you for life. Mark and Megan remained silent while they waited for him to calm down. His breath was coming in sobs, and it had started his pal off, too.

After a few moments, Mark said, 'You said you had remembered something else.'

The two boys looked at each other. Sam spoke first. 'He spoke to Dylan. I didn't take it in at the time, but then we were talking about it today and it came back to me. He was speaking when he approached Dylan, well he ran at him. It was something like, "You wee shit, you said you were a good shot. Fucking liar." And then he added, something about only getting one chance but I didn't catch it all.'

'What about you, Sajeed? Did you hear anything?'

'I didn't hear the last bit, but I heard the bit about being a good shot. It didn't make sense to me. Dylan never held a gun in his life. Ask his parents.'

Alex sat back in his seat, stunned. It was true, then. That poor lad had been killed because of a passing resemblance to a would-be killer. Now what? One death, one murderer and they were no further forward in catching either him or his intended victim. If there was one thing he was sure of, it was that there would be another attempt to kill Kai Anderson, and who knows, the guy who got it so wrong in killing the wrong man could also be a target now for the gang if they did hold to the premise of 'you only get one chance'. Time to visit Kai's mother. He wanted to see for himself her reaction at the news.

He took Megan with him. They had to knock on the door several times before it was answered. A worried-looking woman stood in front of them.

'I've told youse already. He's not here.'

'Mrs Anderson? It's important we speak to you.'

The woman looked at Alex as if he were dirt.

'Got a warrant, have you? Like the last time? Not that you found anything worthwhile then. Like I said, you're wasting your time here.'

Time to step in. 'Mrs Anderson, I'm Detective Inspector Alex Scrimgeour. It's vital we speak to you. Your son is in danger.'

'Is that right, aye?' Her voice was sceptical, but she bit her lower lip to stop it trembling. He'd swear she knew more than she'd revealed so far.

'I'm afraid so.'

She sighed. 'You'd better come in, then.'

The door opened and they followed her inside. The living room was small and dominated by a large TV screen. Alex and Mark sat on one of the two sofas. Mrs Anderson remained standing.

'Where is your son? We believe he's in danger,' said Alex.

'This is a trick isn't it, to get me to grass on him?'

Alex took out his phone and scrolled through to the photo of Dylan McNeill that had been released to the press. He held it up to her.

'Have you seen this young man before?'

She squinted at it. 'Aye, that's the poor lad that was chibbed last night near the station.'

'Yes, it is. Does he remind you of anyone?'

Her face paled. 'What do you mean? What are you getting at?'

'Please answer the question.'

She picked at her fingernails, cleaning out real or imaginary dirt from beneath them. 'He looks like our Kai but when he was younger, like.'

'We thought so, too,' said Alex.

'Well, spit it out, man. You're obviously wanting to say something.'

'There were two boys with Kai when he was killed. Both of them have described exactly what happened. They were walking home from a night out at the pictures. The attacker came out of nowhere, ran straight at Dylan and stabbed him. As he did so, he said, "You said you were a good shot. Fucking liar." What does that suggest to you?'

'How should I know?' She didn't look at them.

'Shall we tell you what we think, Mrs Anderson?' said Megan. 'Earlier that day, we put out a photo of who we wanted for the attempted murder of a police officer. As you are aware, your son is wanted in connection with that. We think that poor, unfortunate boy was stabbed in a case of mistaken identity. It could be your Kai lying on that mortuary slab, Mrs Anderson. In fact, I'll go one further. It was supposed to be Kai.'

Kai's mother said nothing, but her glare was like Medusa's, meant to kill. Fortunately, they were living in Scotland, not ancient Greece. Alex took over. 'I'm sorry, I can see this is a shock to you, but if you know where Kai is, you need to tell us. It's your best chance to keep him safe.'

'You can keep him safe? That'll be right. Where you gonnae do that, then? The big Bar-L? That place is as safe as a fucking bear pit. He went in there a stupid young boy, when he was barely nineteen. A six-month sentence for selling drugs. All that happened in there was that he met more thugs, got into worse company.' Her voice was shaky, she was close to tears, all trace of Medusa gone. She went on. 'He was trying to break away from the daft things he'd done but instead he got drawn in deeper. Once these gangs get their claws in, there's no going back.'

'What are you trying to tell us?'

She looked away. 'I've said too much already.'

'Do you have any idea the danger your boy is in?' Alex tried but didn't manage to keep the frustration out of his voice.

'Of course I do,' she was crying now. 'But can't you see? There's no way out for him. If he hands himself in, he'll go to the jail. If he stays in hiding, he's at least got a chance. Maybe he'll get himself down to London, hide out there.'

'He's in London, is he?'

'I don't know! I wish I did. I wish I could protect him. But if he goes to jail, he's dead. They've got people everywhere, these gangs. Bloody everywhere.'

Unfortunately, it was true. Alex and Megan continued to try to persuade her, but she wouldn't reveal his whereabouts. All she would say was, she didn't know. Alex didn't believe her but thought if Anderson did get in touch with her, she'd be advising him to move to London. It was a huge city, after all. Easy to get lost in. He'd end up living on the streets, homeless, friendless and no doubt on drugs. What a life. It left Alex feeling like shit. What he did, what everyone did, was put an Elastoplast on a fatal wound. The problems were so huge, they were insurmountable. He stood up to indicate the meeting was at an end.

'Thank you for your time, Mrs Anderson. I can't emphasise strongly enough that we believe your son is in grave danger. And perhaps you and your husband as well. Take care, will you?'

She let them out of the house without another word. Her face was grey and pinched. In spite of everything, her attitude, her lack of cooperation, his heart went out to her. He hoped her other children, if she had any, wouldn't get drawn into it.

He gave Megan a lift back to the station, barely responding to her chat. After he'd dropped her off, he set off to Kate's. There was to be no socialising for him that night. All he wanted was to get home and go to bed. His throat was sore and if he wasn't wrong, he had a fever.

Chapter Six

THE NEXT MORNING, Alex lay motionless in bed. His throat was on fire, his heart fibrillated like a butterfly caught in a net. His smart watch told him his pulse was one hundred and twenty, twice his normal rate. The sheets were scratchy against his tender skin, giving him pinpricks of agony. No doubt about it; he had a fever. His head felt as though his brain had been removed and replaced with one of the countless thick, grey clouds that dominated the Scottish sky. Damn. The last thing he needed was a dose of flu or worse, Covid. There was a knock on his door, Kate.

'Dad, it's past eight o'clock. You'll be late for work.'

He managed a croak in reply. The door flew open, and Kate came in.

'Stay back,' he warned. 'Flu, or Covid.'

'I'll get a test,' said Kate.

It was negative. Alex had managed to avoid it through the worst of the pandemic. It must be flu. He hoped he hadn't passed it on to anyone at work, or worse, to his mother. He hadn't been to see her for a couple of days so with any luck she'd be all right. Where had he picked it up? He couldn't think where he'd been in the last few days. Actually, scrub that. He couldn't think, full stop. His mind was as fuzzy as a bear's backside. Kate brought him a cup of tea and a slice of toast. He took the tea gratefully but eschewed the toast. 'I'm not hungry,' he said.

Once he'd drunk the tea and taken two paracetamol tablets he lay down, turned over and went back to sleep.

Kate hadn't bargained for her father being ill. She hoped he was well enough to be left alone as she had arranged to meet three of Callum Peterson's friends later. She wanted to ask them about the newspaper article. She had a bad feeling about the two so-called friends of whom his parents had been unaware and who claimed he was suicidal. Surely his real friends would have met his parents? Perhaps they had and didn't want Callum's parents to find out. But why? Mr and Mrs Peterson were adamant they'd known all his friends. No. It didn't add up, and she hoped she'd be clearer about what was going on once she'd met his friends.

Before she left, she went through to Alex's room to ask if he needed anything, but he was asleep. She'd risk going out but left a note telling him to phone her if there was anything he needed.

She'd agreed to meet Callum's friends in a café near their school in the west end. They were all in sixth year and on study leave. It would cost her in coffees, but she hoped it was going to be worth it.

When she got to the café, it was full of young people. She looked round for a group of two boys and a girl and spotted them up at the back. She went over to them and asked, 'Lucy, Jack, Samia?'

'That's us,' said Lucy. 'Would you like a coffee, tea?'

'No, please. Let me. What are you having?' They all had drinks in front of them so declined her offer. Kate went to the counter and ordered a tea. She wasn't going to risk coffee after the nausea the other day. The pregnancy test remained untouched in her bag. She didn't want to think about it.

Back at the table, she thanked the three teenagers for meeting her.

'You have exams coming up, don't you? It's good of you to speak to me like this.'

'No worries,' said Samia. 'We'll do anything to help. This whole business has been a total nightmare.'

I bet, thought Kate, though she didn't voice it. Teenagers feel things so deeply, and this, the suicide of one of their friends, was bound to affect them badly.

'There are a few things I need to ask you about, but first of all I'd like to get a picture of what Callum was like. Was it a surprise to you, his death?'

'Total, utter mindfuck,' said Jack, before catching himself. 'Sorry for the language.'

Kate waved away his apology. 'It's fine. Go on.'

The three friends talked at length about Callum. It was obvious they had been very close. She took notes throughout, wishing she'd thought of recording their conversation, but they were in full flow, and she didn't want to interrupt. Her hand was getting sore. She let them talk, and as the stream of information began to lessen, she decided to ask them about the report in the newspaper.

'Thank you for talking so freely about your friend. He sounds remarkable. When I spoke to his parents, I mentioned

I'd seen a newspaper article where two of his friends contradicted what you're saying. They said he was suicidal. Did you see that article?'

They glanced at each other before Jack said, 'No, none of us had seen it. Callum's dad rang me and asked about it, but I'd never heard of either Ailie Brand or Sean Gibson.'

Samia agreed. 'We asked around, but nobody knew them. They weren't pupils at our school. Lucy's friendly with a lot of the St Saviour's school pupils and they'd never heard of them, either.'

Lucy added, 'I've got loads of friends there, some of them were mates with Callum, too. They looked at me blankly when I asked about this Sean and Ailie. Do you have a copy of the article?'

Kate handed over a copy. She'd thought they might want to see it and had taken an extra copy with her. The three teenagers studied it, making little sounds of disbelief and outrage as they did so.

'It's nonsense,' said Samia eventually. 'Callum loved music, that much is true, but the rest is garbage. He never once mentioned wanting to study at the Conservatoire. Becoming a doctor was his sole focus. Like, I've known him since primary school and it was, like, all he ever talked about. Well, not all, but you know what I mean.'

Jack and Lucy agreed.

'After Callum's dad told us about these two, we spoke to everyone we knew. We asked a few of the teachers in case they recognised the names. We thought they may have been ex-pupils. But none of them had ever heard of these two chancers.'

Lucy in particular was getting agitated. 'I don't know who these bastards are, but God help them if we find out.

I'm sure Callum didn't kill himself. The question is, who did?'

'Perhaps it was an accident?' suggested Kate.

For a moment they said nothing.

'Did you know he was drugged?' said Jack eventually.

Kate looked at him in astonishment. He sounded so sure of himself.

'What makes you think he was drugged?'

'The post-mortem report said he had taken Ketamine and Rohypnol as well as alcohol. We think someone spiked his drink and then pushed him over the edge.'

Kate was baffled. 'His parents mentioned drink but not drugs.'

The teenagers looked at each other.

'They're ashamed,' said Jack. 'Obviously they were devastated when the post-mortem results came in. They refused to accept it and demanded a second one but the results were the same, and it was concluded that he had killed himself while under the influence.'

'And is that not a possible explanation? I've been reading up on suicide and it's not unknown for people to kill themselves on impulse, especially when alcohol is involved.'

'That's the thing, though. Callum would never take drugs,' said Jack.

Kate wasn't convinced. She knew how good teenagers were at hiding secrets from their parents.

'Are you sure? I won't disclose this to his parents if you don't want me to. I understand it might be hard for you.'

'No!' They spoke as one.

Samia went on, 'You don't understand. He was a total health freak. He didn't drink alcohol. He looked after himself, know what I mean? He would never have taken Rohypnol or Ketamine.'

'What do you think happened then?'

'He must have been pushed. There's no other explanation.'

'That's impossible,' said Kate. 'I mean, for him to have been pushed. That would have shown up on CCTV, surely. And then there's the witnesses.'

Jack leaned forward. His face was earnest and open. 'But there was no CCTV. It was out of order. Broken the night before. Yes, two witnesses said he jumped, but one of them was the guy who was with him, someone we'd never heard of. What was his name again?' he turned to Lucy.

'Paul something. Quinn, no wait. It was Quig.'

'Yeah, that's it,' said Jack. 'He said he'd got talking to Callum on the subway, said Cal was talking about ending it all, so this guy, Quig, decides to stay with him, and then out of the blue Cal jumped up at Bridge Street station and rushed off the train. Quig followed him and his account is that he was trying to hold Callum back but couldn't.' He paused. 'But what if he actually pushed him?'

Kate looked at their faces. They were so young, so naïve, so desperate to believe their friend hadn't taken his own life. She'd have to go gently with them.

'Wasn't there another witness though, who said he jumped?'

Samia took up the tale. 'There was, but he was at the other end of the platform. He said there was a struggle with Quig shouting something like "don't do it". But that could have been a cover for him pushing Callum. With the amount of drugs in his system it would have taken very little. And this so-called struggle to restrain him. It's the perfect cover, don't you see?'

Jack added, 'Apparently, he gave a witness statement and then disappeared. When Callum's parents tried to see him to thank him for helping Cal, he was no longer at his address. He'd gone to London, his flatmates said.'

Christ. This was a lot to take in. Kate offered to buy them another hot drink, but they declined saying they had to get back to studying. They chatted on for a few more minutes reinforcing what they'd already said, before Kate stood up.

'Thank you for meeting me. I'll keep in touch.'

Kate returned to the subway to make her way into the centre of the city. She didn't know what to make of what she'd been told. Why had Callum's parents not told her about the drugs and why hadn't they mentioned trying to contact Quig? Perhaps they weren't completely convinced that he hadn't killed himself. She had an appointment with the journalist, Sheila Morton, who'd interviewed Ailie and Sean. She felt uneasy about leaving her father, so she sent a quick text to see if he was OK and was relieved to get a positive response.

Fifteen minutes later, she was in Princes Square. Kate had booked a table in one of the restaurants there for one o'clock. She was early, so she looked round the shops in the gallery beforehand, thankful there wasn't a baby shop to distract her. When she got to the restaurant, Sheila was already waiting. She indicated to the bottle of wine beside her.

'Don't want to drink alone. White OK for you?'

Even if she hadn't suspected she was pregnant, Kate hated drinking at lunch time – it gave her a headache – but

The Fallen

she smiled, saying, 'That's very kind, thank you. A small glass please. But lunch is on me. You're doing me a favour.'

'Not at all. It's great to get out of the office for a couple of hours. You're freelance, right?'

They chatted on, exchanging bits of gossip about the few journalists they knew in common. It was what Kate missed above all now she wasn't working in the college – the interaction with colleagues. Hell, she even missed her old boss, Gus McDonald, aka the Cheeseburger to the rest of the department. Sheila had worked with him, too, at *The Herald*, and she had several hair-raising tales to tell.

'Did you hear how he got his nickname?' asked Sheila.

'I'd always assumed it was down to his surname.'

'Well yes, partly. No, after a night out he insisted on going to McDonalds for a Big Mac to "soak up the beer" as he put it. Six cheeseburgers later, he puked the whole lot up over the floor in the restaurant. Cost him a fortune to pay for the cleaning. Serves him right the greedy bastard.'

Kate took a sip of her wine. She'd found her old boss to be a pain at times, but she was glad the unpleasant story hadn't followed him down south. She hoped he didn't know the anecdote continued to do the rounds. Sheila carried on drinking, oblivious to Kate's discomfort.

When she finished her lunch and was halfway through her third glass of wine, she leaned back in her chair and said, 'Well, this is all very nice isn't it, but you wanted to question me about those teenagers I spoke to regarding that boy's suicide. Why?'

Kate didn't prevaricate. 'Everyone I've spoken to about Callum's death is convinced he wasn't suicidal. His parents, his friends. People who knew him well and they're adamant they didn't know the two people you spoke to.'

Sheila emptied the bottle into her glass. 'Mm. Well do we ever really know someone? They might be wrong. Teenagers do have secrets, you know. I certainly did.' She drained her wine. 'Shall I get another bottle?'

'Not for me, thanks. I have to drive home.' Kate crossed her fingers at the lie, hoping she wouldn't be found out, but Sheila had spoken to the waiter and ordered another large glass of wine for herself. 'Next time, be like me, ditch the car,' she said. 'Anyway, you were saying... fuck, what were you saying?' her eyes were glassy with drink.

'This morning, I spoke to his three best friends out of the scores of friends he had. They were at school together, they studied together, hung out together, and not once do they remember him mentioning a Sean or an Ailie. They've asked everyone they knew, including teachers, in case they were ex-pupils. Nobody's heard of them. They're not pupils at either of the two local schools. So, where did they meet Callum?'

Sheila thought for a second. 'Well, the girl said he was keen on music, perhaps they had the same music teacher.'

'Callum had violin lessons at school and his parents paid for private piano tuition. I asked them to check with his piano teacher, and no, she'd never heard of them, either. Where did you find them?'

Sheila drew her shoulders back. 'What are you implying, I made them up?'

Kate laughed. 'Of course not. But seriously, how did you get an interview with them?'

Sheila puffed out her cheeks. 'Let me think. I asked around the school the day after Callum killed himself. There were lots of kids hanging around and I spoke to some of them. I wrote up the story, and when I sent it in, the editor said he'd had an email from other friends of Callum's who said he was suicidal, so I'd better meet them to hear what they had to say.'

'OK, so do you have their contact details? How did you get in touch with them and where did you meet?'

'Whoah, so many questions. Let me think. Alistair sent me a copy of the email, so I wrote back to them, and they suggested meeting in the John Lewis café. But here's the thing. Before I came to meet you today, I pinged off an email to the address I had, and it bounced back. Didn't exist.'

Interesting. 'Do you have the email address?'

Sheila checked her phone and wrote it down for her. 'For all the good it'll do you,' she grumbled.

'Do you remember what they looked like?'

'Young,' said Sheila. 'I'm sorry, I'm not good with faces. Or names, for that matter. What's yours again?' They both laughed.

'Actually, come to think of it, they were a bit rough round the edges. I doubt they were the type to be friendly with middle-class doctor wannabes.'

'Callum was friendly with kids from all sorts of backgrounds, according to his parents.'

'Mm. Oh well, it's a mystery. God knows who they were, eh?'

Kate was sorry when the meeting ended. Despite the malicious story about Gus, Sheila had been good company, and it reminded her how she needed more female friendships, something she hadn't managed to hold on to after she'd moved to Glasgow. She missed her friend, Laura, but because of the pandemic, they'd only managed to meet up twice in the past two years. Conor's sisters were lovely, and Kate got on well with them, but they had their own friends, and Kate didn't want to impose too much. Perhaps she'd join a gym or go to an evening class. She fancied pottery or woodwork. A practical class. She'd think about it. It was only two thirty, so after a brief phone call to check on her father, she decided to go to the Mitchell Library, twenty minutes' walk away, to see if she could dig up anything else on the suicide cases. They held copies of Scottish newspapers, on film, and in many cases, in hard copy, too.

She settled herself in, amazed to find the city had such a brilliant resource. Admittedly, the carpet was a little too outré for her taste, but the seats were comfortable, the tables wide with plenty of room on which to spread your papers, and although there were a lot of teenagers there, the ambience was one of studiousness and hard work.

She searched through the main newspapers for the names of the deceased around the relevant dates. There wasn't as much as she thought there would be. With two of the victims, the two Asian boys, there was little more than a brief, factual paragraph. Kate read through the first one, taking notes. The boy's name was Bilal Assam. His parents were also adamant he wouldn't have taken his own life, especially his mother. All but one of his friends said he had never discussed taking his own life. The one friend rang alarm bells. A girl called Ailidh, no surname. Was it another spelling of Ailie, Gaelic perhaps? She'd ask Conor later. Perhaps this was the same girl who'd said Callum was suicidal. It was a strange coincidence otherwise.

Kate was more confused than ever. Had these teenagers killed themselves – it was the obvious explanation – or was there a more sinister reason behind their deaths?

The Fallen

It took her over an hour to get home. Traffic at that time of the evening, especially around Charing Cross, was grim. Conor met her at the door, his face creased with worry.

'Your dad's not well. He says he's slept all day. He won't eat or drink anything. Aren't you supposed to keep hydrated if you have flu? Can you speak to him?'

Kate knocked on his door and went into the room. It smelled of stale sweat. Alex was flushed and there were beads of perspiration on his forehead.

'Dad, are you awake?' she asked.

'Huh? Yes, I'm awake,' he mumbled. 'I'm fine.'

'You are far from fine. You look awful.' She refrained from saying he smelled terrible, too. 'Are you able to get up? Have a shower and I'll change the sheets while you're doing that. Then we'll get you something to eat. I have home-made chicken soup in the freezer. How about it?'

'No, I don't need anything. Need to sleep. Don't want to get up.'

'OK, you don't have to get up. I only thought you might be more comfortable having a wash and a clean bed to get into. But you have to eat.'

He struggled to sit up. 'I'll take a cup of tea.'

'I'll be right back. Don't you go back to sleep.'

When Kate returned to the room he wasn't there. She took the opportunity to whisk the linen off the bed and into the washing machine. It would take two minutes to change the bed, and then at least he'd have fresh sheets to lie in. He came back into the room, in clean pyjamas, as she was wrestling with the clean duvet cover.

'I took your advice and had a shower,' he said. 'The stink was unbearable.'

'I didn't want to say,' grinned Kate. 'I'm sure it'll make you feel better.'

'It has,' he admitted, getting into bed. He took a sip of his tea. 'Oh, that's good.'

'If you don't fancy soup I'll mash up a soft-boiled egg in a cup with butter. Mirren always used to do that for me if I was ill.' As soon as she said it, she regretted it. Mirren, the woman who had inadvertently been involved in her abduction and went on to raise her, was the one sore point remaining between them and she normally avoided mentioning her. But to her surprise, he didn't react other than to say, 'That sounds good.'

After he'd eaten, Alex was keen to hear about her day. He listened without saying anything as she recounted what she'd learned.

When she finished, she said, 'What do you think?'

She'd tired him out. His eyelids were drooping.

'I don't know,' he said. 'Let me sleep on it.'

Dammit, she hoped he'd feel well enough to talk. She didn't blame him though. He was ill, it was hardly a surprise he wanted to sleep rather than discuss the so-called suicides with her. She picked up the dirty crockery and took it through to the kitchen. Conor had gone out for the evening, so she was at a loss as to what to do. She went into her handbag and brought out her notebook. Perhaps she'd read through her notes again. Engrossed in her work, she didn't notice the pregnancy test fall out onto the floor.

It was after eleven when Conor came home. He immediately spotted the test on the kitchen floor and picked it up. 'Kate? Are you...?'

'Maybe,' she replied, sounding snippier than she intended.

The Fallen

'Well, what are we waiting for?' He grabbed her hand. When she didn't respond, he frowned. 'What is it? What's wrong?'

Her eyes were closed but a tear slipped out. Conor sat beside her and put an arm round her. 'Talk to me, Kate. Please don't shut me out.'

She nestled into his shoulder and let the tears come. 'I can't bear the thought of losing another baby.'

'Oh sweetheart,' he soothed her. 'We've been unlucky.'

'And the baby was due last week.'

His arms were comforting. 'I hadn't forgotten.'

'Hadn't you?' Her eyes accused him. 'You never said.'

'Because you didn't mention it. I didn't want to upset you.'

Kate had believed he'd forgotten. How, she didn't know. Every day this month she had imagined what might have been. The due date came and went, and she thought, *I should be in hospital bearing down or whatever it is women do. I should be screaming in pain, gripping Conor's hand, digging my nails into the palm of his hand, all the while knowing it's worth it and that it would result in a beautiful baby.* Boy or girl, she didn't know, but she always imagined a girl.

When it was a week later, she envisaged blissful scenes where she would sit in front of the fire, breastfeeding their child while Conor brought her cups of tea and tasty treats. Every night that week, she went to sleep with that picture in her mind. The snapshot of what should have been.

'Talk to me,' urged Conor. 'Tell me what you're thinking.'

He'd think she was crazy if she told him she was spending her life ruminating about a dead baby, but they'd promised always to be honest with each other. 'I'm thinking about the baby all the time, about what the birth might have been like, whether it was a boy or a girl, what name we'd have given them. I have this picture in my mind of us sitting here like this but with a tiny being resting on your chest. I can't bear it.' She sobbed.

'Oh, Kate. We'll have that one day, I promise.'

'You can't promise anything like that. What if this one dies, too? What if there's something wrong with me and I can't carry a baby to term?'

'Listen Kate,' said Conor. 'You've had two miscarriages, which is bad luck. What was it the doctor said? About one in eight pregnancies end in miscarriage, more if you count the women who haven't realised that they're pregnant. Most of those women go on to have a perfectly healthy baby.'

'Three,' said Kate in a small, barely audible, voice.

'Sorry, what?'

'It's been three miscarriages.'

He stared at her, eyes brimming. 'You never said.'

'It was the week before Christmas.' She broke off and took a deep breath. 'I'd taken the test. You were late home from work, which was lucky as it turned out, because two hours later, before you came in, I started to bleed.'

He took her hand. 'Kate, that's terrible. I hate to think of you going through that on your own.'

Kate was silent. It had been unfair of her not to tell Conor, but she had been so ashamed. She'd been going to keep this pregnancy to herself and not tell Conor until she was safely in the second trimester. What had she been thinking? 'I'm sorry,' she said. 'I should have told you.'

'How far on do you think you are?'

'Further on than before. Eight or nine weeks.' As she said

The Fallen

it, she squashed the little grain of hope that sprung up in her. It was further on than when she'd lost two of the pregnancies.

'But you haven't been sick or anything?'

A small smile escaped her in spite of everything. 'Oh, I've been sick all right. But you've been out at work. This isn't morning sickness, it goes on all day.'

'And I didn't notice a thing.' He stood up. 'Let's get it over with. What will be, will be and if you're pregnant we need to know.'

In the bathroom, Kate took a deep breath before she peed on the stick. She didn't need a test to know she was pregnant, but nonetheless she was nervous. She sat on the side of the bath waiting the necessary two minutes thinking about the other women who'd done or were doing the same thing today. Some would be desperate for the two lines to appear, others terrified. Only a few would be ambivalent like she was, wanting a yes but fearful of what the future might bring. Time was up. She called Conor through and together they looked at the two blue lines announcing her fourth pregnancy.

Chapter Seven

It was three days before Alex was well enough to return to work. He and Kate had plenty of time to discuss the cases she was following, and like her, he was baffled by them. Despite having been sure there was nothing more to them than copycat suicides, he had to admit there were some strange circumstances. Who were the two teenagers who'd claimed Callum Peterson was suicidal when everyone else denied it? Why had Quig disappeared? Kate had asked him about the spelling of Ailidh and he confirmed it was Gaelic.

'It might be a coincidence,' he said to her but without any conviction. It bothered him that the girl appeared to have turned up again, same first name, different spelling and claiming to be a good friend.

A good friend who was known by nobody. Kate told him she'd checked with Bilal's friends and family and met the same story. They'd never heard of a friend called Ailidh. He hoped it was a coincidence but feared there was a more sinister reason. He wasn't sure what, but his antennae were twitching and he was going to dig further while at work. His priority though, was to find out what had been happening while he was off.

Mark brought him up to speed. 'Looks like Anderson shot off to London. No pun intended.'

Alex looked at him blankly.

'Never mind,' said Mark, 'shot.'

"Oh right, very funny. Go on.'

'He was caught on CCTV cameras boarding the overnight bus to London two days after the attempted shooting. Unfortunately, there's no footage of him getting off the bus.'

'How come?'

'It was out of order. The whole system in Victoria Coach Station was down.'

Alex cursed. 'Are there any other stops on the way where he could have got off?'

'Hamilton Interchange and Milton Keynes. We've checked and the driver says four people got on at Hamilton and five at Milton Keynes but no-one got off so we have to assume he's in London.'

'That narrows it down then, though I suppose he might have got off at a service station.'

'The driver says not. He counted everyone back on. Says it's more than his job's worth to forget a passenger.'

Anderson was as good as lost to them. There were what, eight, nine million people in London? No better place to disappear. They might be able to put pressure on his parents though. If anyone knew where their son was, they did. 'What about the murder of Dylan McNeill?'

'We've made progress. On Tuesday a woman phoned in

to say she has a doorbell camera and it had showed a young bloke running south along the road a minute or two after the attack. The quality of the footage isn't good but we're doing door-to-door enquiries in all the nearby streets to see if anyone else saw anything.

'Good, good. 'Have the press been given the footage?'

'Not yet, no. We thought we'd wait and see if anyone else came up with anything better. If they do, there's a chance Crimewatch Live will feature it, in the CCTV round-up section.'

'Right, well if we don't get anything in the next day or two, get in touch with the press with what we've got. We don't want to lose too much time on this.' Alex looked through his notes. 'Has anyone come up with any links between the drug gang and Anderson?'

'We haven't found any links. Anderson was a small-time crook. His drug deals were nothing compared to what has been going on lately in the city. That's not to say he wasn't involved with them, however. He might have kept it well-hidden.'

'I see. Remind me again, when did he get out of the jail?'

'I don't remember off hand, but I'll check for you. Why do you want to know?'

'It might be that while he was inside, he was given a job to do.'

'Right, you mean was he inside at the same time as the gang members? Well, that's easy enough. They were held in Barlinnie before the trial. On remand. Remember?' Mark was frowning.

Fuck, what was he thinking?' Of course he knew that, didn't he? His brain wasn't working properly. 'Right, I'm still suffering from brain fog, sorry. OK, in that case, find out who

The Fallen

he was pals with inside. Or who his enemies were for that matter. Anyone he interacted with. Did he get to know any of the convicted? You know the score. If he wasn't a member before, someone might have got at him when he was a prisoner. Persuaded him to do a hit job either by threatening him or paying him. I'm going out to see his mother again. I'm sure she has more to tell us.'

Strictly speaking, he should be at his desk, but it wouldn't take long to interview Mrs Anderson, and they were short-staffed. Covid was very much around. The severity of the virus might have lessened but its prevalence hadn't. Thirty minutes later, he was at her door, scrutinising the battery-operated doorbell. Was it out of order? He'd rung it twice and there was no reply. Hairs stood up on the back of his head. He was being watched. He looked up in time to see her dodge behind a curtain. Right, this was not on. He banged on the door.

'Mrs Anderson, I know you're in there. Please open the door.' He counted to ten and raised his hand for the second time. She opened the door without warning and almost got his fist in her face.

'All right, all right,' she grumbled. 'I was in the shower and didn't hear the bell.'

'Funny shower that leaves you bone dry.'

She side-eyed him. 'What are you wanting?'

'I need to ask you more questions. You're not in any trouble.'

'Aye, that'll be right. You'd better come in. People round here can't mind their own business,' she shouted at an elderly man who was standing at his upstairs window. 'All right there, Jimmy? Nose bothering you again, is it?' Although there was no chance that he could have heard her, there was no mistaking her body language. He moved away, shaking his head.

'Stupid old fart,' she said and flipped the finger at him a moment too late for him to see.

Inside, Alex updated her on what they knew. 'We have CCTV images that show Kai getting on a bus to London.' He watched her closely. She gave nothing away. He decided to lie to her to see if it got any reaction. 'But it's thought he got off the bus before then. At Milton Keynes.'

'But he's—' she stopped herself from saying more, pursed her lips and threw him a look of dislike.

'You thought he was safe in London, is that what you were going to say?'

Her face reddened.

'Never mind,' said Alex. 'He'll be picked up sooner or later. If not by the police, then by the gang he's got himself involved with. You'd better hope the Met get there first.' She seemed to shrivel when he said this. 'Word is, the gang have found out where he's gone. It would help us greatly if you told us who he's seen since getting out of prison. It'll be a moment's work to find out who he was sharing a cell with and who he palled up with inside. Who he annoyed, as well. It would save time if you tell us now who he was in contact with and who gave him that gun.'

'I don't know nothing.' She didn't meet his glance.

He hated to do this to her, but he wanted to impress on her how much danger her son was in. 'Look, Mrs Anderson, I'm genuinely afraid Kai's in danger if we don't get to him first. They've already killed one boy who happened to look like him and who was in the wrong place at the wrong time. These gangs are ruthless, and from what I've read about your son, that's not him. To be brutally honest, he sounds like a daft wee boy not a hardened criminal.'

Maybe it was the 'wee boy' that did it. Something got to her, and she stifled a sob.

'You're right. He is a daft wee boy. And he's our only wean. I had three rounds of IVF before I got lucky with him. God knows how often me and his dad have tried to get him to give up drugs, get him away from here.' She got up and took a tissue from a box on the mantelpiece. Dabbing at her eyes she continued, 'He was in and out of trouble at school. I always thought he was dyslexic or had that attention thing, what's it called again?'

'ADHD?'

'Aye, that's the one. Wee Alfie next door, he's got it, and Kai was the same at his age. Couldn't keep still for a second. My mother used to say he'd got ants in his pants.' She blew her nose and slumped back in her chair.

'Go on,' urged Alex. He didn't want to lose her now when he was so close to making a breakthrough.

'Primary school wasn't too bad. They made lots of allowances for him, and his last teacher was brilliant, Mrs McCulloch. He came on so much with her. He loved Primary Seven, everything about it. And he was desperate to get to secondary school. We thought he was going to be all right there.'

'Did they not help?'

'They tried. First year was fine, and half of his second year, but then he got in with a bad crowd.' She must have seen the look on Alex's face. 'Don't give me that disbelieving look. You're sitting there thinking, "Aye that's what they all say, but it's true". Her face darkened. 'Have you heard of the Dunmore family? The triplets?'

Every police officer on the southside knew of the Dunmore family. They were notorious in the area. But slippery. They'd never managed to get them for anything serious. One of them was caught with enough cannabis on him to be charged with possession with intent to supply, but it was only a small amount, and he received a community order. And although Jake Dunmore's name came up during the investigation of a sexual assault, there was no concrete evidence, and the case, like so many others, was dropped.

'I'm aware of the name, yes.' He wasn't going to say any more.

'Well, he got in with them. In spite of us telling him to keep away from trouble. I thought he'd be OK. They don't live on the same estate as us, so I didn't think they'd get to him. It's so territorial round here.'

Alex knew only too well. There were parts of Glasgow where teenage boys from a different area weren't welcome. Step foot inside what was considered enemy territory, and you'd had it. It had been a little better in the past few years, but scratch beneath the surfaces, and the prejudices were there for all to see.

Mrs Anderson went on. 'I think they got at him on the bus to school. Offered him dope – for nothing. I'd warned him hundreds of times about it. It's how the drug gangs get to kids. "There's no such thing as a free lunch," I told him over and over, but he didn't believe me. If only I'd found out sooner... ' Tears spilled down her face and she grabbed another tissue. 'Before long, he "owed" them for all the freebies, but oh, it was no problem, so he said. All he had to do was sell a few drugs to his school pals and everything would be paid off.'

'It's an old story,' said Alex. 'And a very sad one.'

'Aye. It wasn't long before social work was involved, and before we knew it, there were endless meetings trying to get a plan in place to help him and us. But it was hopeless. The plans never came to anything due to all the cuts. And before long, those bastards had their claws into him.'

'So, are you saying it's the Dunmores who are behind all this?' Alex was puzzled. They were notorious, yes. But small fry in the scheme of things. If Kai was a sprat, they were nothing but haddock swimming in shark infested seas.

She was holding a piece of Blu-Tack, stretching it out and rolling it into different shapes between her fingers. Alex suspected she'd been a smoker. There wasn't a hint of smoke in the spotless room, but the way she played with the Blu-Tack, like she was making a roll-up, was a dead giveaway.

'No, they got him into it, but they're not the ring leaders by a long shot. I don't know who they are – and that's the God's honest truth,' she said when Alex opened his mouth to protest. 'Kai never told us, even when his dad threatened to beat it out of him.' She wiped her eyes again. 'I'm sick with worry. I've lost a stone in the time he's been out of prison.'

Alex didn't know what to say. He wasn't one to judge but his guess was that as the only much longed-for child, Kai had been over-indulged, never hearing the word 'no' until it was too late, and he was too old and too full of adolescent hormones to take any notice of his parents. Poor sods. He had to go slowly with this next bit.

'Do you know where he is? We think the gang are after him because he failed to kill that police officer.'

She stared at him with huge eyes. He hadn't gained her trust yet, but he was getting there. Softly, softly should do it.

'Do you know anything about the shooting?'

Silence.

Alex leaned forward. 'We think he shot at the wrong man, that he was given poor information.'

She was wary now, her eyes darting round the room as if she was looking to see if anyone was listening. He was on to her. 'Our theory is that Kai was forced into it. Perhaps he owed money. Perhaps he had upset another prisoner. Or he wanted out, and this was what he had to do.' Alex spoke slowly and watched her reactions carefully. Her face remained stony. 'Did they threaten people close to him?' Her eye twitched. 'Was it you and his dad?' He'd got her. He said nothing as she started to sob.

It took time but he winkled the story out of her, making her tea and reassuring her she was doing the right thing. She wasn't convinced, but she told him everything she knew. Alex's guess about the true target was right. It was Mark.

'He was told to get this polis, Nicholson his name is. Kai doesn't know why, but someone's got it in for him. You'd better warn him if you know him.'

Alex nodded at that, making sure not to give any sign he already knew. 'Do you know who told him to do it, who supplied the gun?'

'Probably one of the Dunmores. I don't know, and that's the God's honest truth. As soon as he told me the name of the polis that was him. Shitting hisself, telling me to forget he ever said anything. I tried but I couldn't get him to say anything else.'

Alex was as sure as he could be that what she was saying was the truth. As she spoke, he interrupted only to clarify points, taking down careful notes he'd share with his team later. This was worse than he'd imagined.

An hour and a half later, he was back in front of his team going over what he now knew.

'First of all – this will disappoint some of you, no doubt – I was not the intended target.'

He paused to let this sink in. All eyes turned to Mark. Alex had already warned him of what he was going to say so he was nonplussed.

'What?' he said. 'It was always going to be me, wasn't it? I was the one doing all the hard work.' The strain beneath his cheery grin was all too obvious.

Alex continued. 'It's as I suspected. The drugs gang are behind the shooting. Kai Anderson's mother confirmed he'd told her he'd been ordered to shoot Mark Nicholson. If he didn't, he'd be killed. The only thing we don't have is the name of who gave the order. She was adamant she didn't know, and I got the impression she was telling the truth. Once she'd started talking, she was desperate to tell his side of the story.'

'What's happening with Mark?' someone at the back of the room asked.

'He's staying in a hotel for the time being. Please don't ask which one, this information has to be kept confidential for obvious reasons. We don't want anyone to get wind of where he is.' He looked round the room, noting who looked him in the eye and who didn't. There had been several leaks over the past few years, none of them serious, but he wanted to see where he stood and who he could trust. Not surprisingly,

Megan didn't look up – it was probable she knew already where Mark was. Robbie McPhee was studying his feet. His brother worked for one of the red tops. Mark had told Alex about that a while ago, and the PC had already been warned about passing on stories to his brother. He was worth keeping an eye on. Two other officers didn't look up: Shane McGowan and Chloe Gray. McGowan was scrolling through his phone and Alex told him to put it away. He didn't miss the sneering look on McGowan's face as he pocketed it. What the fuck was his problem? Alex shook his head and carried on with the briefing. 'She gave us no names of gang members other than the Dunmores, who we already know of.'

'Do you believe her, sir?' The question came from an officer who was new to the service.

Alex didn't answer immediately, thinking back to the terror in Mrs Anderson's eyes as she told him what she knew.

'I'm not sure,' he said at last. 'She was terrified so it's possible she didn't want to grass on them in case they got wind of it, but I got the impression she was being truthful. I'll keep the pressure on her and hope we pick up her son in London. She was adamant she didn't know where he was, though I think she was lying about that. My bet is that he's with a relative down there, but she says not. I've informed the Met, but unless we get his mother to come clean, we'll struggle to find him.'

His mood was thoughtful as he got into his car. Life was so hard for some people. Mrs Anderson, or Fran, as he was calling her by the end of their meeting, was a decent enough woman who had been dealt a rough hand with that son of hers. But the boy didn't sound all bad, either. Daft, yes. Spoilt, aye, but Alex doubted he was a real hard man in the way some guys were. Not if what she'd said about the state of him when he'd returned home after taking a pot shot at Alex.

'I shouldn't be telling you this,' she'd told him. 'Kai would kill me if he knew I was talking about it, but it might make you see him in a different light. That day when he aimed at the police officer, he said he'd deliberately missed. He told me he had a clear view of the guy. "He was an old guy, the same age as Dad," he said. "Maybe a wee bit older. He stood outside his flat for ages looking up at the sky. He looked so happy, Mum. I couldn't do it. I missed on purpose." He was crying as he told me. That was when the whole story came out. How they threatened him, how they threatened us all.'

Aye, right. How very convenient to have had a change of heart. If he was honest, Alex's jaundiced view of this tale was shaped by the description of him as an 'old guy'. They'd never given his name or any clue as to his identity when talking to the press. Not even the fact that it had been outside his flat. As far as the papers knew and, therefore, the general public, it had happened in the vicinity of Queen's Park. That vague description was all they gave out, and it covered a large area. His neighbours had all been warned not to talk to the press, and so far, they'd kept a tight ship. Something in the way she told him, though, made him think again. So he reined in his scepticism, smiled and muttered a few words about how difficult it must have been for her. It *was* hard for her; he recognised it in the lines round her eyes and mouth, the greyness of her complexion, and in the way she jumped at the slightest noise.

On his way back to Kate's, Alex stopped off to visit his mother. He hadn't been to see her since before he'd been ill. Thank goodness for Kate and Conor who had been there several times in his absence. To his surprise, his niece was by her bedside, holding his mother's hand as she slept. He gave her a wary smile.

'Gillian, good to see you.'

'I phoned and they said you hadn't been to see Granny for over a week.' The tone of her voice was accusatory.

'That's right. I had flu and I wasn't going to risk spreading it around a nursing home, was I? But Kate and Conor visited every other day.'

She sniffed. Gillian had one of those noses that was always red at the tip as if she'd blown it too hard and too often.

'Well, you might have told me. I don't like to think of her being alone all the time.'

'As I said, she wasn't alone. Kate and Conor were here.'

Another sniff, louder this time.

'I don't understand why you're letting her wither away in here. Dad would never have allowed it. And you living all alone in your huge flat.'

Alex pulled his top lip under his teeth and bit on it to stop him saying anything inappropriate. They'd had words before about this, and although he'd shown her the occupational therapist's letter that said his flat was totally inappropriate for his mother as it was on the second floor of a tenement building, she didn't let up.

'You could have moved into the bungalow with her,' she'd said.

'Well, she's getting the care she needs here.' Alex changed the subject. 'How are you? It's been a while.' He

The Fallen

treated himself to the sly dig. In fact, he didn't remember when she'd last visited. It was months now.

'I'm fine.'

'Still working in Renfrewshire and Inverclyde Division?' Gillian had briefly worked in the same office as him, and he'd never been so pleased to see anyone go. She was dour and humourless. Took after her mother. His brother had been a good guy. How he'd managed to hook up with a woman like Jacqui who moaned the face off you every time you met, he'd never know. They'd divorced when Gillian was thirteen, and Alex's brother, Billy, had had a hard time keeping in touch with his daughter as Jacqui did everything possible to keep them apart. He was dead now, but Jacqui lived on. Thank fuck he'd hadn't seen her in years, not since Billy's funeral where she'd played the grieving widow, although she'd left him for another man. 'Billy was my one, true love,' she'd said to Alex who managed to stop himself from saying, 'Well, you certainly weren't his.'

Gillian smiled, or she bared her teeth at him. 'Yes, I'm an inspector now. Same as you.' A wee note of triumph there.

'Good for you,' said Alex. He couldn't care less if she was chief constable as long as she didn't bother him, or admit to being related to him. Unfortunately, they had the same family name.

The visit continued in this strained fashion until his mother woke up. As was so often the case when she woke, she was confused. She pulled her hand out of Gillian's grasp.

'Who are you? Why are you holding my hand. Alex, who is this woman?'

'It's your granddaughter, Billy's girl,' he said. 'Gillian.' He shouldn't feel triumphant at her not being recognised. God knows, it was rare for her to recognise him, and he visited two, three times a week, but oh, it felt good. And as for what she went on to say!

'This isn't Kate. Where's Kate, I want to see her.'

'She'll be here to see you tomorrow. I told you, this is Billy's daughter, Gillian. Your other granddaughter.' Sometimes when you repeated things to her, she understood.

'Oh,' there was no interest in her voice. Gillian stood up. 'Time for me to go, Granny. I'll see you soon.' She walked away without another word. She must have heard what her grandmother said next, though.

'Who was that woman, Alex? I don't like her. She's got a face like a chewed-up caramel. A right soor ploom.'

'You're getting your sweeties mixed up, Mum.' She'd been referring to a boiled sweet that was bright green in colour and very sour, soordrap as she would have said, but she'd drifted back to sleep. Alex sat on for another half hour in case she woke up again, but she didn't. She spent a great deal of her time asleep now, and often Alex had to wake her up if he wanted to say hello. But he often left her in peace. Who knew how much time she had left? Her ninetieth birthday had been during the second lockdown, and she was now ninety-one. It was a good age, but in all honesty, what was the quality of her life? He'd hate to end up like this, in a home, not recognising his relatives.

What had Gillian been up to? She rarely visited her grandmother. Had hardly done so when her gran was living at home in her bungalow in Crossmyloof, and the visits to her grandmother had halved since then. To his certain knowledge, this was the first time she'd visited since the homes opened up following Covid, and he tried to add up how often she'd visited in the three years Mum had been in Roselands. Five or six times, no more. He suspected Gillian was checking up to see how weak she was. He knew her concern about her grandmother was more about how much would be left for her to inherit than anything else.

Alex had never forgiven her for her reaction when he'd told her about finding Kate after all those years. She'd given a bitter bark of a laugh and said, 'Huh, that's put paid to a good part of my inheritance then." She knew her grandmother's will left everything to her direct descendants. Before Kate turned up, that had been Gillian and Alex. It would serve her right if Kate had a baby, or better still, twins. Gillian Scrimgeour was a nasty piece of work, who'd inherited thousands of pounds from his brother, but it didn't stop her being a greedy cow. He parked the car (a space right outside Kate's flat for once) and put her firmly out of his mind.

He walked up the path to Kate's close, reflecting on how lucky he was. He had a steady job, good health and, above all, his daughter. Fuck, he was getting maudlin in his old age.

Conor had cooked the evening meal, a raging hot vegetable chili Alex suspected would give him indigestion. Didn't stop him wolfing it down, though. It was delicious, and anyway, he always carried a pack of Rennies. When they'd finished eating, he cleared away the dishes, stacking them in the dishwasher. His plan was to go to his room and watch a box set on his iPad, but Kate stopped him.

'Where are you going?'

'Off to watch a Netflix series Mark recommended to me last week.'

'Watch it in the living room with us.'

Alex smiled. 'You do know the old saying, don't you?'

A puzzled frown. 'What do you mean?'

'Fish and visitors go off after three days. I've been here for over a week now. You need space, you and Conor.'

Kate put her head to one side and glared at him. 'We've hardly seen you these last few days. Come and have a drink with us. Unless the Netflix series is more appealing than our company, of course.'

Alex put his hands up in surrender. 'If you put it that way,' he said. 'I'll be right through. Just let me get that nice bottle of whisky from my room.'

Chapter Eight

KATE WAS FED UP. She'd spent the best part of a week on her project about the spate of teenage suicides and had made little progress. When her father came in from work, she grabbed him.

'I need to talk to you and Conor about this article I'm trying to write. Do you have time to talk?'

'Shoot,' he said. He filled up the kettle, made a pot of tea and sat down with them at the kitchen table to listen.

Kate launched into what she'd discovered over the past week. It would be good to hear what he made of it all. On Tuesday, she'd spoken to the journalist who'd interviewed the girl called Ailidh about Bilal. Russell Sinclair, up-and-coming reporter according to his Twitter account. He was younger than her, attractive if you liked that pumped-up gym bunny look, and full of his own importance. He'd swaggered into the coffee shop in Shawlands where they'd agreed to meet. Kate had been on the point of leaving as he was half an hour late.

'Busy, busy. Got a tip from the polis about a – well, never mind.' Russell tapped his nose. 'Sorry, I forgot, sworn to secrecy.' He indicated to a waitress to come over, which to Kate's annoyance she did. Kate had had to wait ten minutes to be served. 'Get us a flat white, darlin', will you? What about you, er Katy, is it?'

Kate glanced at the waitress to see if she had taken offence at the unasked for 'darlin', but the young girl simpered and giggled instead.

'It's Kate. Nothing for me, thanks.' Her voice was icy.

'So, what can I do you for?' His smile was literally dazzling. A mouth full of over-whitened teeth.

Kate suppressed a sigh. What an arsehole. If she hadn't been so keen to find out if he was of any help she would have walked out. 'I'm interested in these teenage suicides. After the death of Bilal Assam, you spoke to a number of his friends. How did you choose who to interview?'

'The usual way. I went up to the school. There were loads of kids hanging around. I asked if any of them knew the dead boy and had my pick of greeting faces to choose from.'

'I'm sorry? Greeting?'

'Aye, you know, wailing, crying. Of course you'll not have heard of greeting weans, you being English and that.'

His description of Bilal's bereaved friends infuriated her. Greeting faces indeed! But she did her best to hide her ire. 'I'm particularly interested in one of them, Ailidh. You don't remember her by any chance?'

The waitress was coming towards him with his coffee, and he waited until she'd gone before speaking. 'Can't say I do, no.' He sipped his coffee and made a face. 'Bog water,' he said. 'Why can't we get a decent cup of coffee anywhere?'

Shit, was this going to be a complete waste of time? 'She was the only one to say she wasn't surprised. In your article she said Bilal had spoken about killing himself, had researched how to do it.'

'Ah, right. I remember now. Yeah, that's it. She contacted me.'

Kate's heart beat faster. 'How did she contact you? Phone?'

'No. Email. Suggested we meet in a café. Fuck. Where was it again? Let me check.' He got out his phone and fiddled with it. A few seconds later, he looked up, triumphant. 'The café in John Lewis, that's where it was.'

It had to be the same girl, similar name, same café. Was she on to something at last? 'Do you remember what she looked like?'

Russell screwed up his face. 'Pretty nondescript. Mousy brown hair, medium height, thin, well skinny really.'

It could be any one of several thousand girls in Glasgow, thought Kate. 'Nothing to distinguish her?'

'She had a tattoo. On her hand. A little heart, blood red, split in two with an axe.'

'An axe?'

'Yes, it was horrible. There was blood dripping from it. A far cry from the usual stuff girls go for. You know, dolphins, bees, butterflies. Twatoos, I call them.' He added, 'Twat tattoos, get it?' as if she wasn't able to work out the mash up for herself.

Infuriatingly, Kate, who had been thinking of getting a bee tattoo, blushed. He spotted it and grinned.

'Don't tell me? A butterfly?'

'No,' she said in a voice that she hoped would put an end to it. He opened his mouth, so she said, 'I don't have any tattoos.'

'But you're thinking of one, a nice wee bee to go on your wrist. With a hive on your other one?'

She screwed up her nose. 'Tattoos are so passé don't you think?' and was pleased to see his face fall. 'Oh sorry, do you have one?'

He didn't answer but changed the subject. 'That's all I can think of so if there's anything else?'

'Do you have the email she sent?'

He flicked through his phone again and read out a string of numbers and letters. It was similar but not identical to the one that was used to contact Sheila.

Kate noted it. There was little point as it undoubtedly no longer existed. It would have been used to arrange that meeting and then immediately deleted. But she'd try it anyway. She had one more question to ask but before she could, Russell got to his feet.

'I have to go now, keep in touch, won't you? I'd like to take you for a drink. You have my phone number. Don't be scared to use it, babe.'

The arrogance of him! I'd like to take you for a drink indeed. She didn't acknowledge his comment but said, 'Before you go, did she mention anyone called Sean?'

'Oh, didn't I say? There was a guy there, too. Pretty sure that was his name. She introduced him but he didn't say a word. He sat there, moping, bit of a wet blanket.'

'He was there? With her in the café? And he said nothing?'

'Grunted a hello, but not another word. Sorry, I must go.' He moved away.

The Fallen

Kate threw down a tenner onto the table – she'd been going to pay anyway but he could have offered – and ran after him. 'Wait, what did he look like?'

'Don't remember. I only remember girls. I'll certainly remember you,' he used the index fingers of both hands to point at her. 'Call me, anytime.'

'I'd eat my own toenails first,' muttered Kate but he had gone and didn't hear her.

Kate finished telling Alex and Conor her story.

'So, what do I do now?'

'What do you think, Conor? Should she go out with him or eat her toenails?'

'I'd pay good money to see that,' said Conor. 'What a first-class twat. Him and his twatoos.'

Kate punched him on the arm. 'Not him, you eejit. I mean what do I do about this Ailie/Ailidh person. What's she up to?'

'Eejit, am I? Good to see you're picking up the local language. OK, serious now. It's not much to go on. Could be kids messing around, or maybe she's a friend of both the youngsters who died.' He scratched his head. 'It's bizarre. What do you think, Alex?'

'There are always weirdos hanging round tragedy trying to get in on the action. And you don't know for sure she wasn't a friend of Callum and Bilal.'

Kate sat back on the sofa. 'It feels bad to me. Why would anyone contact the papers about such a thing if they don't know the person concerned. I'm sure she wasn't a friend of

Callum's. His parents and friends both denied it. As did Bilal's.'

'OK, so this Ailie person is one of the weirdos then. Or it's a prank. A sick one but a joke, nonetheless.'

'Why, though? What's her motivation? Their motivation. Why would anyone do that unless they've got a vested interest in hiding the truth, which is that Callum and Bilal did not kill themselves?'

'Honestly, Kate. I think you're making too much of it. She'll be an attention seeker.'

They sat in silence for a moment. Conor was the first to break it. 'I don't know, Alex. I think Kate's right. It's suspicious.'

Alex wasn't going to concede that easily. 'There were witnesses who saw them fall. You think this Ailie and Sean were involved in their deaths but it's not possible. They would have been seen.'

'You have to admit, it's odd though. Two young people said to have killed themselves and yet their friends say they said nothing beforehand, showed no signs of depression. And apparently the CCTV at both stations was out of order, which is why no one saw it.'

'Coincidence. Listen, Kate, disbelief is one of the stages of grief. Ask anyone who's gone through it. No-one wants to believe their loved one has gone forever. Add in the complication that they did it to themselves and well...' Alex paused to compose himself.

Kate didn't say anything. What was she thinking, bringing this up like this? Alex's wife had killed herself. Her mother! And here she was banging on about these teenage suicides. They'd never talked much about Sandra, her birth mother, not since they'd first met, and Alex told Kate the story of her disappearance. All she knew was that her mother had been having an affair with Alex's best friend, and they'd been in bed together when Kate, or Mairi as she was known as at that time, was taken from her pram in the garden in Jordanhill. Overcome with guilt, she'd killed herself a few days later. Perhaps it was time to talk about it. Kate indicated to Conor to leave the room. Their relationship was so close that they often understood the other's wishes without saying a word. He got up and slipped out of the room. No fuss, no embarrassing explanations or excuses. God, she loved that man.

'I'm sorry,' she said. 'I'm a total idiot going on about this when you're the one with experience.'

Alex stared at the floor, not saying anything. After a few seconds he raised his head. 'I loved her very much. It broke me when I found out she'd been sleeping with Jimmy.'

'Your best friend,' murmured Kate.

'Aye. Best man and all. We were friends for years, did everything together.'

'It must have been awful for you.'

Alex looked at her, his face full of sorrow. 'You have no idea. Jimmy's wife was pregnant and had a miscarriage. Everyone thought it was the stress of finding out about Jimmy and Sandra, but looking back, it could have happened naturally. So many early pregnancies end that way. Anyway, it tipped Sandra over the edge.'

Was this the time to ask more? Kate didn't want to upset her father, but then again, he was already troubled.

'What was she like, my mother?'

For a heart-stopping few moments he said nothing, and Kate cursed herself. She should have left well alone. Then he began his tale.

'We met on a night out. She was with a group of friends, I was with Jimmy, as usual. There was an instant spark between us. I offered to buy her a drink. She said yes immediately, but only if I bought one for all her friends, too. There were seven of them. Cost me a bloody fortune!'

Serves you right! I've always been suspicious of that sort of man. What were you thinking?'

Alex smiled. 'I was thinking she was the most attractive woman I'd ever seen. Not conventionally beautiful, but there was a magnetism to her. Anyway, it was a different time. It's what you did in the late eighties. Flashed the cash.'

'So you bought her a drink, what happened next?'

'And her friends, don't forget. Not that it bought me any favours. They never thought I was good enough for Sandra. We were married within a year. Quiet do. Her parents didn't like me, didn't want her to marry me. But what Sandra wanted, Sandra got.' His face fell.

'Were you happy?'

'I thought we were. I was ecstatic when you came along, and so was Sandra. We doted on you. No baby had ever been so advanced, so beautiful, so clever.' He took a sip of his drink. 'Of course, every parent thinks that about their child. You'll find out yourself one day.' He must have noticed the tears in her eyes because he reached across to touch her arm. 'You will, I'm sure of it.'

Kate brushed away the tears. 'This isn't about me, go on.'

'Now, of course with the benefit of hindsight, it's obvious things weren't all right between us. Your mum had a degree. I didn't. I had a university place but didn't see the point when I got a job with the police. I'd always wanted to be a detective. Sandra liked things that I had no opinion on. She was a real film buff. It was impossible to go to a film without her dissecting it afterwards. It wasn't so bad when we were on our own. She'd talk and I'd listen. I learned a lot about film from her. But there were times we'd go with her friends and that made it different. One of them, God what was her name again? Janice? Janet?' He clicked his fingers. 'Jeanette, that was it. She didn't like me. Even more so than the rest of Sandra's friends. She was always putting me down if I dared to express an opinion about a film, or about anything. She had a knack for backhanded compliments. Some of them stung, when I got promoted to sergeant for example, she said in a very sweet tone: "Congratulations. I didn't think you had it in you." I worked damn hard for that promotion!"

'She sounds a nasty piece of work.'

Alex sighed. 'Och, she wasn't all bad. She loved your mum, wanted the best for her. I think now Sandra hadn't been happy for months, maybe years. We were different people. She was dissatisfied. Wanted more than I could give her. She talked about being a stay-at-home mum, but it wasn't affordable. The house in Jordanhill turned out to be a money pit. We were never done throwing money at it. Dry rot, wet rot, leaky roof and the mortgage rates were horrendous. They rose to fifteen percent at one point.'

Kate pulled a face. 'Oof. That must have been hard.'

'We could have got through it if Sandra had gone back to work. Two wages would have made a real difference to our finances. We never did anything because the money wasn't there. It baffled me. She loved her job, but of course, the affair with Jimmy was underway by then, and she was more interested in when she could meet up with him. I didn't suspect a thing.' Alex stood up. 'I'm going to get another drink. Do you want one?'

'No thanks,' said Kate. 'I have too much to do tomorrow.'

She hadn't yet told him she was pregnant. She and Conor had agreed to wait until she'd had the first scan. 'But help yourself. Conor picked up a nice malt the other day.'

'I'll get a beer thanks.' A minute later he returned to the room. He settled down in his chair and took a deep breath. Kate noticed he was struggling.

'You all right, Dad? We don't need to do this now.'

***

Kate was right, they didn't have to do it, but it was time she knew the truth, thought Alex.

'It's fine,' he said. 'I'm trying to think what to say. This bit's hard. I don't want to be unfair to Sandra, she was your mum, after all, and she loved you more than anything, but you should know what happened.' He took a gulp of his beer.

'The day I found out about the affair, well, it was the worst day of my life. She phoned me at work, hysterical, saying you'd been taken from the garden. I couldn't believe it. She said she'd been exhausted and had gone for a nap. Later, I found out she'd been in bed with Jimmy and not sleeping at all.' He put his bottle down on the little side table. 'I felt sorry for her when she said she was tired. I'm ashamed to say, I left most of the childcare to her. I'd not been promoted for long and worked stupid hours. It's the curse of being married to a police officer.' He shook his head as if to rid himself of the troubling images coming back to him: the arguments, the rages she'd flown into when he'd tried to reason with her that she needed to work, that without her salary they'd fall into debt.

He slumped in his seat, wishing he'd never said anything. This was the most he'd ever talked about that time in his life.

Several people had tried to get him to speak, but he'd remained silent, unwilling to go through it again. His mother, too, had pressurised him, telling him he'd regret it. 'It's not good to bottle things up, son,' she'd said. Get help or it'll poison your life forever.'

It would have, too, if he hadn't found Kate. He'd been well on his way to becoming an embittered, lonely old man.

Kate knelt down beside him. 'This is too painful for you, Dad. Leave it.'

'You'll have to hear it sooner or later,' said Alex, unable to look her in the eye. 'I owe you that. She didn't tell me about Jimmy. I had to hear about him from my boss. That bugged me. Practically the whole service knew about their affair before me. I was horrible to her, and she couldn't take it. She disappeared for a couple of days. I don't blame her. Her parents and I had to put out an appeal to get her home, but I didn't want her home. What she'd done was unforgiveable. And then...' he stopped.

Kate waited for him to compose himself. She said nothing but was by his side, her hand in his.

His voice trembled. 'She came back. The atmosphere between us was poisonous. She was eaten up by guilt and I said nothing to comfort her. And then Jimmy's wife had a miscarriage. It was all over the tabloids in Scotland, juicy gossip for the masses. I remember taking the paper up to her – she stayed hidden in the spare bedroom all day – and throwing it at her, "Two more lives ruined by your selfishness,"' I said. When I went up later, the door was jammed. She'd tied a scarf round the doorknob and strangled herself. Her body was blocking the doorway. I've never forgiven myself.' He put his head in his hands.

Kate put an arm around him as he sobbed but said nothing. He wished she'd speak, even if it was to say something he didn't want to hear. Did she hate him? He thought not, but did she understand? What did she think of them, her birth parents? A mother who neglected her baby and a father who was harsh and unforgiving. He was tortured by this.

After a few minutes he got up.

'I need to go to bed,' he said. 'Sleep this off. I've never told anyone the full story before. It feels good to have got it off my chest. I think.' He stumbled across the room to the door. 'Good night,' he said.

'Good night, Dad,' said Kate.

He hadn't told her the full story, though. He'd take it to his grave. When he'd found Sandra, he didn't check whether she was dead or not, didn't call for help or try to resuscitate her. Instead, he did nothing. For how long? Long enough to ensure that when he did check, she was dead. To this day, he didn't know whether she was already dead when he found her or whether she might have been saved had he acted sooner.

Later in bed, Kate lay awake thinking over what her father had told her. What she wanted to do was discuss it with Conor, but he'd been asleep when she went to bed. Alex's story upset her. She'd known about her mother's suicide and how she'd blamed herself for the disappearance of her child, but Alex's part in it was new to her. She imagined her mother, hiding in shame from everyone. Judged by the tabloids. Grieving for her missing child yet blaming herself. And then, the final blow. How it must have stung, to hear of another woman losing a child because of her actions. It was a desperately sad story, she thought.

Kate didn't blame Alex – how could she – but nor did she condemn her mother. It was best not to judge, she thought, given her own history of an affair with a married man, and it sounded as though her parents hadn't been a great match. What misery we bring to others, she thought, in the pursuit of our own happiness. Both her mothers had been single-minded as they'd strived for what was missing in their lives. Her birth mother sought love, her adoptive mother, a child to replace the baby she'd lost.

Her birth mother's part in Kate's disappearance was clear, but her adoptive mother was also at fault. She'd accepted without question her friend's assertion that Kate was a Romanian orphan when it should have been clear she wasn't. The warning signs were all there: a healthy, lively baby looking so different from the orphans all over the British press at that time, and most importantly, no official papers. Mirren had been so desperate for a child that she had blithely ignored all of this. Her father had always been ambivalent about Mirren, the woman she'd called mum. Maybe he had a point. But the real thing worrying her was how could she be a good mother herself when she'd had such poor role models. It was with this thought in mind that she fell into an uneasy sleep.

The next morning Kate was exhausted. It had done her no good to have had such an emotional conversation so close to bedtime. Conor brought through a cup of tea to her.

'I thought I'd leave you to sleep. You looked so tired. Is everything all right?'

She told him what her father had said the night before.

'It's hard to take it all in,' she admitted. 'Hard to hear that your mother would leave you alone in a pram in a garden while she was making love in an upstairs room. And then that poor woman losing her baby because of all the upset.'

'She might have lost it anyway,' said Conor, echoing Alex's words from the night before.

'We'll never know. According to Alex, the media certainly thought it was my mother to blame.'

'Are you angry with her?'

Kate considered the question. 'I'm not sure. It's hard to be angry with a person you don't know, who's been dead for years. It seems wrong. I suppose it's made me feel guilty. You know, about the affair I had with a married man. It was unutterably selfish of me.'

Conor said nothing. Kate had told him about how she'd thought her previous boyfriend had been going to leave his wife for her. It had shocked him. Although he no longer believed, he'd been brought up a Catholic. It must have rubbed off on him because he had been disapproving when she'd told him. She hadn't been proud of what she'd done, and to be fair, she hadn't known Jack was married until it was too late and she was in love with him. Conor, though, had made her feel ashamed. It was only with what Alex had told her the previous evening that she'd finally realised what harm affairs could do. She explained this now to Conor who listened attentively.

Conor wasn't one to rush into things. She saw he was thinking things through. He took a large gulp of tea and began to speak.

'There's no way you can compare what you did to what your birth mother did. It's a cliché, but it's always worse when children are involved, and she left you alone in your pram.'

'According to Alex, people did that all the time. They left prams outside shops and everything.'

'Aye, when he was a child, but not in the nineties, they didn't. Can you imagine? Leaving the most precious thing you'll ever have, outside a shop for anyone to run off with.'

'I was left in the garden. In Jordanhill, which, as you know, is a very respectable part of Glasgow.'

'Well yes, but you get what I mean. People don't leave their dogs alone in their gardens these days let alone their babies!'

It was true. Since the pandemic, and its accompanying rush to buy pets, especially dogs, there had been an upswing in the number of dogs stolen. The amount they cost, it was easy to see why.

Kate yawned. She was exhausted from all the different emotions she'd been dealing with. 'I'm tired, we'll talk more later.'

Chapter Nine

ALEX, on the other hand, was relieved to have spoken about his guilt over Sandra's death, even if he hadn't admitted how much he might be at fault. His mother was right; he ought to have spoken about it sooner. Kate seemed unaffected when he saw her the next morning. She was as smiley as ever and chatted easily to him.

Later, he couldn't get the teenage suicides out of his head. He drove to work, thinking about what Kate had said about them. Was she right to be suspicious about the deaths? Were they suicides or something more sinister? As far as he remembered, the first one had been less than two months ago. He thought back to what he knew about it. It wasn't much. It was a girl; he didn't remember her name and there had been little about her death in the papers. He'd heard about the Callum Peterson case however as the parents had been so distraught, unable to accept their child had topped himself. Until he'd heard what Kate said, he'd accepted that it was suicide. Now, though, he wondered.

As the deaths were 'unnatural', they had to be investi-

The Fallen

gated by the police. He recalled officers discussing them. The cases had been closed very quickly. Too quickly, some said. Perhaps he'd have a chat with one of the officers involved. He hadn't been part of the investigations, but with the publicity generated by Callum's parents it, had been hard to avoid knowing all about them.

The first thing he did on reaching work was to seek out and speak to the DS who'd been in overall charge of the investigations. She was very competent, and he was certain she'd be able to give a good account of what had happened.

'Janey, can I have a word?'

'Any time, Alex.' She lowered her voice. 'I heard about the shooting, are you OK?'

'Och, that. It'll take more than a wee ned with a handgun to take me out. No, I wanted to talk to you about these teenage suicides. You looked into them, didn't you? Can I ask you about them?'

Janey looked taken aback. 'Is there a problem?'

'No, not at all.' Alex told her about Kate and the article she was thinking of writing. He concluded by saying, 'I don't want her to waste too much time on it if there's nothing in it. She's freelance, you see, and, well, she might be better concentrating on another story.' He went through what she'd told him. 'The boy's family and friends are pretty sure he didn't kill himself. Could it possibly have been an accident?' He wasn't going to raise the possibility of murder, like Kate had. It was too ludicrous.

'I've got the notes I took at the time if you want to see them,' said Janey. 'Perhaps it would be best to read through them first, and then if you have any questions, I'll be happy to answer them.'

'That would be brilliant, thanks.' Alex left her and went

through to his office. Two minutes later, she appeared with the promised notes.

'This is what I noted at the time so they're a bit rough and ready.' She handed him several A4 sheets, neatly typed and stapled together. Alex took them from her. She had to be joking. His idea of rough and ready was notes scribbled on a paper napkin or on the back of his hand, both of which he'd used at times in the past. He didn't make any comment, though, but took it from her with a fervent thank you.

Back at his desk, he put on his reading glasses, a recent acquisition, and started to go through them. He read the first sheet.

Notes on Jasmine Bell (15/10/2008)

Thirteen-year-old Jasmine walked in front of a bus on 3rd March 2022. She had been waiting in Renfield Street at a crowded bus stop when she walked out into the path of an oncoming bus that was driving past to the next stop. It was rush hour and there were numerous witnesses (nine people came forward and there was the bus driver, too) all of whom confirmed what had happened. She fell under the wheel of the bus, so although the bus wasn't going fast, she had no chance of surviving and died at the scene.

Jasmine had a troubled past. She was the oldest in a family of five children to a mother who herself committed suicide following problems with alcohol. Jasmine, along with her siblings, had been in and out of care all her life, starting when her youngest sibling was a baby and she herself was seven. Her last foster placement had broken down in December 2021 and she was living in a children's home on the southside of Glasgow. It had not been possible to keep the siblings together. Her two youngest siblings, now aged six and seven, had been adopted recently by a couple in Perthshire, and she was extremely distressed at this. Her teachers said she was a quiet girl who struggled at school. Lately, she'd been suffering from depression, and the clinical psychologist who assessed her reported she had thoughts of suicide. No one queried the conclusion that she had killed herself.

Alex put the sheet of paper aside. It seemed pretty clearcut. It was a desperately sad story, but one that was all too familiar. Glasgow had the highest number of children and young people in care across the whole of Scotland. From what he recalled, over three thousand children from Glasgow were in care, over twenty percent of the total looked-after population. This was more than you would expect from population figures. Twice as many, in fact. Glaswegians made up approximately ten percent of the population of Scotland. There was a serious shortage of foster carers within the city and children often ended up far from their families in rural areas. The distances made it hard for them to keep in touch with family in Glasgow. If her siblings had been adopted in Perthshire, then contact with them was likely to tail off. Alex read through the notes again but found nothing to suggest any suspicious circumstances. It niggled him however that she had no one to advocate for her, no one to say, 'Wait a minute, what about this?' There was nobody to say she was not suicidal, and that, for Alex, was the saddest thing of all. But what could he or Kate do? Would her article make a difference to anything? It was clutching at straws to suggest anything other than the poor girl had killed herself. He put her case aside. His phone rang as he was about to start reading the second lot of notes. He picked it up.

'DI Scrimgeour.'

'Alex, it's me, Mark. I think I'm being followed.'

'What? Where are you? Have you called it in?' Alex beckoned to a passing PC and put the call on loudspeaker. 'Take notes,' he said.

'I'm on my way to pick up Angus at his nursery. I don't want to go there in case I'm right and I am being followed.' He sounded out of breath.

'Are you in a safe place?'

'I'm in the car trying to find somewhere. I thought about going to Govan Police Office, but I don't want to put anyone in danger.'

Alex indicated to the officer to pick up a phone. 'You got that, phone Govan and alert them to Mark coming in.'

'What about Angus,' said Mark. 'I need to pick him up. The nursery closes soon.'

'I'll go and get the wee man. Phone the nursery and tell them I'm on my way. Don't, whatever you do, tell them you think you're being followed. Do you have a registration number for the car? And a description?'

'They're two cars behind. I haven't managed to get the registration, but it's a white BMW. Not sure of the model, but at a guess, I'd say it's an X5. They've been following me for over half an hour. Since I spotted them, I've taken a bizarre route, so I'm positive they're following me. They might be going to attack me, or they might be trying to scare me. If it's the latter they've succeeded.'

Alex's heart went out to Mark. He must be terrified, though he'd never admit it. There was a definite tremor in his voice though.

'Hang on a second,' the PC was trying to get his attention.

'Sir, Govan say Mark should go there now. They need the make, colour and registration of his car. Mark should to go to the main gate, stop at the main entrance and flash his lights as a signal. Once he's through the barriers they'll drop them and have an additional barrier of police cars.'

'Did you get that, Mark?'

'Aye.'

'What are the details of the car you're driving?'

There was a brief silence.

'I'm in my own car.'

'Fuck's sake, Mark. You were meant to be in an unmarked car.' The plan had been for Mark to be picked up at home and taken to work where he would then use one of the car pool cars during the day before being dropped off back at the hotel.

'You don't have to say it. I'm an eejit but I don't like driving unfamiliar cars.'

'OK, keep yourself safe. I'll get your details to Govan. Remind me of your registration again.'

Once he'd passed these on, Alex put down the phone. He was shaking. What must Mark be feeling? He took several deep breaths to calm himself before setting off to pick up Angus.

The manager of the nursery was waiting for him and called him into her room. 'Is Mark all right? He didn't say why he couldn't pick up Angus, but he sounded dreadful as if he was frightened?'

'Really?' Alex made sure he sounded sceptical. 'He's fine, thanks. Maybe a cold coming on? Or overworked, as we all are.' Alex wasn't going to say anything else. The fewer people who knew about him being followed the better.

'Oh right,' her mouth turned down, as if disappointed to be deprived of what she'd hoped was juicy gossip. 'Well, tell him we're asking for him. Gus is through in room two. He should be ready for you.'

Angus ran straight into Alex's arms for the big swing he loved. Alex twirled him round and the wee boy squealed with delight.

'Gain, gain nuncle Alex.'

Alex obliged twice more until his back gave an ominous twinge and he put him down. 'No more for the moment, wee man. Come on, let's get you ready.'

'My going to your house, nuncle Alex?'

Shit, he hadn't agreed what to do with him once he'd picked him up. 'Mm,' he mumbled. 'Let's eat first. McDonalds?'

'Yes!' shouted Angus. 'My have a happy meal! Wiv a toy.'

'Of course,' said Alex. 'Me, I'll have a double cheeseburger.' Kate wouldn't approve but who was going to tell her?

Alex bundled Angus into the car before he remembered he had no child safety seat with him. He'd picked up Angus many times before, but it had always been planned well in advance and Mark had transferred the child seat to his car. Shit, what was he going to do?' He lifted the bewildered child out of the car and went back into the nursery.

'You don't, by any chance, have a spare car seat, do you?' he said to the keyworker. 'I've gone and forgotten it, like the idiot I am.'

'We keep a couple for emergencies like this. Follow me,'

she led him to a store cupboard where she picked out a grotty looking seat and handed it to him with a defensive, 'It's perfectly safe,' when she saw his face.

Alex thanked her and took it from her without further comment. In the back of his mind, he thought he remembered reading you shouldn't use second-hand car seats, or was it that you weren't allowed to sell them? He strapped Angus in. What else was he to do?

The meal in McDonald's went well. What was in the burgers to make them so attractive to children? Angus wasn't a fussy eater, but Alex had heard other officers talk about their children who'd eat only crisps or pizza, devouring happy meals and even demanding another once they'd finished the first. While Angus was finishing his fries, he phoned Mark, feeling a huge relief when he picked up.

'We're in McDonald's in Helen Street I thought it best to get something to eat first.'

'Yes, of course. Good shout. I'm in Govan office. The car didn't follow me in. I managed to get its registration, and it was stolen, of course. No further word about it, but no doubt it'll be found tomorrow, burned out in waste ground. There's a poor sod out there who's going to be well pissed off. It was a 2020 registration.'

'Listen, Mark. We need to get you to a safer place than the hotel you're in. Somewhere out of Glasgow. I've been thinking, how did they know which car was yours to follow? The other thing is, if they attacked me by mistake, they must have known you were staying with me. But how could they? I'm beginning to think there might be a leak.'

'You're not serious,' said Mark. 'From the police?'

'Not necessarily, but it's possible. Think about it. I'm not on the electoral register. Well I am, but not the one open to everyone. Neither were you when you lived with me. So how did they know where we lived? And your car number wouldn't be easy to find, or your car, unless they knew your movements. Or worked with you. When did you become aware of being followed?'

Mark thought for a second before answering. 'It wasn't long after I left the station. I'd got as far as Polmadie. As for my address, only you, Karen and the nursery knew for sure I'd moved on from your flat. I didn't tell anyone else. No one else knew until last week when you got shot.' He slowed down as the reality hit him.

'Exactly,' said Alex. 'We can't rule out someone's feeding them information. And the next piece of information might be your new address. They might not be doing it deliberately. It's so easily done, a casual remark, a parent at the nursery saying to staff, 'I didn't know Angus's dad lived in the west end.' And an innocent reply, 'Oh no, he's in Paisley Road West now.'

'Christ,' said Mark. 'I've only bought the place. I can't move.'

If we don't catch these bastards soon, you might have to, thought Alex but he didn't say anything. That was a problem for another day. Their priority was to find Mark a safe haven for tonight and the next few days.

'Right,' said Alex. 'Here's what we're going to do. I'll come and pick you up now and take both of you back to Kate's. Who do you trust to pick up your stuff from your hotel and drop them off at the Govan office?'

'Megan's sound.'

Ok. But don't tell anyone where you're going. Not even Megan. I mean it. Trust no one. Phone the hotel to let them know she's picking up your stuff. I want to travel while it's still light so I can spot if we're being followed. I should be with you shortly.'

When he'd finished, he phoned Kate to explain what was happening.

'It'll only be for the one night. We'll get him booked into an Airbnb for the next few days. He'll have to take time off until we've got to the bottom of this.'

By the time Alex and Mark got to Kate's, it was after eight o'clock and Angus was dropping off to sleep. Mark lifted him gently out of the car seat and carried him upstairs. Kate had borrowed a travel cot from Conor's brother. It was in Alex's room where Mark and the toddler were going to sleep while Alex slept on the sofa in the living room. He left Mark to put Gus to bed and updated Kate and Conor on what was happening.

'I've told no one he's here and I'm going online now to book that Airbnb. He's totally pissed off at having to take time off, but I'll give him paper work to do so he doesn't have to use up any of his annual leave.'

Dinner was subdued. He had refused anything to eat as he was bloated from the fast food he'd eaten earlier. He wished he'd waited to eat with the others. They were having salad, so much better for him, and it looked delicious. Old habits and all that. He hadn't had the willpower to resist a cheeseburger. It was months since he'd had one as he'd been eating healthier. Now he had hideous indigestion, and he'd swear his trousers were tighter than they'd been this morning. He wouldn't make that mistake again, he thought as he popped another indigestion tablet into his mouth.

Kate and Conor went out to give them a chance to talk privately. He owed them, big time. They'd been brilliant since he'd had to move in, never a complaint or a hint that he wasn't welcome though he had caught Kate grimacing once when she'd had to clear away his empty glass from the living room yet again. He'd have to watch out for that. A weekend package at a hotel up north where they could notch up a couple of Munros would be a good shout. Conor was a keen hillwalker, and Kate had also found a passion for it after her years in the much flatter home counties. Alex poured a malt for himself and Mark. 'What a day, eh?' he said, leaning back in his chair.

'No shit,' said Mark. 'But what the fuck am I going to do?'

'I've booked you an Airbnb in Edinburgh. You and Angus are going through there for the next wee while. I'll clear it with her upstairs tomorrow. Mark opened his mouth to protest but Alex held up a hand to stop him. 'I'll give you paperwork to do so you don't have to take time out of your annual leave.'

'Will this follow me round for the rest of my life, do you think?'

'No,' lied Alex. This was no time to prevaricate. The man needed reassurance, and he was sure they'd get to the bottom of what was going on. 'Let's look on the bright side and assume we'll catch them. We didn't get to the high heid yins last time, but we will get them. The drug squad is on their case right now.'

'And if you're right and there is a leak in our office? What then?'

'I don't know. I know it's not the answer you want to hear but it's the truth. Anyway, it could be the nursery who leaked your address—"

'Or Karen,' interrupted Mark. 'She hates me now.'

Alex sipped at his drink. 'Don't be daft. No way would she do that. Have you tried talking to her about this?'

'Fuck, no, and I'm not going to. It will only worry her.' Mark added a little water to his malt. 'Or maybe I should. What do you think? What if they go after her or the kids?' His voice rose in panic.

'I've got a couple of officers keeping an eye on her place. And you do have nosy neighbours. That wee cul-de-sac, it's ideal for old busybodies like that man across the road you were always beefing about.'

'Right enough. It's a burglar's nightmare that place.'

'Aye, they're safe enough there, I think. Besides, you haven't been living with Karen now for the best part of two years so they might not know about her connection to you.'

'I hope you're right.' Mark sipped his drink. 'Oh, this is good.'

'Isle of Jura for a change.'

'I'll remember. Anyway, this leak, if there is one. Who could it be?'

Alex swirled his whisky, watching it slide like liquid gold around the glass. He hated having to do this to Mark. 'We need to face it,' he said. 'It could be someone in our office. Maybe in our team.' He mumbled the last part as though unwilling to voice it even to himself.

'No,' Mark was quick to dismiss the possibility.

'Any better ideas?'

Mark brooded in his chair. 'No,' he admitted at last. 'But what makes you so sure?'

'First thing is, I'm not sure. Not at all, but we have to look at all the possibilities. How could the gang have discovered my address? How did they know when I, and by that, I mean you as well, left for work each day? My neighbour said the gunman had been there since before seven thirty that morning, and that's when we normally left for work. I suppose one of the gang might have been watching you and following you, but if they'd done that, they'd be aware of your change of address. The obvious answer is it came from someone you're acquainted with. Someone who knew your routine, when you went to work, when you came home.'

'It's Occam's razor,' said Mark.

'You what?'

'Where there's a number of possible explanations, the simplest is the best.'

'What's that got to do with Occam whoever he is?'

'Not sure. He was a philosopher I think.'

Alex didn't often regret his lack of an education but now was one of the times he did.

'Well, yes. Occam's razor it is, then. A fancy name for gut instinct. Whatever it is, something funny's going on, and if it is a police officer, then all I can say is, fuck it, we'll get them no matter what.'

Chapter Ten

ALEX HAD RARELY HAD such a bad night's sleep. Not since those early days after the loss of his daughter and wife had he tossed and turned so much. Then, it was anger against himself and his wife that kept him awake. He should have known about Sandra's affair, he should have bitten back those bitter words. But then he'd think *she deserved them,* and all the anger would come back. Now, the fear that someone in their ranks had betrayed Mark had rooted itself in his mind. Why was he worried? It could be nothing, it could have been a slip of the tongue from one of the nursery staff. Trouble was, they had no idea who the top guys in the drugs gang were. Not a whisper. They might not be from the southside. They might not even be from Scotland, let alone Glasgow. When Mark had uncovered the foot soldiers last year, they'd all been offered deals for names, but the stupid bastards refused to give up any information. In Glasgow, there were many areas where there was a culture of never grassing on anyone.

At half past three, he gave up trying to sleep. He got out his notebook and made notes about what had struck him. Two possibilities for action were forming in his mind. If they got hold of Kai Anderson before the mob did, they might have a chance of getting him to speak, to try and winkle out whether anyone was leaking things to the gang. The more he thought about it, the more he worried about a corrupt police officer. He had no real suspects in mind as yet, but he'd be watching, and he'd set a trap. The first thing to do would be to find out if anyone was living above their paygrade. There were a few flash cars in the carpark. Who did they belong to? He noted down a couple of questions, but it didn't help ease his worry. He was desperate. All this would take time they didn't have. What he needed was a break, space to think things through.

At six o'clock, he finally dropped off to sleep only to be woken by Angus plonking his bum on his face.

'Angus, get back here at once. It's too early for Uncle Alex to get up. Sorry Alex.'

Alex grunted.

Angus let out a plaintive wail. 'My wants a swing.'

'Uncle Alex is too tired, come on.' Mark tried to lift his son, but he struggled to lift him cleanly off, and Alex ended up with a foot in the balls.

'For ffffancy's sake,' he yelled, coming to his senses in time to stop himself teaching Angus his first swear word. 'Oh sh... sugar.' There were tears in his eyes. Angus started to cry in earnest, sensed that he was in the wrong. 'Oh, come on now, wee man. I'm fine, I'll live. Look...' Alex pulled a funny face, and sure enough, Angus gave him a watery smile. 'That's better, now how about a swing?'

The Fallen

Ten minutes later, they were pals again, and Alex got ready for work. For once, he didn't turn up his nose at Mark's offer of coffee. He was in desperate need of a strong drink to get him through the day. Once he'd finished his breakfast, he took Mark aside.

'Get your things together, enough for a few days, and I'll drop you off at Queen Street Station so you can get the train through to Edinburgh. I've cleared it with the owner of the flat for you to get early entry. There was no one staying there last night, so he was happy to do that for us.' More than happy to get an extra night's rent for sweet fuck all but that was his business not Mark's. 'It's up to you, but I'd lie low, if I were you. Go out, by all means, but don't draw attention to yourself, wear a beanie or a hoodie—'

'A beanie? It's spring. That would definitely show me up.'

'OK, then, a baseball cap or a hoodie. Enough for them not to immediately spot you, though I don't think they'll suspect you're not in Glasgow. A pair of glasses, maybe.'

'False beard? False nose?' said Mark and they both burst out laughing.

'Christ, what are we like?' said Alex when they'd pulled themselves together. 'This is serious, Mark. I don't want to be left with your wean to bring up.'

'As if,' scoffed Mark, but his eyes were worried.

'You'll be fine. Remember to keep your phone on and phone me at least twice a day. If I'm abrupt, it'll be because I'm not alone. Now, get ready and we'll leave in ten minutes.'

It took less than five minutes for Mark to get his things together. Megan had picked up his belongings from the hotel and dropped them at Govan, and he was effectively already packed. After he'd seen them off at the station, Alex went into work. He had a couple of things to put into motion. First of all, he'd watch out for any unusual interest in where Mark was. It didn't take long for the first query to come in. From Megan. Was this suspicious or not? He hoped not.

'Sir, where is DS Nicholson?'

'Why are you asking?' said Alex.

Megan blushed, 'I wanted to find out how he was after yesterday.'

'He's fine,' said Alex, more brusquely than he intended, annoyed at himself for suspecting a wee lassie like her. He remembered his argument with Kate over a year ago and adjusted his thoughts, a young woman like her. God, was it sexist not to consider a woman? 'Don't you have work to do?'

Her blush deepened and he could have kicked himself. Clueless, that's what he was. She was a friend of Mark's, and if Mark trusted her, he should, too. Well, he had an idea of what to do next. He was going to tell a few people that Mark was in his flat, hiding and see what transpired. He'd do his best to ensure Megan and a couple of others didn't find out, and then, if anything happened at the flat, he'd know he was right to be worried about a leak. Time to get to work.

An hour later, he called a mini team meeting, ostensibly to share information about where they were with finding Kai Anderson. He was going to lay a false trail there, too, by claiming there'd been a sighting of him in Manchester. But the real reason was to tell them about Mark's experience of being followed yesterday. He omitted those he knew to be trustworthy and settled on inviting four officers he wasn't sure about. He'd discreetly asked around about the cars in the car park. Three stood out as being ultra expensive. Two of them belonged to civilians, so he dismissed them immediately. A civvy wouldn't have access to anything of interest to a criminal gang. That left the three-year-old Range Rover. Alex only had a vague idea of their cost but knew they weren't cheap. He googled the price and gasped. New ones were round about the hundred thousand pounds mark. A hundred grand for a car! Those around the age of the one he'd clocked were about fifty thousand. It belonged to Shane McGowan. He was a recent graduate recruit, but Alex knew nothing else about him. How the fuck did he afford that? Generous parents? A lottery win? Either was a possibility, he conceded, but this was suspicious. The one thing he was sure of? A PC's salary went nowhere to cover the cost of such a car. The others he wasn't one hundred percent sure of were Robbie McPhee, Chloe Gray and Ewan Sinclair. Robbie had form for leaking things to the press and had had to be warned about it in the past. It was one thing to pass on information to the press, though, and another to deal with criminals, and he was pretty sure Robbie wouldn't do that. He was an idiot but not a bad one. He wanted to be certain, though, belts and braces, rule him out. Chloe was a snippy little thing. He didn't trust her; it was a gut feeling he had. She showed no trappings of wealth, but he wouldn't put it past her to be cunning enough to keep rich pickings under wraps. Finally, and this one worried him a lot, DS Ewan Sinclair. Last year, Ewan revealed he had gambling problems. He claimed to be going to Gamblers Anonymous, but he might have lapsed, and he would be vulnerable if he had. He hoped it wasn't Ewan. At heart, he was a decent bloke, but Alex wasn't going to take the risk. He had to do this. The first thing to do was to establish whether there was a leak. Once he'd done that, he'd think about how to proceed.

First of all, he wanted updating on the various tasks he'd

set them. Ryan had collated the neighbours' statements, but there was nothing of interest there. Chloe had been through the CCTV footage, but although Anderson had been picked up on several cameras, there was nothing showing him meeting or talking to anyone else. Bugger. It would have been good to pin him to the Dunmores, but no such luck. Ewan had been on leave, so had nothing to report. Only Shane had anything of interest. He'd got a couple of names from Barlinnie: Kai's cell mate and also another prisoner he'd allegedly been friendly with. He looked at his notes.

'Uh, their names are Steven McNicholl and the cellmate was Ian Barr.'

'Good, good. I'll send a detective to talk to them later today.'

'I can do that, sir.'

'OK, sure. Take another officer with you, though. Report back to me with what

you've got.' Alex talked them through the alleged sighting of Anderson then added, 'Before you go, you'll have noticed that Mark's not here. He was followed yesterday, and we've decided it would be best for him to work from home for a few days. He's going to lie low in his flat. Don't worry,' he said, as murmurs reached him of *jammy bastard, getting to work from home,* 'I've given him plenty of paperwork to do while you lot carry on skiving.'

They laughed, all except PC Gray. She never laughed at his jokes, or anyone else's for that matter. It came to him *that* was why he didn't like her; she wasn't a team player.

'I'd appreciate it, though, if you kept it to yourselves for now. Not one word. I mean it. Otherwise, everyone will be wanting to be a target so they can stay home.'

Alex watched closely to see if there was any untoward

reaction to this news, but they were hard to read. Maybe he'd got it all wrong and the information about Mark wasn't coming from here after all. He returned to the pile of paperwork on his desk, questioning whether he'd done the right thing. He hoped this would work. Babysitting Mark wasn't on his list of things to do, in any version of his world. This had to be sorted out and soon. His phone rang and he cursed. He never got a moment to complete things. There was always some interruption or other.

'DI Scrimgeour,' he said, trying but not succeeding to sound alert and interested.

'Alex, can you come up to see me? Now." It was Pamela.

'I'm busy at the moment. Can't it wait until this afternoon?'

'Now,' she said and cut him off.

Fuck, what now. Alex got himself out of his office and upstairs. He wasn't in the mood for a bollocking, which no doubt, Pamela intended to give him. He knocked on the door and she called to him to enter.

Her head was bent over paperwork, and she didn't look up. Alex sat down in the seat in front of her desk. She continued to write. Alex sighed heavily. This sort of passive aggressive behaviour was typical of her, and it pissed him off big style. She didn't blink an eye. Alex looked at his watch. He'd give her five minutes, and then he was off. One of his officers was in danger, and he had no time to play her silly power games. Another glimpse at his watch. Three minutes left. He coughed. His temper was rising. Perhaps it would be best to leave now before he exploded. Ah, she was looking up. He caught her glance and narrowed his eyes. She must have seen the annoyance in them because she put down her pen.

'When was I going to hear about the incident with DS Nicholson?' she asked.

'I was in the middle of a memo to you when you called.'

'I see. And what would this memo say?'

'Do you want me to go back downstairs and write it, ma'am?' He used the term "ma'am" deliberately, knowing she hated it. She'd let slip once it made her feel old.

'No, you might as well tell me now you're here.'

Alex stopped to consider what he might say, all the while wondering how much she knew. Well, there was only one way to find out. 'Yesterday, DS Nicholson called in to say he thought he was being followed. As you know, we now think that the gunman who shot at me was supposed to kill Mark, so I took it very seriously.'

'You told him to stay at home.' It wasn't a question.

Alex made an indeterminate noise. He'd gone above her to get clearance about putting Mark in an Airbnb so it must have been one of the four who told her the false information. It was a leak but to the wrong person.

He hazarded a guess. 'Did Shane tell you?'

She was taken by surprise by the question. 'No.'

Damn. 'Who was it then?'

'It doesn't matter who told me. Anyway, I called you up here to say it was a good call. Mark's safest at home for the time being. Well done for acting on your initiative.'

Alex was speechless. Should he tell her he'd already got authorisation from the chief superintendent? Not to tell her risked her finding out some other way, so on balance, it was best to come clean.

'Actually, I got clearance from the chief superintendent. Mark isn't at home. He's in an Airbnb for the next few days to give me... us time to figure out what's going on.'

The Fallen

'Right. And so?'

'I thought I'd tell four of the team he was working at home.'

Pamela frowned. 'You passed on false information to members of your team? Can I ask why?'

'I thought it better not to say where in fact he was.'

'I see,' she propped up her chin with her hands. 'Alex, do you suspect someone of giving out confidential information?'

'Yes.' He waited.

She sighed. 'I've been suspicious for a while that someone was passing out snippets of information. To the press, I mean. Nothing more sinister than that. What made you think something was wrong?'

He had no option but to trust her. 'It struck me yesterday that the gang would have had to have known what car Mark drives in order to follow him. He was definitely being followed. He noticed the car, stolen of course, not long after he left the station. It then tailed him for more than half an hour. Who was it? They must have had the registration of Mark's car and got a car to wait near the station and then follow him. It might have been to find out where he lived or they might have been going to carry out another attack yesterday. I'm assuming they don't know his address, as Mark only moved there recently. He hasn't got round to telling many people. He says a few people he works with are aware he moved but don't have his new address. His son's nursery is one place that might have leaked it. Not necessarily deliberately. People talk, and all it takes is one person to agree that, yes, Mark has moved to Paisley Road West, and they've got a way in. I thought I'd try to rule out people here first.'

The shock was visible on her face. 'You think there's an officer passing on information to the gang? This is much worse than I thought. I imagined you were talking about leaks to the press. Do you have any individuals in particular who you suspect?'

Alex gave her the names of the four officers he suspected. 'I might have got it wrong, but there's a reason to suspect every one of them.' He went through them before continuing, 'We can keep a watch on Mark's flat, and if anything happens there that's suspicious, we're on to them. If not, then they can be ruled out and I'll think again. Was it one of them who tipped you off about Mark working from home?'

'No. It was Megan Webster,' said Pamela.

'Oh, right.' His suspicions about Mark and her being in a relationship must be right. He'd have to speak to her now and ensure she didn't let on anything of what she knew. He said as much to Pamela, and she picked up the phone immediately.

'Megan? I need to see you now. Immediately.'

Poor Megan. She wasn't long in the job and would be terrified at being called up to the superintendent's office. But when Megan came in, she looked far from intimidated.

'What can I do for you?' she said.

Alex raised his eyebrows. Pamela saw this and smiled. 'Megan is my husband's niece,' she said. 'But don't go telling everyone.'

This was turning out to be an interesting day. Alex asked Megan how she knew Mark was going to be at home. As he suspected it had been Mark who told her.

'What exactly did he say?'

Megan screwed up her face. 'He said he was working from home because of being followed yesterday. Oh, and he also told me not to come round to the flat.'

'And have you told anyone this?'

'Only Auntie Pam. Sorry, I mean DCI—'

Pamela waved her apologies aside. 'You definitely haven't said anything to anyone else? Are you in a relationship with Mark?'

'No, we're friends, that's all.'

'Good. I mean, that's good that you've not told anyone. Although I hope you're not thinking of a relationship with him. He's far too old for you. And relationships with people you work with are a big no-no.'

'He puts it the other way, says I'm too young for him.' Megan blushed and Alex noted it. He'd been right in thinking she had a crush on Mark. He'd better warn him.

'Does anyone else know you're friendly with Mark?'

'I suppose so. It's not a secret.'

'And you definitely haven't told anyone other than your aunt about him working from home. Think carefully, Megan. It's very important.'

'I'm sure.'

'Right, I want you to keep it to yourself what Mark told you. Don't tell a soul. If anyone asks, say you don't know but tell me immediately, and be aware of their reaction. You can return to work now.'

Once she was safely gone, Alex spoke to Pamela. 'I told Mark not to say anything to anyone, but at least he didn't tell her where he actually was going.'

'Good thinking. Who does know where he is, by the way?'

'Only Mark and me. The chief knows he's going to an Airbnb but not where it is.' He took a chance, unsure if what he said next might offend her. 'And I think it should stay that way.'

'Agreed. Good, now we wait. We'll have to hope your

instincts were right, and one of those four is the culprit. If you're right, it narrows it down considerably, and we can look into them. If not...' she didn't finish the sentence.

Back at his desk, Alex was on tenterhooks waiting to see if anyone had taken the bait. But nothing. At four o'clock, he spoke to Pamela again. Might as well make the most of her being in a cooperative mood.

'Is there any way to find out if there's been any burglaries in Cardonald today? Would it be possible to ask for an update on all crimes reported, however small?'

'Mm, could do. Leave it with me.'

An hour later, she came back with the response. 'Nothing, well there's been a few crimes reported, but nothing to suggest anything untoward in Mark's flat, anyway.'

Shit, it looked as though it was back to the drawing board. Alex made his way back to Kate's where he'd be able to take a phone call from Mark in privacy.

Mark was fine, he reported. Bored stiff and tired from having to work and look after a toddler at the same time. 'I'm going to have to take him out tomorrow,' he said. 'I'll go crazy if I have to spend another day indoors with him. If I have to sing *The Wheels on the Bus* one more time or row, row, row the fucking boat, I'll kill myself.'

'That's an unusual title for a child's song,' laughed Alex.

'Oh there's a lot more like it. I found an actual children's book called *Go the Fuck to Sleep.*'

'No way.'

'Aye, there is, and there's another about eating. Not that I'd need that for Gus. He's a human dustbin.'

Alex laughed. 'Look after yourself, Mark,' he said before signing off.

After dinner, he settled down with the notes about the alleged teenage suicides. Kate and Conor were round at Conor's parents' house, otherwise he would have shared them with her. He spread them across the kitchen table and began to read. The next on Janey's list was Bilal Assam.

Notes on Bilal Assam (16/2/2007)

Fifteen-year-old Bilal Assam was seen to jump or fall onto the subway track at Kelvinbridge underground station on 7th March 2022. He was struck by a train coming into the station and died at the scene. The post-mortem concluded he had died from multiple injuries consistent with being struck by a train. There were traces of Ketamine and Rohypnol in his body, and it is thought he took this as a relaxant before killing himself. He was coming home from his chess club (All Glasgow Youth Chess), which he attended every week. He was their best player but had lost the club championship by half a point. Two of the club members said he was upset about this, but others were not so sure. Witness A said: 'I don't want to speak ill of the dead, but Bilal was a bit arrogant, and he didn't like being beaten by a girl.' Others in the club said this was nonsense. He had immediately congratulated the girl with no hint of rancour. The girl herself, Witness F, said: 'Bilal was a good sport. We were rivals. I wasn't as good as he was, and more often than not, he won, but I've improved recently, and he made a silly error [she went on to detail what this error was but I didn't understand a word] and I beat him in our game. Overall, I was half a point ahead of him and I won the championship. I'd say he wasn't in the least bothered by it.'

His parents were understandably devastated by his death. He was the only boy in the family, and expectations of him were high. The father said he wanted to be a lawyer to fight injustice. Both parents were enraged at the suggestion he'd taken drugs as it is against their religion, and they insisted on a second post-mortem. By the time it was done, there was, of course, no trace of Rohypnol in his blood and this placated them a little. They saw this as a reason to doubt that he had taken Ketamine with his father saying: 'You got it wrong with the Rohypnol so this must be wrong, too.' It was explained to him that K remains in the body much longer than Rohypnol, but they wouldn't be shaken in their belief that two post-mortems were wrong. His mother was incomprehensible in her grief but was adamant he would never kill himself: 'It is against our beliefs. It is not possible.' She repeated this a lot when being interviewed.

Two people claimed to have witnessed the actual incident. It was late in the evening, and the station had been quiet. Their accounts differed substantially. The first witness said he stumbled down the stairs as if drunk and 'fell into the path of the train'. No trace of alcohol was found in his body, although, as stated above, there was Rohypnol and Ketamine. The second witness, however, claimed to have spoken to him on the platform, as he was crying. She asked him if he was OK and to use her words: 'He said something along the lines of "I can't do it. I can't take it anymore".' She tried to reassure him, but he became aggressive, and she moved away. She was at the other end of the platform when he jumped into the path of the train (her words). She had no recollection of anyone else on the platform at the time. Unfortunately, the CCTV wasn't working as it had been vandalised. This left two possibilities, accident or suicide, as there was no suggestion of a third party being involved. On the third day of the investigation, Bilal's father came to us to say he had found a suicide note on Bilal's computer. A copy of this is attached to these notes. In addition, although extensive enquiries were made, the witness who had reported seeing Bilal stumble down the stairs was nowhere to be found, and it was concluded that he had given a false name and address and was, therefore, unreliable. A report was sent to the Procurator Fiscal, and the death was deemed by him to be suicide. Bilal's mother never veered from her claim that Bilal did not kill himself.

Alex looked at the copy of the suicide note. It was brief and to the point.

Dear Mum and Dad, I can't bear it

He studied it for a few seconds. It didn't ring true as a suicide note. There was no signature, no full stop at the end of the sentence. It could have been a statement about anything. Perhaps he no longer wanted to play chess or attend the private school that had high expectations of their pupils, or there were tasks at home he wanted to get out of. Anything. There was nothing to suggest he was about to go to a violent death. Why did he not print out the confession or add more to it? Well, he was no expert, but its composition left him uneasy. He put the paper aside. It was as confusing as ever. Unsigned suicide note, two conflicting witness statements. The only thing that was clear was that there was no sign of foul play.

No sooner had he picked up the notes for the next case than his mobile rang out. It was Pamela. She was breathless.

'I've had a call from the Govan office. A young man was caught putting a petrol-soaked rag through Mark's door. A neighbour heard shuffling on the landing of the close and came out to see what was going on. The perp had a lighter in his hand ready to fire up the rag and the neighbour wrestled it from him. He's a boxer, would you believe? The neighbour, I mean.'

'Did he manage to stop him from escaping?'

'He did that. Gave him a doing. The perpetrator is at the Queen Elizabeth getting a plaster on his broken arm at the moment, but the doctor says once the orthopaedic technician's finished with him, he's fit to be questioned. I've asked for him to be sent to Govan. I don't want anyone in our bit hearing about this until we've had a chance to question him. I know it's late, and you've been working all day, but I think it would be best if you did the interview.'

Alex looked at his watch. It was after ten, he'd planned an early night after the poor sleep he'd had on the sofa. He was knackered, he wasn't convinced he could put two words together, but he'd make sure he did. Rage filled him as he thought of the lucky escape Mark and his son had had. There was only one way out of a flat and that was where the cunt had tried to set a fire.

'I'll be there in twenty minutes,' he said.

On his way there, he thought about what to do next. The obvious thing would be to divide them into two groups and go from there. With any luck, he could narrow it down to two people within the next couple of days. He'd discuss it with Pamela to see what she thought. But it was a strange coincidence that four people thought Mark would be at home on the night his flat was attacked.

Chapter Eleven

KATE BUMPED into her father as he was coming out of her flat.

'Where on earth are you going?' she said as he squeezed past her at the door.

'Work,' he said and set off down the stairs without giving her a chance to ask any more questions.

'I'm worried about him,' Kate said to Conor, once they were inside. 'He mentioned this morning that he barely slept last night, and now it looks as though he's in for an all-nighter at work.'

'He's tough as old boots,' said Conor. 'He'll outlive us all.'

'But he drinks too much, and his diet isn't great. It improved a lot when Mark was living with him, but now he's gone, I'm worried Alex will go back to his old takeaway habits.'

'Get him to come over here a couple of times a week for a meal.'

'You don't mind?'

'No, of course not. He's good company, and he's your dad. Of course he's welcome.'

Kate thought for a second before saying, 'I always feel uneasy about the link between our two families. It's taken time for him to come to terms with the part Mirren played in my abduction.'

'But she didn't play a part. That's the whole point. It was Josie who stole you, not Mirren.'

Her doubts from the evening before nagged at her. 'True, but why did she accept without question the story about me being an orphan from Romania?'

Conor put on the kettle before answering. 'She was desperate for a child to love, but anyway, it's all in the past. Why are you bringing it up now?'

'Oh I don't know. I feel it's always a bit awkward when he comes round and your family are here.'

'Well, they feel guilty that they didn't do enough to help Mirren at the time, and perhaps if they had, the whole thing might have been avoided.' He didn't look at her as he popped teabags into their mugs.

'Alex did blame her for a time, but I don't think he does now.' Kate hung up her jacket. 'Anyway, this is getting away from the main point, which is that I'm worried about him.'

Conor hugged her. 'Please, try not to worry. I don't want you stressing about this. Not at this time.'

She leaned into him. 'OK, I'll try to tone it down. Now, where's the cup of tea you promised me?'

The notes Alex had been reading were on the kitchen table. Kate picked them up and put them to one side but when she read the front page she looked at them more closely. Not for a moment had she thought he was taking her concerns seriously. Yet, here was the proof. He'd gone to the trouble of speaking to someone at work, a police officer who knew the background to the so-called suicides. Was he going to show her these? Was he allowed to? She doubted it, but the temptation was too much. She put aside her qualms and picked them up. Conor put a cup of tea at her side and left her to it.

An hour later, she was no clearer as to what was going on. The picture was confusing with all four young people having witnesses to their deaths suggesting they'd jumped or acted in a way that suggested intention. Once or twice, there was a dissenting voice, mentioning a stumble or stating that he "looked as though he had been pushed", but much of the evidence was clear: stepped out in front of a bus, looked round before jumping and shouted *I can't take it any more* before jumping in front of a subway train. Was she on the wrong track in seeing these as suspicious deaths? Had she been overly influenced by Callum's friends and family? It was difficult to avoid thinking this. The notes on one young girl were pretty unambivalent. Surely, she, at least, had killed herself? She put the notes aside, all optimism about the possibility of a story gone. She was too tired to think this through at the moment. It was time for bed.

The following day, she had an appointment with the GP about her pregnancy. Her stomach churned as she sat in the waiting room. By the time her name was called, she was shaking. Why on earth was she was so nervous? Part of It was fear she was wasting their time. The waiting lists for the NHS were at an all-time high since the pandemic. The media was full of horror stories about cancer treatments stopped or never getting the chance to start. And here she was taking up time to talk about her fears about having another miscarriage.

However, she needn't have worried. Dr Patel turned to her with a warm smile when she entered the surgery.

'How can I help you, Kate?'

'I'm pregnant,' said Kate.

'Congratulations. Now I expect you've done a pregnancy test already, but we like to double check, in any case. Have you brought a urine sample?'

Kate handed over the miniature whisky bottle that was the only suitable container in the flat.

'Sorry,' she grimaced.

'No worries,' said Dr Patel. 'One patient brought in a sample in a screw-top wine bottle once. They'd filled it up to the top!' She looked closely at Kate. 'I see from your notes your previous pregnancy ended in miscarriage. Is this worrying you?'

'I've actually had three miscarriages,' said Kate.

The doctor frowned. 'We only have a note of one,' she said.

'I'd literally only done the test both times when the miscarriages happened.'

'So, you'd have been six weeks pregnant or so?'

'Yes, about four weeks I think,' said Kate. 'I know early miscarriage is very common but...'

'You're worried. That's perfectly understandable.' Dr Patel leaned back in her seat and looked at Kate over her glasses. 'Now, as you've had three miscarriages already, you'll be at a high risk of having another one.'

Kate swallowed. It was what she expected but it stung, nonetheless. 'What does that mean?'

'It means we'll keep a closer eye on you than normal. It would have been good if you'd come to us after the other two because then we could have looked into what went wrong.'

Kate blinked back tears. 'I'm sorry. It was so early. Not even my partner knew about the last one until recently. I...'

Dr Patel rushed to reassure her. 'No, no. I'm not blaming you. It's perfectly understandable. Talking about it makes it more real, doesn't it? Now, first things first. What was the date of your last period?'

Kate told her, and after a brief examination, the doctor announced she was around eleven weeks pregnant.

'We'll get you an appointment at the ante-natal clinic as soon as possible and also get you booked in for a scan.'

'Is there anything in particular I should or shouldn't do?'

'There's nothing in particular you can do to avoid an early miscarriage. By and large, they're caused by an abnormality of the foetus. I'm afraid all we can do is wait and see.'

She'd heard more reassuring words in her life, but Kate had thought this would be the case, so she wasn't surprised. She thanked the doctor and left, buoyed a little by the fact she was further along than she'd thought. More than a quarter of the way through. Surely, this time? She wished she'd passed the first trimester mark so she could tell Conor's family. Kate wasn't a believer, but it would be a comfort to think of all those prayers being said. His great aunts, in particular, would be saying rosaries every day of the week. Whatever a rosary was. Kate had only the faintest of notions. From what she had gathered, it involved lots of prayers.

Outside the surgery, she looked at her watch. Half past ten. She'd go back to the flat, see if Alex was there. He hadn't been in when she left. Surely, he hadn't gone into work.

When she got home, she spotted his car outside. Good,

The Fallen

he wasn't in work. If he had any sense, he'd be in bed catching up with his sleep. She went into the flat quietly so as not to wake him, but she needn't have bothered. He was in the kitchen making himself a bacon roll.

'That's not good for you.' He jumped as she crept up behind him.

'Ha, I know but after the night I've had!'

'Sit down and I'll finish off here.' Kate took over. 'Crispy bacon?'

'Yes, please, and a fried egg as well.'

'At least let me poach it.'

'No chance, I want it fried.'

Kate broke an egg in the pan and finished making her father's breakfast. He'd already made a pot of tea, so she poured them both a cup and sat down. 'So, what's with the grand exit at ten thirty last night?'

Alex took a gulp of his tea and filled her in about the attack on Mark's flat.

'Fortunately, there's no damage to the flat. They got the guy that did it, so I was there to interview him. We think someone might be passing info to the gang – I'd told a few select officers Mark was working from home and had to stay put. This bloke claimed he was given his orders to "light up" the flat, as he put it, and was adamant he knew nothing more. Hours I was there, and I got nothing out of him.' He looked despondent. 'This is bad, Kate. One thing the wee shite said was that whoever it is behind these attacks, they won't rest until Mark has been killed. He said he was told to see to it or else. He was terrified but unfortunately not frightened enough to confide in us.'

'Are you sure it's this gang behind it? Why would they wait until the trial was over?'

Alex's mouth was full. When he'd finished chewing, he said, 'It's beyond me. It's definitely someone in that gang, but whoever it is, they're hiding behind the foot soldiers.'

'Has Mark any ideas? Suzanne maybe?'

'Suzanne as boss of an organised crime group? I don't see it myself.' He wagged a finger at her. 'You're obsessed with that woman.'

Kate laughed. 'I am. I'm sorry. Have you spoken to Mark? How did he take it?'

'Yes, I phoned him earlier. He's taken it better than you'd expect given he and wee Angus could've been killed, but he's pretty angry. At least there's no damage to the flat.'

'I don't blame him. What's going to happen now?'

'We reached the twelve hour cut-off for questioning, so we've applied for another twelve hours to see if we can get anything else out of him. I've been ordered to get some sleep. Two nights with only two hours sleep at most. Not done that for a while!'

'Do you really think there's a leak in the police? What makes you think that?'

Alex stretched in his chair and yawned. 'Sorry, Kate. It'll have to wait. I'll have to get to bed. I'll get a few hours' sleep, and with any luck, I'll be back at Govan to do the last couple of hours before he's charged.' He picked up the pile of notes he'd left on the table and frowned. 'Have you been reading these?'

Kate blushed. 'I'm afraid so. Sorry.'

'Mm,' said Alex. 'My fault for leaving them there. But you shouldn't have.'

His eyes were drooping. He was nearly asleep. Kate stood up. 'You're right. It was wrong of me. Don't worry, I won't use anything I read there. You need to get to bed, though.'

'All right, all right, I'm going.' Alex yawned loudly as he left the room.

His dirty plates were still on the table. Much as she loved having him stay with her, Kate wished he'd clear up after himself. Once she'd put them in the dishwasher, Kate poured herself another cup of tea and took it through to the living room. She was uncertain what to do for the rest of the day. Hearing about the attack on Mark's flat had horrified her. She'd phone him later after Gus was in bed. She didn't have any interviews lined up for today, so was at a loose end. A plan, that's what she needed. She thought again about what she'd read in the notes Alex had brought home. Was there a pattern? There was nothing obvious. Three boys and a girl. Different sexes and races. Two of the boys were of Asian origin. Apart from Jasmine, they were all from comfortable backgrounds. The parents of Bilal, the first boy to die, were in business. They owned three restaurants in Glasgow and lived in Kelvinside. The parents of the other Asian boy, Deepak Varma, were doctors, as was Callum's mother. Like Bilal Assam, Deepak had been a pupil at a private school. Not the same one though, and there was nothing to suggest they knew each other. Callum and Jasmine attended state schools. Alex had left the notes on the table again. Kate knew she shouldn't, but she picked them up to have another look. Deepak's notes were on top.

Notes on Deepak Varma (2/4/2004)

Deepak was two days off his eighteenth birthday when he jumped or fell from Jamaica Bridge in the centre of the city on the 31st March 2022. It was late at night, and he had been out with friends from his school. They'd left the club they'd been visiting shortly after two a.m., but he got separated from them around Queen Street station when the group stopped to go into a kebab shop. The general consensus was he was in a mood because he'd failed to pull. Initially it was thought the event was an accident but two days later a suicide note was found in his computer.

Kate stopped reading. This was too much of a coincidence, wasn't it? And convenient, too. Unsigned notes in a computer. The one from Bilal Assam had been brief. She hoped she'd be able to find out what Deepak's said. She'd have to ask Alex if he knew. Would he help her though, now she'd read the notes against his wishes? She continued to read.

Deepak had been on the waiting list for CAMHS. His parents said he'd been depressed since failing to get an unconditional offer to study law at university, although he did have one conditional offer. However, he was convinced he would not get the results needed, and his mood had been low for several weeks. School friends were contradictory and said he hadn't wanted to go to university anyway. They said he wanted to set up an IT business, but his mother, in particular, had wanted him to go to university. The procurator fiscal concluded it was suicide.

Kate put the notes back. This was becoming more and more confusing, and she was concerned she was wasting her time with this. So far, she had nothing to go on. Nothing else about the mysterious pair who claimed suicide when everyone around was denying it. There were only the briefest of newspaper reports about Bilal, Deepak and Jasmine. Callum's was the only death to get more than a couple of lines, possibly because it was the most recent, but more likely because his parents had made a fuss. She read through the notes a second time focussing on finding links, but these were few and insignificant. She tried drawing a Venn diagram to see if there was any space where they all intersected. Nothing. They didn't live in the same area, they didn't attend the same school, they didn't have friends in common, and they had different interests and different careers in mind. There must be a link, but whatever it was, she couldn't see it.

No more interviews arranged, nothing to go on, no ideas. She hated the thought she might not finish this article – it had seemed like a promising pitch – but it looked as though, this time, she'd gone down a dark alley with no way out. It was infuriating. Well, she either sat here and moped or she could get on with something else. On a whim, she decided to take the rest of the day off. She'd go into town to buy new clothes. She hadn't done any shopping for ages. After scribbling a note to Alex, she changed into jeans and a T-shirt and got herself ready for a trip into the city centre. John Lewis had a good selection of franchises, she'd try there first. Raincoat on – the weather forecast was ominous – she ran down the hill to Cathcart Road to catch a bus. For once, she was lucky, and a bus came immediately. Less than half an hour and she'd be in the centre of Glasgow. She put her ear pods in and clicked on her favourite playlist on Spotify.

John Lewis was quiet, and she browsed happily for half an hour, choosing various tops and dresses to try on. She kept well away from maternity clothes, she wasn't going to tempt fate. On her way to the till with a pile of clothes, though, she stopped and considered what she was doing. She was pregnant, so why did she have tight-fitting dresses and tops in her arms? She was called forward to the till but turned away at the last moment bumping into the woman behind her in the queue.

'Sorry,' she muttered, 'forgot something.'

It took only a few minutes to return everything to its place on the rails. Now with money burning a hole in her pocket, she forced herself to leave the department store before she was tempted to look at baby things. She'd go and visit her grandmother instead.

Her grandmother was asleep when she visited. This was becoming more and more common. Alex had mentioned that she'd been asleep when he'd seen her the night before last. Kate sat beside her for fifteen minutes before standing up to leave.

'You off, then?' said one of the care workers, a young man called Billy.

'She's asleep. I don't want to disturb her.'

Billy's smile was sympathetic. 'Yes, she's asleep most of the time now.'

Kate's grandmother stirred then and opened her eyes.

'Oh, she's waking up.' said Billy. 'I'll leave you to it.'

'Hello, dear. Is Alex with you?'

'No, he's at work, Gran.'

'He works too hard.'

'Yes, he does. How are you?'

'I'm tired, Sandra dear. I want to sleep.'

Kate studied the careworn face. She never knew what to say or do when her grandmother confused her with her mother.

'Oh, silly me. I'm getting confused again. It's Kate, isn't it?' She closed her eyes. 'You were such a bonny baby.'

'Yes, Gran, it's Kate,' said Kate. On impulse she added, 'I'm pregnant, eleven weeks. You're going to be a great-grandmother.' But there was no reaction. Her grandmother was asleep once more.

Chapter Twelve

AFTER A FEW HOURS' sleep, Alex was ready to face going into work. He bought himself a fish supper on the way, telling himself Kate would never find out. He arrived at Govan police station bloated and ashamed at yet another lapse. What made it worse was the PC who indicated to him on his way to the interview room that he had tomato ketchup on his chin. He dived into the gents to check there were no more mishaps to be seen. The way his luck was going, he wouldn't be surprised if there were coffee stains on his shirt or a bogey poking out of his nose.

Little progress had been made with the arsonist in the time he'd been away. He got a brief update from the DS who'd been carrying out the interview.

'His lawyer has advised him to say "no comment" to everything. It's a waste of time. We should charge him and get on with something more productive.'

He was right but Alex had to have one last go at him. He went through to the interview room and settled himself into his chair. He nodded to the lawyer in acknowledgement

The Fallen

before saying to the accused, 'I hear you can't comment on anything.'

'No comment.'

Alex laughed. 'It wasn't a question, son.'

'No comment.'

'And neither was that.'

'No comment.'

This wasn't funny. Alex turned off the tape. 'You're a friend of Kai Anderson, aren't you? And don't say a word, because that was a rhetorical question. But then I don't suppose you know what that is.'

The boy – he was nineteen – but looked five years younger, yawned and shrugged. His lawyer tapped a biro on the table.

'Do you have any further questions for my client?'

Alex ignored him. 'Kai's in deep shit after messing up that job. He had to get out of Glasgow. I suppose it'll be the same for you. He was on the first bus to the big smoke. Word is, your boss doesn't like failure, and you, well, what you did was hardly a success, was it?'

'Is this relevant?' The lawyer's face was tight with irritation. 'And that tape should be on, as you well know.'

Alex switched the tape on again. 'Interview resumed at four thirty-six p.m. How long have you been a member of that drug gang?'

'No comment.'

This was going nowhere. He should charge the wee shit now and get home. He was due time off after his all-nighter. A tap on the door stopped him. He switched off the tape again.

'Excuse me,' he said.

Outside, a worried looking sergeant spoke to him. Alex's stomach churned when he heard what he had to say.

'OK, thanks.'

Back in the interview room, he studied the boy who'd tried to burn down Mark's flat. He looked exhausted and less cocky than he'd been the night before. Alex addressed the lawyer.

'You might like time alone with your client once I've said what I'm going to say.' He then turned to the boy, 'Your friend, Kai Anderson has been found. Dead, I'm sorry to say, and believe me, I truly am sorry. I spent a long time talking to his mother. She was in despair over her son. Her only child. Can you imagine what that despair looks like now?' Alex paused, the boy had tears in his eyes. 'I can see how upset you are, Liam, so I'll leave you to talk things over with Mr Jamieson here. I'm going to have to go and speak to Kai's mother now.'

Alex had a female police officer with him. He didn't have to be the one to break the news to Kai's mother, but he owed her that respect. When they reached the house he sat for a moment, wanting to put off the dreadful moment.

'Sir?' said the PC, 'Shouldn't we go in?'

Alex sighed. 'Yeah. Let's get it over with.'

When Mrs Anderson answered the door, he saw in her eyes that she knew why they were there. Fair play to her, she didn't make a fuss but said in a subdued voice, 'You'd better come in.'

Once inside, they all sat down. Her face was white and strained looking.

The Fallen

'My husband will be home in a few minutes, we should wait—' she broke off at the sound of a key in the door. 'That's him now.'

Kai's father was slower off the mark than his wife had been. 'What's all this then? Have they caught the wee bugger at last?' No one replied, and his eyes widened with anguish when realisation washed over him. 'Oh no, no. It can't be. Tell me it's not true.'

'I'm very sorry, Mr and Mrs Anderson, but a body has been found in Bellahouston Park and we have good reasons to believe it's your son."

'What reasons?' Mr Anderson stared at them, the fear obvious in his face.

'A bank card with his name on it as well as his driving licence were found on his body.' Alex paused. 'I'm very sorry. Of course, he will need to be formally identified, and an officer will take you to do that later.'

'But he's in London. It can't be him. Fran, phone your sister.'

His wife looked at him in despair. The tears that had been absent were now pouring down her face. 'Sharon phoned me first thing this morning, said she tried to dissuade him, but he disappeared last night saying he was going home. I've been on edge all day waiting for him to appear.'

'Oh, Jesus Christ. What are we going to do?' Mr Anderson put his head in his hands and let out a howl that chilled Alex, it was so despairing.

The rest of the visit passed in a blur. Alex made them tea at one point and he and the police officer waited until Fran's mother came round to offer support. Before they left, Fran pulled him aside.

'It's Liam Brown you've got in custody, isn't it? He was

one of Kai's best friends. Can you give him a message from me?'

Alex listened carefully. 'I'll pass that on, Fran.' He took her hand. 'Once again, I'm so sorry for your loss. Someone will be in touch soon to take you to formally identify him.'

Tears were streaming down her face. 'Please, don't let it happen to Liam, too. I don't want anyone else to get hurt.'

Alex and the woman police officer left the grieving family.

Back in the car, Alex said, 'It's been years since I had to tell a family about a loved one dying. It doesn't get any easier.'

Truth was, it was more difficult the more times you did it. That one had been particularly bad. The Andersons were an ordinary family who found themselves in the middle of a tragedy. Alex felt sick as they drove back to the station in silence. He was thinking mainly about the parents and their grief. They weren't bad people and, from the sound of it, Kai hadn't been a bad lad, just a stupid wee boy who got in with the wrong company. It happened so easily. In his experience, not all criminals were intrinsically bad, thoughtless, yes, and impulsive and frequently with horrendous life experiences that had traumatised them. Whoever was heading up this drug gang, though, they came close to evil. And evil wasn't a word he habitually used. Who could have murdered Kai? One of the Dunmore triplets, perhaps? Now, they were a bad lot. But who would tell the truth about them? They didn't tolerate grasses, that much was clear from how Kai, and now this other kid they had in custody, behaved.

When he got back to the station, the lawyer met him with a grim smile on his face. 'That was a nasty trick you played on my client there.'

Alex managed to refrain from swearing at the man. The wee shite wanted his face flattened, so he did. 'What are you talking about?' he asked, keeping his rage under wraps. It wasn't the lawyer's fault Kai was dead.

'Pretending his pal was dead, murdered, so as to get a confession out of him. Well, your wee plan hasn't worked. I've told him what I think is going on, and you'll get nothing from him.'

Count to ten, don't punch him in his fat fuck of a face. Alex moved closer to him and was pleased to see a hint of fear on Jamieson's face as he moved back.

'Mr Jamieson, Kai Anderson is dead. He came back to Glasgow this morning, we think on the overnight bus from London, and this afternoon, he was found dead in Bellahouston Park. Stabbed. Who knows what he was doing there, but the other gang members sniffed him out, and they'll sniff out Liam as well, when he's released later today.'

'You're lying,' spluttered the lawyer. Where the fuck had they found this guy? He'd not come across him before, and he was much less amenable than most of the lawyers Alex dealt with.

Alex turned his back to him. 'Have it your own way, but I have a message to deliver to Liam, so if you'd like to follow me, we'll resume the interview.'

The colour had come back to Liam's face and some of his cockiness, as well. The lawyer had done a good job on him.

'Liam,' said Alex after he'd switched on the tape, 'I've come from seeing Kai's parents. His mum was very keen that I should pass on a message to you.'

The sneer on Liam's face wavered for a second then returned. 'Go on, then,' he said.

'She told me about how you were his best friend at school,

never apart, even though Kai was older than you. "Never apart," she said. "They used to go up to the reccie after school and play football for hours. They were rascals, don't get me wrong but it wasn't until the drugs got them that things went downhill. Before he went to London, Kai told me how it was he'd got Liam into the drugs and how he regretted it."' Alex paused and looked closely at Liam. His face was unreadable. He went on. 'She said you'd resisted at first, told Kai how you wanted to stay fit for football.' There was a sharp intake of breath from Liam. Alex was getting through to him at last. He couldn't help himself; he shot a triumphant look at the lawyer who glared at him. 'And then one day after he'd mocked you, you agreed, and, bang, that was you. In with the big boys. "If you see Liam," she said, "Tell him how sorry Kai was. Tell him to get out of Glasgow. Kai would have been all right if he'd stayed in London. They wouldn't have found him there. But Glasgow's too small. Tell him."'

Liam was motionless for a moment, then his face crumpled as he turned to his lawyer. 'You told me the polis were bluffing, and Kai wasn't dead. You're fucking shite, so you are.'

'No, no. All I said was, be careful what you believe.'

'Aye, well, I believe him, not you. The only way he found out those things about me was from Kai's maw. He's spoken to her all right. Get the fuck out of here. I don't want you as my lawyer.' Liam put his head down on his desk and sobbed.

'Liam, are you sure you don't want a lawyer here?' said Alex. 'You are entitled to one.'

A muffled reply. 'Get him out of here.'

'I'll be available if you need me,' said Jamieson. He picked up his briefcase and left.

Alex turned the tape off. 'Shall I get us a cup of tea?'

The Fallen

A shake of the head, then, 'Do youse have any ginger? Irn-Bru?'

'I'll see what we have. Have you had anything to eat? Shall I get you a McDonald's or a pizza?'

'I don't think I can eat anything.' He wiped his nose on his sleeve and reconsidered. 'Maybe a poke of chips?'

Alex left the room and asked for a bag of chips, Irn-Bru and a cup of tea to be brought to the interview room. He decided to give Liam a little time to himself. He was shaken up by what had been revealed, that much was clear. Despite what he'd done, Alex felt sorry for him. Perhaps if he thought things through, he might tell them something. But the future didn't look good for him and in two hours' time, once he'd been charged, he'd be released, and who knew what was going to happen then.

While he was waiting, he phoned Mark to update him. 'Mark, how're you doing?'

'Dying of boredom, mate. Any news?'

Alex told him what had happened.

'Jesus, they're ruthless that lot, aren't they? That poor kid, He should have stayed in London where he was safe.'

'Homesickness, according to his aunt. Ach, Mark, the parents. They were destroyed. Kai was their only child. It was unbearable, know what I mean?' He didn't wait for an answer but continued. 'Anyway, I'd better get back and see if Liam wants to say anything other than "no comment". If not, I'll have to charge him and release him. The Procurator Fiscal says there's enough to charge him with attempted arson, but as no one was in the flat at the time, it's not a serious enough charge to remand him in custody. No matter what, I doubt he'd be safe there, but he certainly won't be safe out in the community. I'll speak to you later if there's any updates.'

When Alex went back into the room, Liam had composed himself. He was picking at the chips, his appetite clearly gone. He pushed them aside when Alex sat down.

'I'm feart,' he said.

'Do you want to tell me what happened? Remember, you're under caution, and I will have to tape it. I can get you another lawyer.'

'No, I want to get it over with. Way I see it, I'm fucked, like Kai was. It was like what Kai's maw said—'

'Hang on, let me get the tape going, and I'll need to get another officer to sit in.' Once that was done, he told Liam to carry on.

'Kai took the piss out of me because I wouldn't try drugs, but I wanted to be a footballer. All my friends did, but I was good. I had a trial for Partick Thistle a couple of years ago.'

'Good man,' smiled Alex. 'They're my favourite team.'

'Aye, well, turned out they didn't want me after all, and that, combined with Kai's taunting, brought me in. I can tell you who the heid honchos are in Glasgow, but you'll have to protect me.'

Alex was taken by surprise. He'd thought the guy would say nothing.

'OK. That's above my pay grade, I'll need to speak to someone.' He switched the tape off and left the PC with Liam. Two minutes later, he was on the phone to the superintendent, and then the Procurator Fiscal. 'I think we can get to whoever is behind this gang if we go with this.'

'All right,' said the PF. 'We'll go for a lesser charge citing duress as a mitigating factor, if he agrees to give evidence against them.'

Alex returned to the room and explained to Liam what would happen. 'So, if you agree to give evidence against whoever's in charge in Glasgow, we can charge you with a lesser offence. Arson is an extremely serious crime. Doesn't matter if it's unsuccessful. The prosecution will argue that although the flat was empty, serious psychological harm was done to your intended victim, and you could end up with twelve years in jail. But if there are mitigating factors and no serious harm was done to the victim, then it would be reduced considerably to two years or so.'

'Fuck,' said Liam. 'Aw, shite, I'll tell you what happened.' He took a deep breath. 'Have you heard of the Dunmore triplets? Jake, Sam and Sonny?'

The Dunmores again. 'I have, aye.'

'They're in charge in Glasgow. They get the drugs from down south and the Dunmores are in charge of distribution here. They specialise in getting youngsters involved, some are only wee kids, eleven or twelve years old. And they're terrifying. You must know that, right? Nobody dares cross them, not the polis, nobody. Recently, they've got much worse. It started with that daft bird and the bloke who killed her man. I don't know the details.'

Alex did. This was exactly what he'd thought. It was the case Mark had given evidence in. Eighteen months ago, a young woman had conspired with her lover to murder her partner who was a member of a rival drugs gang. They made it look like a fight outside a pub. What followed, was an outbreak of revenge killings as two gangs fought to gain leverage over the other.

'Go on,' said Alex. 'What else do you have?'

The triplets were nicknamed the triple Krays because of their ruthlessness. No one was prepared to stand up to them.

They had terrorised their entire neighbourhood, and beyond. Alex listened to Liam without interrupting him. There was no stopping him, and what he said was very interesting indeed. There was a link to Barlinnie. Kai's mum had been right in saying that. It appeared that someone inside was either running things himself or giving the orders to people on the outside. Liam remained adamant he didn't know any more. All he said was he'd heard it was "an old bloke"', and eventually, Alex admitted defeat. But he had enough to get a start. And he'd begin by finding out who Kai's associates were when he'd been inside.

Chapter Thirteen

THE PHONE CALL took him by surprise. It was the middle of the night, and he was dreaming he was hiding drugs in his flat. The ring tone of his personal mobile rang out with the dulcet tones of Angus chanting "Alex, Alex" in his ear. He woke up confused, baffled as to what the child was doing in his bedroom and whether he might find the drugs, before he remembered he'd changed the ring tone on the day Mark and the toddler had moved out from his flat. He'd forgotten all about it because he rarely used his own phone. Few people knew his personal number and even Kate phoned him on his police issue one as he was more often than not, working.

'Yes?'

'Mr Scrimgeour, it's Julie Bremner, I'm night manager at the nursing home. Your mother... well, you should come as soon as possible.'

For years, he'd been expecting and dreading this moment. 'I'll be there in fifteen minutes.'

He leapt out of bed and started to get dressed. He could barely stand he was so tired and as he was going into the

167

kitchen to get a glass of water he stumbled over a bag of shopping Kate had left there and cursed. Damn, he hoped he hadn't woken Kate and Conor.

'Dad? What are you doing?' Kate came out of her bedroom, hair standing on end. Her face was flushed with sleep.

'It's your gran. The nursing home have called for me to go in. I don't understand it, she was fine when I saw her two nights ago.' But as he said it, he thought of how she'd been awake for so little time, of how the care worker he'd spoken to had said she'd slept all day, of how many times he'd experienced the same thing over the past few months. She'd been slipping away, and he'd been too busy to notice. 'I'd better go,' he said.

'We'll come with you,' said Kate. 'No, no arguments,' as he opened his mouth. 'Conor will drive. You're knackered and I'm not having you driving when you're exhausted.'

He wanted to argue but found he couldn't. 'Thank you,' he said. 'But be quick.'

Five minutes later they were on their way. It was after three in the morning and there was no traffic on the road. There were only the traffic lights to slow them down and they got to the home in fourteen minutes.

'I'll wait in the car,' said Conor.

'No, Conor, you have work in the morning.' said Alex. 'Best go home and try to get back to sleep. We'll get a taxi home.'

The night manager was at the door and took them to her office to explain what was happening. 'Your mother is comfortable, but she took a turn for the worse before bedtime last night. She has pneumonia. She's been refusing to get out of her bed the past week and won't sit up in bed. Unfortunately, that increases the risk of lung infections.'

'Has she seen a doctor?'

'Yes, she gave your mum antibiotics, but I have to warn you, she's very ill.'

Alex had often wondered how he would feel when this moment came. It was so long since she'd been the woman who'd brought him up, the woman who used to take him and his brother, Billy, to the park to play on the swings, who read to them at bedtime until they begged her to stop because they were too old and it wasn't cool to have a story read to you. They wanted to read books for themselves. That woman was long gone. So, too, was the woman who had welcomed him and Sandra home from hospital with their first and only child. She'd cleaned their house from top to bottom, stocked their freezer with enough meals for a week, and then after a cuddle with little Mairi, as Kate then was, took herself off home.

The care home manager carried on talking, but Alex was lost in his memories, good and bad, and barely heard her. Having to tell his mother Mairi was gone was one of the worst moments of his life. She had doted on her granddaughter. Her face had gone stony when she found out Sandra's part in it.

'I'll never forgive her, son. What was she thinking? And with Jimmy of all people. Bastards.' It was the first time Alex had heard her swear. She'd been strict with him and his brother when they were growing up, never allowed a hint of a swear word, threatening to wash out their mouths with soap and water if they ever muttered a curse. Alex smiled to himself. That had all changed with the Alzheimer's. Her younger self would have been horrified if she'd known she would use such language in her old age. After Mairi disappeared, she'd never been the same and it was one of the biggest regrets in his life that she didn't fully understand Kate and Mairi were one and the same person. She sort of knew Kate was her granddaughter, but often she forgot and would become confused, asking if Alex had married again. Thinking of these things reminded him he hadn't informed Gillian. He interrupted the manager.

'Did you phone my niece Gillian?'

'Yes, I did. She said she would come in the morning. I did say it might be too late by then, but she didn't reply.'

It didn't surprise Alex that Gillian had refused to come. She'd hardly visited when her grandmother was alive so why would she come when she was dying? All the same, he was relieved she wasn't here. Her passive aggressiveness was hard to take at the best of times. It would be intolerable now. It was fitting and right that only he and Kate were here.

The night manager broke into his ruminations. 'Do you want to go along to her room now? One of the carers is with her.'

As soon as he saw her, Alex knew his mother had little time left. He'd always been amazed at how nurses and doctors were so confident in their assessments of a dying patient. It was in their face. Or rather it wasn't. The muscles of her face had relaxed, and her skin was paler than he'd ever seen it. Her breathing was shallow and intermittent. Alex touched her hand, it was cold, and he resisted the urge to rub it to warm it up though he held it as tight as he dared. He didn't want to hurt her. The carer offered up her seat and went to fetch one for Kate. They sat at either side of her bed. 'Talk to her,' said the carer. Play a favourite tune. Hearing is

The Fallen

the last sense to go.' She went to the door. 'I'll leave you alone now. Call me if you need anything.'

What did you say to a dying person? One who was no longer the person they'd once been? One who didn't recognise you from one moment to the next? He looked at Kate in despair. Tears were running down his face.

'Gran,' said Kate. 'It's me, Kate, your granddaughter. I wish we'd got to know one another better.' Janet stirred and muttered something that sounded like *Where's Mairi?*

'It's all right, Mairi's here with you and Alex is, too. Alex is your son, my father. He's a bit of a grump but he's a great dad. I love him and I love you, too, Gran.'

Alex felt better now Kate had spoken. He took out his phone and put on a piece of music he remembered her playing a lot when he was a child. *Wonderful World* by Louis Armstrong. It played softly in the background as he spoke to her.

'Mum, you're OK. You don't need to fight anymore. It'll be fine, you can let go.' He had no idea whether it would be OK. Religion must be a comfort, he thought. Imagine if you did get to see the people you loved once again. Might get a little complicated, though, for those widows and widowers who got themselves new partners. What was he doing? He wasn't concentrating on what was important – his mother. He listened carefully, there hadn't been a breath for several seconds. Then it came, a long sigh followed by silence. He counted to thirty. 'I think she's gone, Kate.'

'Should I get the manager?'

'No, let's sit here with her for a while.' Louis Armstrong came to the end of his song and Alex switched off his phone. 'Those were lovely words, Kate. She adored you as a baby. I don't think she ever got over your kidnap. She was never the same afterwards.'

'It's not surprising. It must have been devastating for her, for you.'

They sat lost in their own thoughts for half an hour or so. Alex was the first to stand up. 'We'd better tell Mrs Bremner now. And I should phone your cousin.' They walked slowly along the corridor to the office.

The manager was sympathetic but brisk. Alex appreciated her matter-of-fact manner as she outlined to them what they needed to do. The GP for the home would come round later in the day to issue the death certificate. Once they had that, they could get in touch with a funeral parlour. She recommended the Co-op as very efficient and reliable and gave them a leaflet outlining all the things they had to do. Thank goodness, he thought. He had taken in hardly anything she'd said. By the time he got round to phoning Gillian, it was five to seven.

'Gillian, it's Alex. It's bad news, I'm afraid. Your grandmother died at five o'clock this morning.'

There was silence for a few seconds before she spoke. 'It's seven o'clock now, why have you waited all this time to tell me?'

He looked at his phone in disbelief and took a deep breath before saying anything. 'There were things to do, Gillian.'

'All of them more important than telling her only granddaughter?'

Alex found it hard to keep the anger from his voice, but he managed and was proud of how calmly he spoke to her. 'You're not her only grandchild as you're well aware. And you were given the chance to come but you said you'd be there first thing this morning instead.'

'I didn't realise she'd die so quickly.' Her voice was high with indignation. 'And I'm the only grandchild she ever knew.'

She wasn't being rational, grief did that to you, so Alex kept his temper and refrained from saying what he thought. As he did so, though, he couldn't imagine ever forgiving her for the way she was speaking to him. However, this wasn't the right time to get into an argument with her, much as he longed to.

'We need to meet to discuss the funeral arrangements. I'll contact the Co-op to arrange the funeral, but we need to discuss the details.'

'The Co-op? How common. Granny would have been appalled at the thought.'

Was she deliberately trying to pick a fight? In fact, years earlier, before the dementia had taken her from them all, his mother had written down what she wanted but Alex didn't raise that now. Instead, he said keeping his voice level and calm.

'Well, as I say, it's details now that are important. Where and when do you want to meet?'

Five more awkward minutes of conversation followed and, at last, they agreed to meet at Alex's flat in the afternoon. Kate asked him about this as they waited for the taxi that they'd called to take them back to her flat. 'Why not ask her to mine?'

'It's time I went back to my own place and now I know for sure it was Mark who the gang were after and not me, there's no reason not to.' He filled her in on what Liam had told him.

When he'd finished speaking, she looked him in the eye and said again in a firmer voice, 'Why not ask her to mine? What's the real reason.'

Alex felt foolish as he told her. 'I don't want her finding out where you live. She's so jealous of you, it's unreal. Who can tell what she might do or say.'

Kate frowned. 'Don't be daft, Dad. What's she going to do? Scratch my face with those talons of hers?' Gillian treated herself regularly to manicures. Last time he'd seen her, they were long, pointed and a deep, crimson red. The nails of a woman who never did housework.

Alex didn't think he was overstating his case. Gillian was nasty and he wasn't going to take any chances. She wouldn't hear from him where Kate lived. 'I don't trust her,' he muttered.

'Do you want me to come with you to meet her?'

'No, best to do it myself I think.'

When they got back to Kate's flat, he phoned his work to say what had happened.

'I won't be in for a few days,' he said to Pamela when he finally got hold of her. 'My mother died last night.'

'I'm sorry to hear that, Alex. You must take as much time as you need. The death of a parent, it hits hard. She might have been old but she's your mum.' There was no hint of snarkiness in her voice today.

Taken aback by her kind and sincere words, Alex thanked her and rung off. It was time to go home now and prepare for what was undoubtedly going to be an uncomfortable meeting.

The Fallen

He'd hardly had time to take off his jacket and put the kettle on when his doorbell rang. He padded through to answer, thinking it was unlike Gillian to be so early. However, it was Alice, his neighbour from downstairs.

'Alex, you're back. I saw your car. I'm so pleased.' She stepped inside without waiting for his invitation. 'How are you? We've all been so worried.'

'I... um, this isn't a good time, Alice. I—'

'Oh, I'm sorry.' She stepped back. 'It was, well, it's not every day there's a shooting in the street. And then you disappear for over a week to God knows where. We've all been worried about you.'

It had been remiss of him not to keep his neighbours updated, and he apologised before saying, 'Alice, I'm sorry but my mother died during the night, and I have to meet with my niece in half an hour to discuss the funeral arrangements.'

Her face fell. 'I'm so sorry,' she reached out and rubbed his arm in an attempt to comfort him, but Alex wasn't used to physical contact and pulled back. 'If there's anything I can do, Alex. Anything at all.'

'Thank you,' he managed. 'But I think we'll be fine. I should have told you and everyone else about the case. I'm sorry, I wasn't thinking straight. It turns out I wasn't the target, so no one here needs to worry about a return of the gunman.' Alex had been going to keep the information that the gunman had been murdered in Bellahouston Park yesterday to himself, but she was way ahead of him.

'He's dead, isn't he? The man who tried to shoot you? It was on the news last night with a photo of him. He was a dead ringer for that photofit put out by the police.'

He didn't deny it but neither did he confirm it.

'It's OK, don't say another word. Obviously, you're not

allowed to talk about it. I shouldn't have asked. Well, once all this is over, you must come down for a drink. It would be good to get to know you better. And Alex,' the hand reached out again, 'I'm so sorry about your mother.'

This time he managed not to draw back from her. He made a non-committal noise and moved towards the door, hoping she'd take the hint and go. At the door, she hugged him. Christ, what was he to make of that? It was too much. He stood stiffly, not reciprocating. Alex had never been a hugger, and he hardly knew this woman. Alice released him with a last pat on the back. 'I'll see you soon.'

There was no food in the flat of course. Nothing to offer Gillian. Another black mark against him. He should have stopped off at the shops on his way over. It was now twenty minutes before she was due at the flat. He should be able to make it to the wee supermarket at the Monument to the Battle of Langside if he was quick. He put his jacket back on.

Gillian was early. Just his luck. She was standing on the steps outside the close when he came back with his provisions.

'Sorry, there was nothing in the house. I've been living at Kate's since I was shot at. Did you hear about that?'

Gillian didn't reply. She followed him upstairs in silence. Alex had to stop himself from sighing heavily when they got inside.

'Coffee?' he asked.

'Is it freshly ground?'

'No,' he didn't elaborate. 'Tea then?'

'A glass of water will do.'

He ran the tap and got out a glass, which he filled. When

he handed it to her, she looked at him as though he had offered her a dead mouse.

'Don't you have bottled water?'

'Shall we get on with this?' He sat down at the kitchen table.

Gillian sat down, made a show of pushing the water aside before she took a notebook out of her bag. She immediately began to talk. 'There's a nice little church near to where I live. It will be perfect for the service. Does she have a burial plot? Because if not, then that's a priority. I've been thinking about hymns, too, *The Lord is my Shepherd* of course and—'

'Hang on, Gillian. Mum left clear instructions for what she wanted.'

'Oh, right.' Her nose wrinkled. 'Was she compos mentis when she did it?'

'When she was given the diagnosis of Alzheimer's she sat down with me and your dad and stated explicitly what she wanted: Cremation in Linn Crematorium, reception at House for an Art Lover, ashes to be scattered in Pollok Country Park. There's more details of course, but that summarises it.'

'Yes, but you said she had the diagnosis. Surely, she wasn't up to it.'

'She was. It was at the beginning of her illness.'

'And do you have proof of all this?'

Alex rubbed his forehead attempting to erase the headache that was threatening him. What had happened to Gillian to make her this way? She'd been an undemanding child as far as he recalled. Admittedly he hadn't known her well. He'd eschewed get-togethers with his brother and sister-in-law after the twin tragedy of his daughter's disappearance and wife's suicide, and by the time he was up to socialising, they'd separated, and his brother hardly ever got to see Gillian. Billy had re-married but it didn't last long. The woman had two children from a previous relationship, and although he knew no details, they'd never accepted Billy in spite of all his efforts. Efforts that meant that Alex had to take on more than his fair share of responsibilities with regard to their mother.

'I do, yes.'

'I'd like to see it.'

Alex looked through the file in front of him; the file his mother had made up when she still had good cognitive functioning. What was it she'd said to him? 'I want the arrangements to be clear cut so there's no arguments after I've gone, so I've written down all my wishes in my will. You'd better see you carry them out or I'll be back to haunt you.' Had she guessed Gillian would be difficult. If so, she'd never said a word against her. But it was a possibility. She might have reasoned that Gillian took after her mother. Mum had never liked Jacqui much.

He and Billy had argued with their mum about her desire for a humanist celebrant. She'd been a member of the Church of Scotland all her life, though she had stopped going when Mairi disappeared. 'Yes, I'm sure. I want nothing more to do with the church. I stopped believing when Mairi was taken. I prayed and prayed she'd be returned to us and what did I get? Nothing. So, no. At my funeral I want nothing about God. He ignored me so I'm going to ignore him from now on.'

Alex wasn't a believer, but he'd never had much time for those who claimed to have faith but lost it as soon as something bad happened to them. He'd said as much, but there had been no convincing her of the poor logic of her thoughts.

Truth to tell, both he and his brother had discussed her ability to make these decisions at the time, but the consultant they spoke to assured them she was cognitively able. And he certainly wasn't going to reveal their doubts to Gillian now.

He took out the Will and handed it to Gillian. 'It's all in there. In fact you can keep that, I have several copies. As you can see, I'm the executor and the estate is to be divided between her living direct descendants including those *in utero* at the time of her death.'

'What does that mean?'

'You, me and Kate will share her estate three ways unless of course either of you is pregnant in which case the child will inherit an equal share once born.'

She frowned. 'Don't I get my Dad's share?'

'The estate will be shared between living descendants.' With an effort Alex spoke calmly. He was not going to get into an argument with her. But Gillian had moved on to another topic.

'How much is left?'

'Sorry?'

'How much money is there?'

'I don't think it'll be all that much. The fees for the nursing home were many thousands of pounds a year and they ate into much of what she got from the sale of the bungalow.'

'She must have had savings.'

Alex was exhausted and unable to think straight. There are some other investments but to tell the truth I haven't looked at them. There was enough money readily available to pay for another six or seven months and I was waiting for—'

'For what? For her to die? How do I know you haven't been dipping into her savings yourself?'

Alex stood up. 'I think you should go, Gillian, before you say anything more. You're upset, so we'll leave it there. Your grandmother's money is all accounted for, every single last penny.' You're welcome to inspect the accounts, of course.'

He was pleased to see her blush but didn't expect what she said next. He'd thought she'd apologise for her crassness, but no.

'I think that would be best. I'll have a look at them after the funeral.' She stood up and without another word, walked out of the flat.

Thank goodness she'd gone. Gillian had never been easy to deal with, but this was a new low. Once the business with the will was over, he doubted he'd ever see her again. It saddened him that his only niece disliked and mistrusted him, but there it was. To distract himself from these thoughts he tidied up the kitchen before starting on his list of things to do. Before he could though, his mobile rang out.

'Mr Scrimgeour, is Krzysztof, the plumber. I come tomorrow if OK?'

Shit. The fact that the plumber was due to start on his bathroom tomorrow had completely fled his mind with all that had gone on in the past week. For a moment he considered putting him off but quickly decided not to. He'd waited four months for this slot. Krzysztof, who was Polish and highly skilled in his trade, was in demand, and it might be six months or more before he was available again. Everything was stacked up ready and waiting in the hall and it would all be done in a week, and best of all, out of the way before the funeral.

'Yes, Krzysztof. That'll be fine. What time will you be round?'

'Eight o'clock. And please, call me Kris. Is easier for you, I think.'

'Ah, OK. I'll see you then.' Alex put the phone done. He'd make himself a coffee and then start on the organisation of the funeral. First things first, he'd collect the death certificate and then get the death registered.

Chapter Fourteen

It didn't take long to arrange the funeral. It was a great help to have his mother's wishes written down so clearly. There was no need to search for music or through poetry books for readings. It was all there in her perfect copperplate script. A meeting with the funeral director set everything in motion, and within a few hours, the crematorium had been booked for a fortnight hence, the booking had been made for a reception at the House for an Art Lover and an appointment made with his mother's lawyer to discuss her will. He put a notice in *The Herald* and phoned her closest friends. All that remained to do was to meet the humanist celebrant to pass on details of his mother's life and to sort out his mother's possessions. He phoned Gillian, taking a deep breath when she answered in her usual abrupt manner.

'It's Alex, Gillian. I've as good as finished all the arrangements now. The cremation is at Linn Crematorium two weeks tomorrow at two p.m. followed by a reception at House for an Art Lover from three p.m. onwards. It's a simple coffin, as Mum requested, and no flowers except family ones. Donations to be sent to the Alzheimer's Society or there's a JustGiving page I've set up."

'Fine,' she said. 'I'll see you then.'

'Hang on a second,' he said, worried she was going to cut him off. 'There's a couple of other things to discuss. The celebrant wants to meet us so as to get a sense of the sort of person Mum was. I thought if we got together, Tuesday or Wednesday next week? When would suit you?'

'I'm busy,' she said.

'All week?' Alex didn't bother to hide his disbelief.

'Yes, all week.'

Aye, right, he thought. No way was she busy every evening for a week. 'Well, is there anything you would like me to tell the celebrant, any memories of your gran you'd like to pass on?'

'No.'

Alex counted to ten in his head. 'Nothing at all? You're happy for Kate and I to meet the celebrant without you?'

'You might as well. All my wishes have been completely ignored.'

His hand was balling into a fist. 'It's not up to us, Gillian. Mum set out what she wanted.' She didn't reply so he carried on. 'Well, if you're sure. There's one other thing, though. Kate has offered to go through Mum's possessions, sort out clothes for charity and so on. Perhaps you'd like to help?'

'No. Although there are one or two pieces of jewellery of Gran's that I want.'

Alex noted the peremptory 'want'.

'I'll ask Kate to put any valuables aside and we'll discuss what you can have. But anything personal should be shared between you.'

A sniff. 'We'll see about that.' And with that she hung up.

The arrangements were made, so Alex decided to go back to work the next day. It was better that way. Otherwise he would have too much time on his hands and might start to brood. Silently, he thanked his mother for her foresight in leaving all her papers in such good order. She'd gone through it all: savings accounts, investments, insurance policies and handed them over to him. What a contrast to when his brother died. Billy had died suddenly, and that made it all so much more difficult. It happened not long after the break-up of Billy's second marriage, and he was only fifty. A heart attack. It was a shock to everyone, not least his second ex-wife who was stunned to find she'd been left with nothing. What did she expect, thought Alex. A medal for infidelity? She'd left Billy a few weeks before and assumed he hadn't got round to changing his will. In fact, it was the first thing he did when he discovered her affair with a younger man. Alex remembered thinking at the time that he and his brother hadn't had much luck with their women. Nothing but faithless wives. It was a shock to Leanne to discover Billy had left her nothing. Half his estate went to Gillian, and the rest was shared out between various charities. She'd been fuming.

Although Billy left a will, the rest of his papers were in disarray and took a great deal more sorting out than his mother's estate. Alex had been the executor for his will, too, and he recalled sitting in Billy's kitchen going through his papers. There were bills to be paid, bank statements to be gone through, bank accounts to be found. Billy had no decent filing system, and it had taken months to sort everything out. In addition, there were the two bitter, feuding ex-wives nagging him all the time. One was bad enough but Jacqui although she knew she had been left nothing was keen to see Gillian get her hands on her rightful inheritance.

No, this time was much easier, no house to sell, no mobile phone contracts and broadband to cancel, no utility companies to contact. Alex grimaced as he remembered a phone call he'd had with a hapless young woman at the energy company when Billy died. Most companies he'd contacted had a department that dealt specifically with what to do when a customer died. Not this one. The girl had been clueless. She tried to put him through to a supervisor, but God knows why, she continued to try to chat to him on the phone while he was waiting instead of putting him on hold.

'What sort of day are you having, sir? A good one, I hope.'

Alex had been stunned. It was all he could do not to swear at her. 'I told you not five minutes ago about my brother dying. What sort of day do you think I'm having?'

She hadn't replied. Later, he thought of complaining to the company, but it wasn't the girl's fault. Call centre workers had little training. Though a little common sense wouldn't have gone amiss.

Anyway, he was mostly done with his mother's affairs. A few phone calls and it was sorted, all bar the investments. But his lawyer would deal with them. Although he'd dealt with probate himself with Billy's estate, he'd hand this one over to his lawyer given the difficulties with Gillian. It was better this way. The lawyer was optimistic it shouldn't take long. But it hadn't stopped Gillian phoning him to find out when she might expect her inheritance. His mother was barely cold. What a contrast to Kate, whose only questions had been to ask what she could do to help. Gillian also tried over and over to get him to say how much money there was.

'I've no idea,' he'd said. 'The investments were made a

long time ago. I don't imagine they're worth too much. But there is a life insurance policy so there should be money from that.'

There was a long silence. Alex decided to wait. Eventually she spoke. 'You're claiming the investments are worth nothing to cover up how you've mismanaged her affairs.'

'Well, I've handed it all over to my lawyer, so she's dealing with it all.' He'd put his phone down before he said anything he might regret. He could have added that the main reason he'd handed probate to the lawyer was to avoid this sort of accusatory conversation with Gillian. If she had been more trusting, they could have saved a few thousand pounds. But he kept his peace. When this was over, he need never see her again.

Little had happened in the two days he was off. Liam Brown was trying to strike a deal with the procurator fiscal, but from the sound of it, he wasn't getting what he wanted. The trouble was, the only names he had were those of the Dunmore triplets, but he didn't have any concrete evidence to give them, and therefore, had no bargaining power to speak of. He said he didn't know the name of the man who'd instructed him to set fire to Mark's flat. He'd been given instructions on a burner phone, so there was no trace of who had called him. All he could say was that the man sounded old. There were no handy text messages for the tech department to try to follow up. Nothing. It was a disappointing outcome from what had originally been a promising lead. Liam had been released but was staying with relatives in Aberdeenshire as it was thought he'd be safer there.

Alex hated to admit it, but they were stuck. Shane McGowan reported back from his visit to Barlinnie to interview Kai's cellmate and another prisoner who was said to have been close to him.

'Nothing much to report there. Both are non-starters as far as gang members go. The guy, McNicholl, is ancient and on his last legs, and the other one's inside for fraud. No connection to the gang whatsoever.'

Damn. They needed something concrete. Mark was getting restless. He'd phoned the previous evening begging to be allowed to come back to work, but Alex was sure it was too risky and told him to stay put. He was astonished, therefore, when, in the middle of writing a memo to all staff about the need to take annual leave in a timeous manner, Mark walked into the room.

'What the fuck?'

'Nice to see you, too,' said Mark.

'What are you doing here?'

'I had to get out of Edinburgh. They're that fucking po-faced there. Never crack a light, the lot of them. I'd have ended up doing myself in.'

'What have you done with the wee man?'

'Karen's got the day off and she offered to look after him. Only for one day, mind. I'll need to sort out child care for tomorrow.'

Alex put his head in his hands. He breathed slowly to calm himself. 'Do you not realise how serious this is? There's a hit out on you and now you've brought Karen into it? I mean. Fuck.' Mark glared at him, but Alex was in his stride and didn't hesitate. 'You're a stubborn bastard. I told you not to come back, but, no, you know better. Fuck. Wait there, I'll need to inform DCI Ferguson you've returned to work. He strode out of the room without another word. Furious didn't begin to describe him.

'Come in,' Pamela's voice rang out.

He went into the room.

'Alex,' her voice rose in surprise. 'I didn't think you'd be in for a while yet. I'm so sorry to hear about your mother.'

'Thank you, but I'm better at work. It will take my mind off everything. I've also got the builders in to install a new bathroom, so it's better to be out of their way.'

'Hmm. Would it not have been better to postpone them? It's hard dealing with builders at the best of times and with your mother...' she tailed off.

'They come highly recommended. I've been waiting months for them to start, and I've no intention of going back to the end of the queue. You can't move in my hallway for tiles and plasterboard.'

'Well, if you're sure you're fine to be back at work, I can't stop you.'

'I am but I will take two or three days off around the funeral.'

'Yes, of course. When is it?'

'In a fortnight.'

'So, how can I be of assistance?' For once she sounded as though she actually wanted to help.

'Mark Nicholson has returned to work,' he said, not bothering to hide his annoyance. 'I'm worried.'

Pamela tutted. 'Bloody idiot. What on earth was he thinking? Tell him to get his arse up here now.'

Alex's rage was waning, and he regretted his impulse of telling Pamela. He didn't want Mark getting into trouble. The poor sod had enough on his plate as it was. There was nothing for it but to leave. He slipped out of the room, subdued.

Downstairs, he told Mark to go to see her. Unsurprisingly, Mark didn't look thrilled by the prospect.

'Come and see me when she's finished with you.'

Mark grimaced and set off. It was a full hour before he returned.

'What did she say?' asked Alex.

'In a nutshell, keep my head down.'

'That's it?'

'More or less. In between the haranguing. Fuck, I thought you could give a good bollocking, but you've a lot to learn compared to her. She told me to book into another Airbnb, but in Glasgow this time. Mustn't tell anyone where it is. She's going to try to find another solution for looking after Angus. Says she's got the name of a good childminder, totally trustworthy.' He had the grace to look apologetic. 'You're right. I shouldn't have brought Karen into it. I wasn't thinking straight.'

He looked ashamed enough for Alex to feel compassion.

'Look,' he said. 'It isn't too late to go back to Edinburgh. We'll see about getting a childminder there. I honestly think it's best if you stay away from Glasgow for the time being.' As he said this, though, he was thinking about his interview with Liam and how he had said the gang was everywhere. Maybe it didn't matter where Mark was. The important thing was keeping it from those who could harm him.

'No offence, Alex. But I want to be back here, in Glasgow where I belong.'

'What about – no, forget it.'

'What?'

'No, it's a daft idea.' Was it though? Mark's affair with

Suzanne was old news. Perhaps it was a goer. He hesitated before going on. 'Didn't Suzanne say you could use her flat?'

'I, well, yes, she did. But I don't think it's a good idea, do you?'

'I think you're right. But at least consider it. Otherwise what are we going to do with you. I'm getting my bathroom done so my place is out, but I'll ask Kate and Conor if they'll put you up for the night. But not a word to anyone. Right? If anyone asks, you're going to that hotel on Paisley Road West. That way we might be able to set up a trap. No, hang on.' He held up his hand. 'I have a better idea. I already have four people in mind who might be a leak. I was suspicious already but am more so now. They were the only ones that I told about you allegedly working at home. Within the day, someone tried to light up your flat. Let's try and narrow that down further. We'll tell two of them you're staying there, and tell the other two you're staying out in Giffnock. There's a hotel there, isn't there? Let's see if it brings anything nasty to the surface.'

'But what if doesn't? What if it's none of them?' asked Mark.

Alex rubbed his forehead. 'Oh God, Mark. I could be barking up the wrong tree, and, yes, be imagining the whole thing, but what if I'm not? We've nothing to lose.'

'Maybe, but whatever happens, I won't use Suzanne's flat. I am not going to be beholden to her.'

Three hours later, the trap was set. He'd told McGowan and Gray that Mark would be staying in the hotel on the Paisley Road and said to McPhee and Sinclair that Mark was going to the Giffnock one. In both places, there would be a little surprise waiting for anyone who relied on whoever the informant was. As for the informant, if there was one? They were one step closer to being discovered, and when they were, they'd be in deep shit.

Chapter Fifteen

KATE WAS delighted when she opened the door to Mark and Alex. 'Of course, he can stay here. As long as you need, Mark. It'll be great to have Gus so close by. She wasn't happy to hear Alex had gone back to work so soon, but he placated her by promising to take more time off around the time of the funeral. She understood why he wanted to work. It didn't do to have too much time to think when you were grieving. She knew that from losing Mirren, her adoptive mother, but on the other hand, it would have been nice to be able to spend more time with him. He worked far more hours than was healthy.

She had agreed to go to the care home early in the morning. When she offered to help Alex with the funeral arrangements, he told her they were all under control. The only thing left to do was to go through her grandmother's personal items and sort them out.

'It would be a great help if you could do that,' he said.

'Will Gillian want to help, do you think?'

Her father's face closed up. 'No.'

'Have you asked her?'

'Of course I have,' he snapped. 'Sorry, that came out badly, I phoned her earlier today and asked her, but she refused. All she's interested in is getting at Mum's jewellery. And she's being difficult about the funeral arrangements.'

'How so?'

'Your grandmother noted down exactly what she wanted. It's there in her handwriting, but that doesn't matter to your cousin. Your grandmother wanted a cremation? Too bad. Gillian knows better, It should be a burial. A humanist service as requested by Mum? No, no. Gillian's minister will take care of it. The type of coffin, the music, the readings. Anything she can object to, she does. Even what to do with the ashes.' The strain showed on his face.

'What does Gillian think should be done with them?"

'She wants them buried in the cemetery and a gravestone put up. Is that possible? Mum was adamant she didn't want to be buried.'

'Why not give Gillian her way on this?' asked Kate tentatively. She was glad there had been no one to argue with when Mirren died. She and Mirren had planned the funeral together down to the readings and music being used.

'If I give in on one thing, she'll see it as weakness and go for my jugular.'

'Surely not.'

Alex had looked at her with what she thought was pity. 'Oh Kate. Your cousin is not a nice person. I suspect it's because of her money-grabbing mother who made my brother's life a misery until they divorced and then did everything in her power to stop his access to his daughter. One of the worst things she did was tell Gillian her father didn't want to see her when in fact Billy was desperate to keep in touch.'

'That must have been upsetting for Gillian.'

'I suppose so.' Alex didn't look as though he believed it or wanted to believe it. 'It certainly upset Billy. He adored Gillian and he was distraught when she wouldn't speak to him. Two whole years, I think it was. And then by the time he was finally allowed access, Gillian was fully under her mother's influence and believed every lie she was told. Needless to say, the poison dwarf made sure Gillian kept in touch with Mum. She wasn't going to risk Gillian losing her inheritance.'

'But surely there was a possibility your brother might have disinherited her? Wasn't it risky for her mother to do that?'

'That sort of thing wasn't in Billy's nature, but anyway it's not possible under Scots law.' Alex didn't go on to explain, and Kate didn't press it. Her father was exhausted and becoming emotional at this talk of his brother. When you lost a loved one, Kate thought, you lost not only them but also the people who'd already gone, all over again. Each fresh bereavement brought back the pain of earlier ones.

She went to the care home immediately after talking to her father. They were keen to get the room back as there was a long waiting list for places, but, in any case, it was foolish to pay for an empty room. It would have been good if there was someone to share the tasks with, she thought, looking at her grandmother's belongings spread out in front of her. But she knew now it wasn't going to happen. Her father had made that clear. Kate had only met Gillian once, a brief meeting in the care home when they'd turned up by accident at the same time. Gillian had been distant and aloof, and Kate hadn't taken to her. She assumed the feeling was mutual, although she'd done her best to present a friendly face.

Best get on with it. Kate had to decide what went to charity, what was for recycling and what could be kept. The jewellery had to be kept for now as her father said they would be shared between her and Gillian. Kate didn't want any of it. Gillian could have it all, as far as she was concerned. She wasn't going to squabble over a dead woman's baubles.

While she worked, she listened to the radio. Occasionally, one of the care workers popped a head round the door to check how she was doing, but essentially, she was on her own. It would have been nice to have company, someone to advise her whether an item of clothing was worth keeping or not. A woman friend, was what she needed. She sat back on her heels and tried to think of ways of meeting more friends. The news came on, and she moved to turn off the radio, but when she heard the words 'presumed suicide' she stopped herself and listened.

A teenage boy was fatally injured today after falling onto the track at St Enoch Subway station. A train was drawing into the station when the teenager is said to have jumped. He was pronounced dead at the scene and has not yet been identified. This is the fifth such teenage death in seven weeks. In Edinburgh, the first minister is set to make a statement about drug dea—

Kate turned the radio off. She took out her phone and did a Google search to try to find out more, but she found nothing other than what had already been said on the radio.

She sat back in the armchair. This wasn't right. It wasn't a coincidence, she'd swear to it. She had to get to the bottom of it. She took out her phone and dialled Alex, but he didn't pick up. No wonder, he must have so much to do, although he claimed it was all under control.

She wandered through to the kitchen in the home and made herself a cup of decaffeinated tea. She'd read in one of her pregnancy books that caffeine wasn't good for pregnant women and also that there was more caffeine in tea than in coffee. She didn't believe it. Tea never had the same kick as coffee. Anyway, she wasn't taking any chances with this pregnancy. Tea made, she took it back to her room to drink as she didn't want to make small talk with any of the carers or residents who were liable to pop into the kitchen. Besides, she had decided to phone Sheila Morton, the journalist who had written the article about Callum, to see if she knew anything more, and she needed privacy to do that. Newspapers were always a good source of information about what was going on. If only she could get a job as a journalist. Freelance work was so hard on many levels, not least the lack of human contact.

Kate scrolled through her phone until she found Sheila's details. She was reluctant to contact another journalist, knowing as she did how ruthless they were where a half-decent story was involved. But it would be good to find out basic details such as where the boy went to school, where he lived. She hesitated before dialling the number. Was this the right thing to do? Sheila might steal the story and then where would she be? No, she had a good feeling about Sheila, they might become friends, and she needed a friend at the moment. If only Laura would move up here or visit for a few days, not that there was the least possibility of that happening. Whenever Kate asked her, she was met with a barrage of questions about Scotland. More often than not about the midge population. Laura claimed to have been scarred for life by camping holidays in Scotland when she was a child.

Right. She reached into her bag and brought out her phone. She'd do it. A few seconds later Sheila's unmistakable gravelly tones were in her ear.

'Kate, great to hear from you. Fancy lunch again soon? I owe you, don't forget.'

It was a relief to be on the receiving end of such a welcome.

'Lunch would be great,' she answered, 'but I'm calling for another reason. A favour.'

'I knew it was too good to be true. You want the lowdown on this latest suicide?'

'Am I that transparent?'

'I'm afraid so. But as it happens, I'm more than happy to share what I know with you.'

Kate's heart was beating faster. 'Really?'

'Sure. Look, I'm over in the southside this afternoon. Why don't I meet you there? I've got my oxygen mask ready.'

Kate laughed politely. There was an age old rivalry between the west end and the southside with each claiming they needed support if they had to move from their preferred area to the other for whatever reason. To an outsider like Kate, it was tedious. 'Well, there's plenty of places to meet, but why don't you come to my flat and I'll make us a light lunch.'

Sheila agreed at once. 'Give me your address and I'll be there by one o'clock. Does that suit you?'

'Perfect.' Kate gave her the address. She finished off what she was doing with her grandmother's belongings and loaded the bags destined for the charity shops into the car. She'd come back in the evening. Another couple of hours should see it all sorted, and they could let the home get on with getting the room ready for the next resident.

On the way home she picked up a couple of strawberry tarts from a bakery for dessert. They'd have a Caesar salad for their main course; there was leftover chicken in the fridge, and it would make a nice light lunch. Once home, she set to work, making sure the flat was spotless. She wasn't going to put up with any jibes from a Wendy, as the southsiders called those from the west end. She had no idea whether they had a similar nickname for southsiders. Suzys maybe?

At one o'clock precisely, the doorbell rang, and Kate buzzed her in. She went to the door to welcome her. Sheila had brought a bottle of Prosecco with her and Kate's heart sank. She didn't like drinking during the day anyway, but it was unthinkable now when she was pregnant... Ah well, she'd pour herself the smallest glass possible and keep topping up Sheila's. With any luck. she'd be so pissed she wouldn't notice. Kate forced a wide grin.

'Sheila! How lovely to see you. Come in.'

'Bloody hell, I was only joking when I said I needed oxygen. I've been on the number four bus for hours and then I had to walk. Up a hill! What a beautiful flat though and the view! It's well, wow.'

The tenement stood on a hill up from the main road and overlooked the entire city giving views to the north including the Campsie hills and beyond. Kate looked round her living room. It was a lovely room with the original cornicing, a bay window where the windows were almost the full height of the room and working shutters. They'd put in oak flooring with soundproofing underneath so as not to annoy the neighbours, and the effect was light and spacious.

'We like it,' said Kate taking Sheila's jacket. 'We're eating in the kitchen, come on through. She led the way into the kitchen with its dark blue painted shaker units. It didn't have the same "wow" factor as the living room as it wasn't as big, but Kate loved it nonetheless.

Kate put two glasses on the table and served the salad while Sheila wrestled with the bottle. She managed to open it and poured two large glasses before Kate managed to stop her. Shit. Sheila lifted her glass to Kate's and said, 'Cheers,' before downing half of hers. Good, all the less for Kate to pretend to drink.

'So, Kate. What do you want to know? This salad is delish by the way.'

'Thanks. Anything, really. Name, age, where he lived, who his friends were, that sort of thing.'

Sheila made a face. 'There isn't much. His name is Alfie Barnes, aged fifteen. Don't have his address yet, but, get this, he went to the same school as one of the other teenagers. And his parents are kicking up hell. Refusing to accept it's suicide.'

'Just like Callum's parents.'

'Exactly.'

'Do you think he went to the same school as Callum?'

Sheila's face fell. 'They won't say. The police, I mean. It doesn't matter. It'll be on social media in no time at all. As soon as they release his name.'

'Have you checked?'

'No. Silly me. I've only just realised that's what'll happen.' Sheila poured herself another Prosecco and gestured at Kate with her glass. 'You've hardly touched yours. Come on, drink up.'

Kate raised her glass to her lips and pretended to take a sip, hoping Sheila wouldn't notice. She was in luck. Sheila had gone back to the subject of the latest death.

'What do you think it might mean, if they knew each other? Do you think there might be a link with the others? Or is it coincidence or copycat suicides?'

'Haven't a clue,' admitted Kate. 'It might be copycats, I suppose. There was a case when I was at school down in England. Local boys' grammar school. Three boys in the same year killed themselves within a month of each other. No good reason why.'

'Is there ever?' said Sheila. Her tone had darkened.

'I don't know,' admitted Kate. 'Apart from those boys, and I didn't know them personally, no one I know has ever killed themselves.' She pushed a piece of chicken round her plate, remembering she wasn't telling the full truth. But she'd been a baby when her mother killed herself. 'People do it out of desperation, I suppose. They don't see any other way out.'

'My brother took an overdose of sleeping pills once.' Sheila scrutinised Kate's face. 'We found him in time, don't worry. He survived. He'd got into debt. So, yes, you're right. Often it is as simple as not being able to see what else to do.'

'I'm sorry,' said Kate. 'That must have been awful for you.'

Sheila blinked back tears. 'And for my parents. He was only seventeen at the time. A long time ago. But they've never stopped thinking he might try again. and frankly. at their age, they shouldn't be having to worrying about their adult children.' She picked up the bottle and poured herself another glass of wine. 'Anyway, time to change the subject. I've given you all I've got. What are you going to do about it?'

'I haven't decided yet. It might be significant that this latest suicide victim went to the same school as one of the others. What are the chances? How many secondaries are there in Glasgow?'

'No idea.' Sheila took out her phone and worked with it for a moment. She looked up. 'Says thirty here, and then there's the private schools...' Another pause. 'There's eight of them. I'm no statistician, but it doesn't sound like chance. Perhaps there's something going on in those particular schools.'

'Like what? It must be coincidence.' But Kate had a gut feeling Sheila was right. The problem was to find out what and she had no idea where to start. She had no proof, no clues. Perhaps it was time to change tactic and move to another story. She said as much to Sheila who looked disappointed.

'I had great hopes for you,' she said. 'I didn't take you for a quitter.'

Kate bridled. She was not a quitter. 'We'll see. I haven't given up yet. Now, would you like coffee?'

Sheila excused herself and left the room to use the lavatory. While she was away, Kate jumped at the chance to rid herself of her glass of wine, pouring it down the sink. She managed to get back to her seat a second before Sheila came back into the room, her face slightly pink and her eyes red. Talking about her brother had clearly upset her.

It was late afternoon before Sheila left. Whatever it was she'd been going to do in the southside that afternoon, she hadn't left much time for it. 'Keep in touch, won't you?' she said before enveloping Kate in a too-tight hug.

Despite longing for a friend, Kate wasn't sure she would. The jibe about being a quitter had stung although Sheila made sure to smooth things over. It was more than that, though. She had wasted three and a half hours when she ought to have been working. Sheila was good company, but Kate couldn't afford to waste time like this. At this rate, she'd never get back into journalism, and the thought depressed her more than she cared to think.

Chapter Sixteen

THE NEXT DAY, Kate was at the care home finishing up what she had to do. It hadn't taken long to clear her gran's things, and the only things left to do were to take clothes to the charity shop and to go through a rosewood box she'd found at the bottom of the wardrobe. It looked like a jewellery box, and for a brief moment, Kate considered passing it to Gillian unopened. It was foolish, but apart from her father, Gillian was now her only blood relative, and she didn't want to fight over it. The feeling didn't last long, though, when Kate imagined her father's face if she did. Kate decided she'd take it home instead and spend time sorting through it and thinking about how best to do it. The logical thing would be to take turnabout in choosing a piece, but she'd have a look first. If there was anything that looked especially valuable, it should be included in probate.

She'd just got into the flat when her mobile rang out. She looked at it as she took it out of her bag: Sheila.

'Kate, thanks again for lunch. We must do it again soon,

and this time it's on me. I now owe you two lunches. Anyway, that's only part of the reason I'm calling.'

'Oh?'

'I was in Tinderbox this morning, and I overheard an extremely interesting conversation.' Sheila paused. 'You there?'

'Yes, yes. I'm here. Go on.'

'It was the crime correspondent from one of our rival newspapers. He was talking to a colleague about the latest suicide. I'm putting the last word in inverted commas, by the way.'

This was interesting. 'What did you hear?'

'He said he had an email from one of the boy's friends, a girl called Aileen. Aileen is claiming the boy killed himself. Which, as I said yesterday, the boy's parents are vehemently denying. They're making a hell of a fuss, and who can blame them? This whole thing stinks more than three day old fish. He's going to meet the friend this afternoon to hear her side of the story. Want to come along?'

'What? You've been invited, too?'

'No. I thought we'd earwig.'

'But won't they recognise you? It's too risky, you've met the girl before, and the journalist knows you.'

'They might. You on the other hand, no chance.'

Kate's heart beat faster. 'How would that work?' Kate hated confrontation. What if they twigged that she was listening? She outlined her fears to Sheila who dismissed them.

'You'll be fine. You can sit near them and record them with your phone.'

'Mm.' Kate frowned. She wasn't convinced. 'What if we follow the girl instead? Try to find out who she is.' Sheila started to protest, and she cut in quickly. 'If we get her on her own, she might talk.'

'Look, are you up for this or not?'

Kate put aside her original doubts. This was a lead she couldn't afford to ignore. 'Where are they meeting?' she said. 'I'll be there. With my phone at the ready.'

She met Sheila in the computer department outside the John Lewis café where the other journalist, James Farquer, had arranged to meet the girl. 'Are you sure it's the same girl?' she'd asked Sheila.

'Yes. It's too much of a coincidence not to be the same girl. She's given virtually the same name – Ailie, Ailidh and Aileen. What are the odds, *and* she's chosen to meet him in the same place where I met her. It's her all right.'

Now they stood side by side looking at laptops. Kate needed a new one in any case, so she took the opportunity to try one or two. They'd agreed Sheila would point out whoever arrived first, the journalist or 'Aileen'. The café was quiet, so there should be no problem getting seats near enough to hear their conversation.

Sheila nudged Kate. 'Don't look, but there's James now. He's early. Go and stand behind him in the queue and then sit as near to him as possible. Don't do anything to draw attention to yourself.'

'You're not coming?'

'Best not. He might get suspicious.' Sheila gave her a little push. 'Go on, you need to get close.'

Kate was nervous, but her anxiety fled when she was in the queue. She stood in line waiting for tea, two places behind the journalist. He was young and good-looking but had an air of arrogance that was unattractive. When she heard him berating the server for having run out of oatmeal milk she went right off him. She was hard put not to intervene but contented herself with a sympathetic smile for the girl along with a two pound coin into the tip jar.

Out of the corner of her eye she watched as he looked for a table. Good, he'd chosen one where there was another free right behind him. It wouldn't be hard to eavesdrop from there. She took her peppermint tea and sat down.

By the look of things, the girl was late. Farquer was restless, beating out a tune with a pen on the table. Christ, it was irritating. She took out her phone. No point in recording his arrhythmic efforts. She kept her head down. as if reading her phone, only looking up from time to time. Ah, this must be her. A skinny girl who looked no more than fifteen stood at the entrance looking round. Farquer raised an indolent hand, and she joined him.

'Awright?' she slurred. She sounded as though she was drunk. Kate was worried her phone might have difficulty picking up her words. The girl's voice was quiet and subdued. Shit. She had a notebook with her, so she'd revert to using that in case the recording didn't work.

'Do you want a coffee?'

'Irn-bru'd be good. Ta.' She sat down so she was facing Kate. Kate was careful not to look at her. The journalist went up to get the girl her drink.

When he returned, he got straight to the point. He slammed the drink down in front of her and said, 'OK, what've you got for me?'

The girl sniffed. 'You said you'd give me twenty quid.'

The Fallen

'After I've heard what you have to say. You need to answer my questions, first.'

'Go ahead.' She opened her can and gulped it down, letting out a huge burp as she did so. Kate hid a smile, wishing she could see the journalist's face. He looked the type to think that no one should ever do such a thing in front of him.

'You said you know the boy who died. How come?'

'He went to my school.'

'Right. And how friendly were you with him? You see, I've spoken to his family, and they didn't recognise your name.'

Kate grimaced. He was more on the ball than Sheila and the other journalist had been. Was he going to nick her story? If there was one?

'They're snobs. They didn't want me being friends with him.'

She'd love to see Farquer's face to gauge for herself his belief or otherwise. He'd be sceptical, she was sure of it. And from the sound of his response, he was.

'Right.' He drew out the word. 'So why did they say they'd never heard your name before? That they'd spoken to his real friends and they too had no idea who you were.'

The girl sprang out of her seat. 'You know what? I'm out of here. Who the fuck do you think you are looking at me as if I'm a fucking liar? I don't fucking know why they're dissing me, but I can fucking give a guess. It's because his dad fingered me once and I called him out about it. Dirty old lech.'

Farquar changed his approach. He was losing her. 'Sit down, Aileen. Let's start again. What did you want to tell me?'

207

With a sulky shrug, Aileen sat back down.

'He was up for killing himself, no matter what they say. Told me he was thinking about doing it. I begged him not to. He told me he had a plan. He was going to jump in front of a bus.'

'But that's not what happened, is it? He jumped onto a live rail in the underground.'

'It's basically the same, jumping in front of a fucking huge thing that's going to kill you. It's not as if he said he was going to take a whole load of Paracetamol and then hanged hisself. It's the same fucking thing, you mong.'

The girl, Aileen or whatever her name might be, certainly wasn't shy about saying what she thought. Kate thought back to her own teenage years and how she would never have dared speak to an adult like that. It would have been good to have a tenth of Aileen's gumption. Not to be such a people pleaser. She looked at her phone; it was recording, but she had no idea whether it was going to be of any use. Her shorthand had come in useful for once, and, in any case, she had a good memory for what people said. Farquer was speaking now but his voice was low, and it was hard to hear what he was saying. He sounded threatening, though. He wasn't going to take any nonsense. Kate only made out a few words and gathered that he considered Aileen to have wasted his time. Without warning, Aileen got up and left. Kate sat paralysed for a few seconds. She wanted to get up but feared the journalist would spot her. Fortunately the café was filling up and she took the chance to stand up and offer her table to another woman who was looking around for a place to sit. Once that was done, she sped off in the direction of where the girl had gone and hoped she hadn't left it too late.

Aileen had been wearing an orange top that was fluorescent in its brightness. Kate looked down the escalator to see if she spotted her. There! She was at the first floor and was moving at speed down the moving staircase, pushing past anyone in her way. Several noisy tuts were heard in her wake. Kate jumped on and ran down it as fast as she dared but she got stuck behind a couple of boys who were fooling about.

'Excuse me,' she said to no avail.

By the time she reached the ground floor, the girl was nowhere to be seen. Damn. But Sheila was waving to her. She ran over.

'Where is she?'

'Down there. She's going through the gallery. Look, over there. It's definitely the same girl I spoke to.'

Kate followed her pointing finger. 'I see her. Right, I'm off. I'll ring you later. Lots to catch up on.'

Outside, Aileen was walking towards the west. Did she live in the west end? Kate kept a safe distance behind her. Aileen turned left at Renfield Street. She must be going to get a bus, or maybe she was making her way to the train station. Kate hoped it was the former. It would be harder to follow her on to a train. She was in luck. Halfway down the street, Aileen joined the queue for a bus. But which one would she take?

The queue wasn't orderly. People leaned against the walls of shops scrolling through their phones. Several buses stopped here. Panic rose in Kate's throat. Was the girl local? What if she lived far away, in a part of the city where Kate had never been. She'd been to all the usual touristy places, but Aileen might live in one of those distant housing estates of which Kate had heard so much. She was here now though, nothing for it but to join the waiting crowd.

The girl was inside the bus shelter thumbing a phone

when another teenager joined her, a boy. Damn, Kate had distanced herself from her by staying outside. She had to get nearer to hear what they were saying? She crossed to the edge of the pavement and stood, pretending to examine the times of the buses, all the time straining to hear their conversation. It was hard to make out more than a few words over the roar of the traffic. Kate had read that Renfield Street was one of the most polluted streets in Scotland and she believed it. She made out only a few phrases, but they were interesting, suggesting Aileen had an agenda in meeting the journalist. The boy was getting at her, his voice getting louder in his agitation.

'You've fucked this right up, you stupid bitch. What am I going to say to Jake?'

'Tell him the wanker didn't turn up?' The girl's voice was plaintive. She was pulling at her hair, twisting it in her fingers. 'It's for the best.'

'And what if this bastard writes about you? Are you sure he didn't believe you?'

There was no sign of the confidence she'd shown in the café. She nibbled at her nails then said, 'He asked a lot of questions.'

'Fuck it. Nothing for it but to wait and see. I told Jake it wasn't a good idea to try the same thing again. What did you say your name was this time?'

'Aileen.'

Kate barely made out the word. She daren't look round but she was sure 'Aileen' was regretting her lack of imagination.

'Aileen? First Ailie, then Ailidh. Now this. They're all the fucking same as your own name. What were you thinking, Hayley?'

The Fallen

This was progress. She had a first name, and it wasn't a common name either.

'Here's the bus at last.' The boy held out his hand as a number three bus drew to a halt. Kate made out the destination on its front. Govan. She sort of knew where that was. It wasn't disastrous, at least it was on the southside. She'd be able to get a taxi home without taking out another mortgage. Or perhaps Conor would pick her up. The young couple got on the bus and went upstairs, Kate following them. She was in luck, the bus wasn't busy, and she managed to sit right behind them. Her phone rang as she was taking her seat. It was Sheila.

'Hey there,' she answered. 'Can't talk now. On the bus and the connection's poor.' Sheila caught on straight away. 'Right. What number? Give me it in case...' her voice faded. The connection was poor, she hadn't lied about that.

'Three,' said Kate in the hope Sheila would hear her. Sheila repeated it then said. 'The Govan bus, right?'

'Yes,' said Kate. 'Look, I'll speak to you later.' She rang off, desperate to hear what the two teenagers were saying. They'd been sitting silently but were now chatting again.

'I fucking told Jake it was daft to try the same thing again. Why did you do it?'

The girl side-eyed him. 'You ever tried saying no to him?'

'No.'

'Shut the fuck up then. You don't say no to him, to any of them.' She turned her face to the window. They said nothing and Kate was beginning to wonder if she should cut her losses and get off the bus. This was futile. However, the girl turned to him and began to speak. Her voice was low, and Kate had to strain to hear.

'I wish we'd never got involved in all of this.'

'Me, too,' said the boy. 'But what choice did we have? I mean, what with the way Mum is.'

So they were siblings. Hayley and what? Was his name Sean as he'd told Sheila? She doubted it. He'd been pretty pissed off at Hayley's attempts to cover up her name. Shit, they were standing up, about to get off the bus. Kate stood up, too, ready to do whatever came next. She'd follow them at a distance; with luck, they'd be going home, and at least she'd have an idea of where they lived, although what she'd do after that, she had no idea.

It was raining when they all got off the bus and the two teenagers started to run. Fuck. Kate was scuppered. Running after them would be too noticeable. Why couldn't the rain have stayed off. She walked at her fastest pace and whenever she was sure they wouldn't be able to see her, she ran. But it was no use. These kids were fast and when they turned a corner into an estate, they had disappeared by the time Kate got there. Damn it. All that effort and she wasn't any further forward. She got out her phone to ring Sheila.

Kate wasn't expecting to be ambushed by the two teenagers. She'd finished her phone call and was almost back at the main road, not paying attention when they appeared in front of her. There must be another way back to the main road. Surely she would have noticed them overtake her. They stood in front of her, blocking her way, their faces set and grim. They're only teenagers, she told herself. Children. It's daytime, there are people around, what harm can they do?

'Why are you following us?' said the boy.

Kate put on her best indignant voice. 'What are you talking about? Let me past, please.'

'You were in John Lewis. Next table to me and that wanker,' said Hayley.

'John Lewis? Rubbish. I've been visiting my mum.' As she said it, she cursed herself. Never give too much detail.

The boy leapt on her mistake. 'You were, aye? What street'll that be then?'

'None of your business.'

'You're following my wee sister, so it is my business.' The boy's face was in hers, and Kate looked around for help, but the street was empty. Where had all the people gone? She swallowed, tried not to show she was frightened.

'Who the fuck are you?' He clenched his fists.

She gave in. She wouldn't be able to outrun them, not the boy, anyway. 'I'm a journalist. I wanted to talk to you about these teenage deaths, the kids who've fallen. Why are you lying about them?'

'The fuck? Prove it.'

Kate rummaged through her bag for her NUJ card. 'Here.'

He squinted at it before thrusting it back at her. 'We're not going to talk to any more journos.'

But his sister interrupted with, 'Five hundred quid and we'll tell you the whole story,' she said. The boy looked at her in horror.

'Hayley,' he said. 'The fuck are you saying?'

'I'm sick of this, Lewis. Five hundred quid will get us out of this shithole. Away from Jake and his gang and away from her and her fucking problems.'

'Hayley, she's our mum.' The boy looked as though he might cry.

Kate was torn between staying and hearing more and making a break and running for it. God, they were nothing but kids. Despite her fear she was sorry for them. 'I don't have that sort of money, but if you have a good story, we could sell it together and get much more.'

'How much?' said Hayley.

'It depends on the story. Tell me and I'll give you an idea of how much you might get.'

Hayley shot a glance at her brother. He made a face as if to say *it's up to you*. 'It's about those kids who are killing themselves. We know why.'

Shit. Back to this again. Peddling lies for whatever reason.

'Look. I've spoken to one of the teenager's parents and their friends. There's no way that boy killed himself. I've also seen police notes on the others. And yes, one of them was undoubtedly a suicide but the rest? Jury's out. So, if you have nothing else, I'm off.'

'I've got proof. Look at this.' Hayley had grabbed her brother's phone and was frantically scrolling it. She raised it to Kate's face. 'That's why they're killing themselves. Sex shaming.'

Kate blinked. The photo she was looking at was one of Callum Peterson in a highly compromising position. She pushed it aside wishing she'd never seen it.

'How did you get this?'

Hayley folded her arms. 'Uh-oh. Not another word until we have a deal.'

Kate thought for a moment. 'If, and I mean if, I get a paper to take this story I'll give you thirty percent of what I get for it.'

'Other way round. We'll have seventy percent.'

The Fallen

'Not a chance.' Kate waited.

'Fifty then.'

'Forty. Final offer.' Kate prayed they'd accept. She'd go to fifty but didn't want to lose face.

'Deal.' Lewis spat on his hand and held it out.

'Deal,' said Kate, keeping her hands firmly at her sides. 'Social distancing,' she added when she saw he was about to protest. 'One of us might have Covid.'

'Oh, aye, right enough.'

'OK, where can we go to talk more about this? What about your house?'

The two looked at each other. Hayley shrugged. 'Might as well. It's the afternoon, she'll be out of it.'

'She' must be their mother. Kate didn't like the sound of a house where the main caregiver was likely to be stoned or high this early in the day.

'There's a café across the road. Why don't we talk there?'

Three minutes later they were installed at a window seat. The rain had come on and the window was streaked with water. By the look of things, it was the first drop of water it had seen for weeks. Kate went up to the counter and ordered a tea for herself and cokes for the teenagers. She was desperate for a pee, but it would have to wait for now. They might hoof it if she left them for any time. When she got back to her seat they were arguing.

'Lewis thinks you'll do us over.'

Kate looked her in the eye. 'I always keep my word. If this is a good story and I sell it, you could be looking at several hundred pounds or more. Each.'

'What's to stop us going to the papers ourselves?' Lewis stuck out his chin.

'How's that worked out for you so far?'

That shut him up. Kate turned to Hayley.
'Now, tell me what's going on.'
They both started talking at once.

It was a depressing tale of neglect and poverty – a mother present in body but not there in spirit.

'She's stoned or hammered all of the time,' said Hayley. 'We've brung ourselves up.'

'Brought,' said Kate without thinking and winced when she saw Hayley's hurt look. 'Sorry, I shouldn't have said that.'

Hayley was subdued so Lewis took up the story.

'Hayley's right. She's never been there for us. The only thing she cares about is her next fix. As soon as we were old enough, she had us doing errands for the dealers. Nobody thinks anything of a wean coming to your door. They could be there for a pal. It's not as suspicious as a strange adult chapping at the door.'

They went on to outline how they'd been dragged deeper and deeper into the mire of drug dealing. Asked to recruit pals from school. 'But we were never at school long enough to make friends, so we didn't have any to bring in. So they made a different plan. Catfishing.'

'Really?' said Kate. She couldn't think how impersonating someone online was relevant to the tale.

'Yes. It was aimed at boys. They'd post a photo of a girl online and get chatting with them. Mainly through one of the main social media channels, Instagram or Facebook. It took months to set up. I don't know all the details, but they targeted people in Glasgow. Once they were friends, they upped the ante.'

The Fallen

'In what way?' asked Kate. It was beginning to register with her what was going on.

'The usual way. How are teenagers always pulled in? I've shown you mine now, you show me yours, that sort of thing. But before they get to that stage there's a lot of chat, where do you go to school, where do you live, basic things to get to know someone.'

'How do you know so much about it?'

Hayley scuffed the ground with the toe of one of her shoes. 'I had to spend hours trying to reel them in.' She glared at Kate. 'Don't judge me.'

'I wasn't judging you. I imagine you must have been pressurised into doing it.'

'Pressurised. Aye, that's one way of putting it.' Hayley's eyes were dead.

'Go on,' urged Kate. 'What happened then?'

'You'd be surprised at how much it goes on. And how serious it gets. It starts off harmless enough but then they're enticed into wanking off and all sorts in front of a camera, and if the wrong people get hold of that, you're fucked.'

Kate didn't want to think what 'all sorts' meant but she could imagine. 'I see,' she said.

Lewis's face was dark. 'I don't think you do. They get hold of one picture, then threaten to put it on the internet unless you do more. Bring your wee sister along to the party, for example. You can beg them to stop, but it doesn't make any difference. You're in their power.' A tear rolled down his face and he wiped it away.

Kate took a chance. 'Is that what happened to you?'

He said nothing. Hayley, her head down, nodded and Kate decided not to ask for further details about what had happened to them. She sipped at her tea and changed the

217

conversation's course back to other victims. 'So, once they've got these films and photos what do they do?'

'That's you working for them. Dealing drugs wherever they want you to.'

Was this what it was all about? Drug dealing? Blackmail? 'Can you explain it a bit more?'

Hayley looked at her as if she was an idiot. 'They send you the video or photo, so you know they're not bluffing, and tell you you're part of their gang now and that you'll do whatever they say, deal at school or whatever. If you refuse, then they threaten to send the photos to your parents or put them online.'

'Right,' said Kate. 'But surely they'd involve the police?'

'The polis? You're fucking kidding right? They're in on it as well.'

'Not all of them.' Kate's hackles were raised.

Hayley humphed at Kate's tone. 'You posh cunts are all the same. You don't have a clue about the real world.'

With difficulty Kate reined herself in.

'OK, so they can't go to the police. What happens next?'

Hayley glared at her. Her mouth narrowed into a straight line, and for a moment, Kate thought she'd lost her. Eventually, she spoke again.

'They're told to deal. Recently they've moved on to posher schools, trying to widen their market so they've targeted kids there.'

It made sense. All the young people, except Jasmine, who had been in care, came from middle-class areas. Two went to private schools.

'But surely there were dealers there already?' she asked Hayley.

'Aye, that's right but the schools are on to them, and as

soon as they see anyone near the school who they don't recognise, they call the polis. I should know. Nearly got caught once.' She drained her coke. 'The gang wants dealers actually in the school. Best if they can get hold of a kid who's well respected. That sort of kid'll go under the radar.'

It all made sense.

'You mean like Callum Peterson,' said Kate. 'Star pupil with his life ahead of him. From what his parents and friends said, no one would ever suspect him of being a dealer.'

Hayley said nothing. Kate stared at her.

'What is it? What are you not telling me?'

'It's maybe nothing, but I heard Jake—'

'Shut the fuck up, Hayley.' Lewis jumped up from his seat. 'You'll get us killed. We're out of here, come on.' He opened the door and stormed out. Outside he glared back at them, gesturing to Hayley to get a move on.

What the hell was this about? Kate felt in her pocket for one of the business cards she always carried. She managed to slip it to Hayley without Lewis seeing.

'My phone number's there. Ring me anytime.'

Hayley nodded and put the card in her pocket.

'I'd better go,' she said.

Kate watched her run to catch up with her brother. It looked as though she was pleading with him, but he was having none of it. He looked furious. Whatever it was Hayley had been going to tell her, it must have been important. Damn, she was on to a big story, she knew it, but nothing would come of it if Hayley didn't phone. Nothing for it but to wait and hope.

Chapter Seventeen

IT WAS rotten luck that the builders had picked on the one week in the year when it was hot to redo his bathroom. He should have waited until July when it was bound to rain. Fortunately, Kate had told him to use her shower whenever he wanted. With any luck, they'd be finished for the day when he got home, though they had a work ethic the likes of which he'd never seen. The plasterer hadn't left until nine thirty last night. Alex had offered him tea, coffee, beer and sandwiches, all in an increasingly desperate attempt to get him to leave but it made no difference. Would the man never go? He admired him for working so hard, but jeez, he wanted space to relax, get rid of his cares.

It was past nine o'clock when he got home. He plodded upstairs all but deafened by the banging coming from his flat. At this rate, all his neighbours would be up in arms. He didn't blame them. They had a right to expect peace in the evening. He'd have to raise it with the builders.

Before he had time, though, Krzysztof called him through to the bathroom.

'Mr Scrimgeour, so sorry but I am afraid your cat did this.' Kris pointed to a large turd in the centre of his brand new, very expensive shower tray.

'I don't have a cat,' said Alex as he grabbed a wad of toilet paper and cleaned up the mess. Krzysztof looked appalled.

'So sorry, so sorry. I think it is yours. Cat is here. In big room.'

Alex gave him a wry smile and went through to the living room. Sure enough, there on the leather sofa was a small cat. (How on earth had it produced such a huge turd?). It was sleeping contentedly. Alex lifted it up, no collar. He didn't remember seeing it around the place before. The family upstairs had a cat, but it was black and white, not a tabby like this. Perhaps they'd got another to keep it company. Whatever. It wasn't staying here. He lifted it up and took it to the door. Should he knock on his neighbours' doors and ask? No, it would find its own way back. He shooed it outside.

Krzysztof left soon after, saying he'd be back round at seven the next morning. Didn't the man have a life? Alex had never met a workman like him. Ah well, he'd best get to bed then if he wanted to be up early enough to have a shower before the plumber arrived.

Alex's dreams were vivid that night. His doorbell was ringing. When he went to open the door, he found a large tiger outside saying: 'I've come for my tea.' Alex slammed the door shut but it was too late, the tiger was already inside. He awoke, sweating, to the thumping of his door. Shit, he must have slept in. He stumbled to the door where a cheerful

Krzysztof was waiting for him, accompanied by the small tabby from the day before.

'Quick, get in before that damn cat sneaks in.' Alex ushered Kris inside. The cat miaowed loudly when the door shut, as it realised it wasn't welcome. Too bad.

After a hasty shower, a bowl of Shreddies and a gulped cup of tea, Alex was ready for work.

'I won't be home until late, Kris,' he said as he left, 'so pull the door behind you when you're finished and I'll see you in the morning.' He hesitated. 'Perhaps if you make sure to finish by about seven thirty. I'm worried the neighbours will complain. People aren't used to workmen doing their trade in the evenings you see.'

'No problem,' said Kris. 'Lady upstairs she want work done. I go see her later.'

Mm. Well at least his neighbours would have one relatively peaceful evening.

When Alex arrived at the office, DCI Ferguson called him up to her office. She'd been more pleasant since his mother died, but he remained wary of her.

'Come in,' she called as soon as he knocked on the door. So there was to be no game playing today. No passive aggressive showing of her power over him. He opened the door and went in.

'This is going to take some time,' said Pamela. 'Do you want a coffee?'

'No, thanks.' Alex refrained from saying how busy he was. No point in spoiling the mood. He waited.

'How are you today, Alex? If you need any time off before the funeral, please say. Take as long as you need.'

'I'm fine. It's better for me to have a lot to do.'

'I hoped you'd say that. Quite a bit happened yesterday.'

'Oh, yes?'

'First things first. Who did you tell about Mark going to the hotel on Paisley Road West?'

Had it worked then? He'd been disappointed nothing had happened the first night. Perhaps he was on the wrong track after all.

'I told McPhee and Gray. Why?'

'Well, we booked a room in Mark's name. The hotel rang in to say a woman had called to ask for Mark last night. The hotel told her that he was out and immediately phoned us.'

A woman? So was Chloe Gray behind it after all? 'Did anything else happen?'

'Nothing. We had an officer in the room ready to tackle whoever broke in. We'll do the same tonight. But this time we'll tell the hotel to say Mark's in his room.'

'I think it would be best to leave it,' said Alex.

'What on earth do you mean?' Pamela stared at him. 'This was your idea after all.'

'Hear me out,' he said. 'If we go after whoever this is, we may miss out on the bigger picture.' He had her interest now, that much was obvious by the way she studied him.

'Go on,' she said.

'What about putting a tail on her, or having her phone tapped?'

Pamela considered this. 'If it is her, she's likely to be using a burner. No, I think it's best we go ahead now and get her.'

'Can't you give it more than a second's thought?' The

words were out before he knew what he was doing. Her lips tightened.

'I'll discuss it with my superiors. I'm sure you have work to be getting on with.' And with that, he was dismissed.

An hour later, he was summoned once more.

'That was quick,' he said.

Pamela gestured to him to sit down.

'This isn't about Chloe Gray. What do you know about Mark Nicholson's background?'

What was this? Alex frowned. 'Not much other than that he was brought up in the greater Pollok area and went to Caledonia University.' He could have added that Mark had been an exceedingly angry young man when he joined the force, but she didn't need to know that.

'Hmm. You're not keeping anything back, are you?'

'I don't think so. Mark has never been one to talk about his past.' He had enough to worry about in the present but that was none of Pamela's business. Instead he said, 'What is this about?'

'His father. Has he said anything about him? Anything at all?'

Alex sat back in his chair. 'I don't remember him saying anything about his father, or his mother, for that matter. We grew close when he was staying with me, but all we talked about was his current situation.' He tried to remember the late night conversations, but all he came up with was how he regretted cheating on Karen but wasn't sorry about the fact he had another son now. How if Suzanne reappeared, he'd fight her for custody. Nothing could convince him to give up his son now. But they'd never spoken about further in the past. Or had they? One conversation came to mind. A late night one when they'd both had too much to drink.

'What was your childhood like?' Mark's question had come out of nowhere.

'Oh, pretty ordinary. Mum, Dad, big brother. Of course there's only my mum left now.'

'Your brother died a few years ago, didn't he?'

'Yes.'

'Heart attack?' said Mark. He sipped his whisky.

'Yes. Completely out of the blue.'

Mark was silent for a few seconds, staring into his drink. 'It's hard losing a sibling.'

'You've lost one too? Yes, it is. What happened?'

But Mark didn't want to talk. 'I shouldn't have mentioned it. Forget it.' He'd changed the subject, and Alex had forgotten the incident until now.

'Have you remembered something?' said Pamela.

She was sharp. It must have shown in his face.

'He had a sibling who died. He mentioned it once. But he didn't say how or when.'

Pamela tapped her biro on her desk. 'Alex, did you know Mark's father is serving time for murder?'

Alex's mouth dropped open. 'What?' The word exploded from him. 'No, I had no idea.' His heart was racing. What did this mean? Why had Mark never told him? 'Who was the victim?'

The tapping became more urgent. 'Mark's younger sister. I believe Mark was only nine at the time. His evidence was crucial in getting his father convicted.'

Alex exhaled. 'The poor kid. What happened?'

'It's pretty grim. Apparently, he threw his daughter down a flight of stairs because she wouldn't stop crying. Mark witnessed it. She was left with severe brain damage, unable to walk or talk. Nothing. Mother died of a broken heart, they say.'

'Shit. That's terrible. No, Mark's never talked about it. What sort of sentence did he get?'

'He got the maximum. Life. Apparently, he'd been brutal for years, terrorising his family. He'd always hit Mark in places where the bruises weren't easily seen. His mother reported him to the police once after he beat her up but, in the end, she didn't press charges. She never forgave herself for not having the courage to report him properly. Mark's testimony was that his father had rushed into the bedroom and dragged his sister out of bed by her hair. She was only four years old. Four, Alex.' Pamela fiddled with her pen, her eyes were sad. 'Mark tried to stop him, but he got her out of the room, raised her above his head and flung her down the stairs. Poor wee thing didn't stand a chance. This wasn't an accident or an impulsive push gone wrong. This was a vicious, brutal attack on a defenceless child, which is why the sentence was so long. And he's still there. He was released fifteen years ago, got himself into a drugs gang and has been in and out ever since. He's always in trouble in prison. Always in fights. He's made a lot of enemies there. And got friendly with really bad people.'

Alex was finding this hard to take in. Mark must have had a hell of a childhood. He found it hard to imagine what his life must have been like. But why was Pamela telling him this? He asked her.

The biro between the fingers of her right hand came to a halt. She stopped tapping and twirled it round instead.

'That bloke you interviewed for trying to set Mark's flat alight, Liam Brown – he's come clean.'

'Hasn't he done so already?'

'There's more to the story than we believed. Yes, there's drugs involved. Isn't it always the case? But the order to kill Mark? It came from his father.'

'What?' Alex was stunned.

'Exactly my reaction. Kai Anderson was in his pocket, it turns out. Desperate to get out of the gang he'd been in with. A gang that Mark's father has a lot to do with. Stuart Nicholson told him he was free to go, but first he had to do one last thing. Kill Mark. He was warned that he had to get it right, if not, he and his parents would get it.'

'Jesus.'

'As you know, we've been working in collaboration with the drugs squad. I had a meeting with them late yesterday afternoon. They weren't pleased at this development. Apparently, they have an undercover officer on the job working on child exploitation in the gangs and they're pretty pissed off at this diversion. What was it they said again? Oh yes: "An old has-been gets shot at and he thinks it's all about him."'

Alex bridled. 'Two things, Firstly, it's not exactly my fault, is it?'

Pamela smiled, a look at contentment at having got to him. 'Did I say it was?'

Damn it. He'd taken the bait too easily. 'And secondly, I have never claimed it was about me. Not once.'

'Are you quite finished? Can I continue?' She arched her right eyebrow in an infuriating way. Disdainful. How did she manage it? He didn't reply and she carried on. When she finished, the only possible way to describe how he felt was stunned: What sort of a man was Mark's father? To arrange these attacks on his own son? He gaped at Pamela, who grimaced.

'Yes, exactly,' she said. 'It's unbelievable.'

'Are you sure it's him?'

'I'm afraid so. He's built up a powerful network of bad people, both in prison and out of it. From all accounts, he's a brute of a man. Violent and not afraid to use his fists. He became involved in drug smuggling inside. It's alleged he did a few people a favour by taking care of their enemies and over the years he has built up a nice wee empire. Of course, there's never any witnesses to what he did. Not one with the courage of a nine-year-old boy to testify against him. That's how he's managed to get away with it for so long.'

Alex breathed in deeply. 'Does Mark know about this?'

Pamela shuffled the papers on the desk, not looking at him. 'Not yet, no. I want you to tell him.'

He agreed at once and saw relief flicker across her face. He didn't mind. It made sense. He knew Mark as well as anyone.

'What do I tell him?'

'What I've told you. I think, as well, that his ex-partner should be warned. He might want to do that himself. Or he might want you to do that. Go with his instincts. She should move out of her house for the time being, go to a safe place.' She paused. 'Are you OK with all of that?'

Alex blinked. 'I... yes, of course. I'll get on to it right away.'

'Good. One more thing. Did you contact the prison to see who Kai Anderson shared a cell with?'

'Not me, personally. Shane McGowan interviewed whoever it was.'

'What did he say about it?'

'That the man had nothing to do with the gangs. A Steve McNichol.' His voice trailed off. 'That's a coincidence, isn't it? McNichol, Nicholson.'

Pamela was tapping her biro on her desk in the way he hated. 'I'll say it is. Right, tomorrow I want you to interview Stuart Nicholson in prison. Then we'll take a closer look at Shane McGowan. I'll get together what we have on him. It might be a coincidence, but then again, a quick phone call to Barlinnie will tell us if there's any such person as Steve McNichol. Me? I doubt it very much.'

It was fair to say he felt as though he had been hit hard by a punch to the head. There was a pulse throbbing that threatened to become a headache, and he was light headed, dizzy. Perhaps he ought to have had coffee after all. Pamela had told him to use one of the interview rooms.

'Put up a do not disturb notice in clear view,' she warned him. 'Mark might need time to process all of this.'

He went downstairs immediately to seek out Mark. 'Fancy a coffee?' he said.

'No, thanks. Too much work.'

'It can wait. Grab yourself a coffee, and one for me while you're at it and come to interview room two. I need to talk to you.'

Mark began to protest, and Alex cut him off. 'Now! I mean it.' Mark rolled his eyes and got up from his desk. 'This better be important.'

'It is,' was Alex's terse reply.

It was over. He'd told Mark. Mark hadn't moved while Alex went through the tale of how his father was trying to get him killed. When Alex had finished, Mark had said nothing. He sat in his chair staring ahead, his face blank.

'Are you OK?'

'Fuck. What do you think? I thought the cunt would be dead by now. Never thought for a minute he'd be behind all this. Fuck.'

'Did you not keep in touch with him?' As soon as the words were out of his mouth, Alex regretted them. Mark's eyes narrowed.

'That bastard killed my sister. She didn't die immediately, but the little girl she was he destroyed by picking her up like a bundle of washing and flinging her downstairs. So, no, Alex, I didn't keep in touch with him.'

Christ, he was a fool, he should think more before he spoke. 'Do you want to tell me about it? It must have been very traumatic.'

Mark was silent for several seconds, trying to control his emotions.

'That's one way of putting it,' he said at last. 'My mum never recovered. She blamed herself, saying she should never have gone out that night, or that she ought to have left him years ago.' Mark put his head in his hands. 'The thing is she was right. She shouldn't have gone out then. And she should have left him years before. He was a brute. He hit me, Mum and Mandy. If anything went wrong in his life, he took it out on us, his family. The people he was supposed to love and protect.' He looked up at Alex, tears brimming in his eyes. 'Did your da beat you up, Alex?'

'The odd skelp on the legs, but I think it hurt him more than it hurt me.'

'That's what I thought you'd say. That bastard put cigarettes out on my mum. Pressed them into her arms. Up at the top, near her shoulder, so the scars weren't visible. So, when I got the chance, I told the police what he'd done.'

'You did the right thing.'

'Did I?' said Mark. 'The right thing to do would have been to kill him.'

'You were a child. You don't mean that.'

There was a vacant look to Mark's eyes as he gazed at Alex. 'I do.'

Alex went on to break the news that Karen, too, might be in danger. And their children. Mark didn't take it well. To Alex's horror, he started to sob.

Alex sat in awkward silence unsure what to say. 'Come on, now. It'll be alright. You'll see.' He cringed inwardly at the meaningless words.

'Will it? How am I going to tell her I've put her and our children at risk again. What sort of father am I? A fucking useless one. I've done nothing but put our family into danger. First that fucking sister of Suzanne's tried to kill us all, and now this.' In an attempt to get back at Suzanne, Julie Campbell had set fire to his house and then kidnapped Mark and Karen's youngest child. His face paled at the memory. 'What am I going to do?'

'I'll come with you,' said Alex. He should be going to Barlinnie now, but this wouldn't take long, and Karen had to be told. 'This is not your fault. You didn't choose your father.'

When they drew up in front of the house Mark had shared with Karen, Mark didn't make a move but sat on in the passenger seat staring ahead. Alex nudged him.

'Come on, son. Let's get it over with.'

Karen opened the door with a scowl that changed to a neutral expression when she saw Mark was not alone.

'Yes?' she said. 'What do you want?'

'Can we come in, Karen?' said Alex.

Immediately, her hands flew to her face. 'Dear God, is it one of the kids?'

'No, nothing like that. But we need to talk to you, urgently.'

They followed her into the house. It was the total opposite of Alex's flat. A small living room crammed with furniture and toys. But in spite of the clutter, it was cosy and welcoming. They sat down on one of the sofas, pushing aside a half built Lego castle.

'Tell me,' she urged. 'What is it?'

To her credit, she didn't interrupt when Mark was telling her what had happened. She sat rigidly on the sofa, her face stony throughout. He finished by saying, 'You'll need to move out of here for a while. It might not be safe here. Where will you go?'

'None of your business,' she snapped.

Alex stepped in. They had to know where she and the children were going to be so they could at least check up on them from time to time.

'I'm sorry, Karen, but I'm under strict instructions from my boss to find out where you're going to be. We can't offer full protection, but the local police will keep an eye on wherever it is you go.'

She pushed back her hair from her face. 'Oh God, I don't know. What am I going to do? The children should be at school. Do I take them out? And my work, do I go into work? This is all such a mess.'

Alex said nothing, feeling it might make things worse if he spoke. Mark leaned forward and took her hand. 'What about your parents?'

Karen glared at him, and he retreated. 'They already hate you. What would I tell them?'

'An emergency flood, work getting done in the house?'

'They'd only fuss. Dad would want to come over and check how the work was going. Mum would be offering to help to tidy up. You know what they're like. And then I'd have to tell them, and it would be worse because I hadn't been honest with them.'

'Do you have any friends who could put you up?' asked Alex.

'No. None of them have much room in their houses. Though there is...' she stopped.

'Who?' said Mark. His face had darkened, and Alex suspected what was coming next.

'Craig, my friend. He might be able to put me up.'

Mark looked thunderous but said nothing. Thank goodness. It could only make things worse. Alex had an idea.

'Look, isn't it a holiday weekend this week? Why don't you take the children away for a few days. It'll be covered by the department.' Mark opened his mouth, but Alex shot him a warning frown. Alex would pay for it. 'That way you're not beholden to anyone.'

She looked relieved, and Alex wondered what this new relationship of hers was like. She hadn't exactly leapt at the chance to go and stay with this Craig, whoever he was.

'If you're sure. That would be good. A lodge for three nights at one of the caravan parks on the Clyde coast costs around four hundred pounds.'

'Write down what you need, and I'll get on to it,' promised Alex.

'And after this weekend, what happens then?'

Fuck knows, thought Alex but he stopped himself from

saying it. If it wasn't all over, she and the kids could come and stay with him for a while as a last resort.

'Let's worry about that later,' he said. 'I'll find a solution.'

Outside, Mark turned on him. 'What are you playing at? No way will the boss sanction paying for a lodge, and I can't afford it.'

Alex ignored his objections. 'I'll take care of it. Now, I need to find a place for her to stay.'

Mark protested all the way back to the station, but Alex was determined and when he was in that mood it was best not to cross him.

Back at work, Alex searched online for a lodge to meet Karen's needs. It didn't take long – there was a suitable one at Wemyss Bay. It wasn't outrageously expensive – and once he'd phoned Karen to give her the details, he called the local police in North Ayrshire to fill them in and ensure officers would check in on Karen while she was there over the weekend. He hoped this would all be tied up by then, and she could go home once more.

On the way home, he stopped to pick up a fish supper. He'd have a beer or two to go with it. This was the last time, he promised himself. The weight was piling on again, but he was too tired and fed up to cook.

There was no sign of Kris or any other workmen when Alex got home. Thank the lord. All he wanted was to sit in front of the telly with his takeaway and relax, or he'd listen to music. He was in the mood for Ella Fitzgerald. He searched through Spotify for the playlist he'd made and put it on now while he got his meal together. The fish supper was tepid, so he put it aside. If he remembered correctly, he had leftover samosas in the fridge. He'd heat them up along with the fish and chips – fuck! What was that? A blur of fur rushed past him to the front door. That damn cat – again. It was mewing to get outside. Little shit. He opened the door, and it promptly turned round and ran into the living room. Alex knew he should get it out, but at the moment, he couldn't be arsed chasing it round the flat. He'd get it in a minute. Better check on progress in the bathroom.

It looked as though it was nearly finished. What an improvement on what was there before: a bog standard bathroom suite with small white tiles and flowery borders, dating from the nineties. Now the sleek look achieved by the anthracite coloured tiles, wall hung toilet and freestanding basin on a custom-made unit made it right up to date. And his pride and joy, the walk-in shower to replace the bath. Brilliant – oh fuck, what was this? Not that damn cat again! Right in the middle of the shower tray.

Half an hour later, supper eaten and with the bathroom cleaned, yet again, he managed to get the cat safely out of the flat. Alex settled on the sofa with a bottle of fifteen-year-old Bowmore at his side. He had just poured himself a generous dram when the doorbell rang. For a moment, he considered not answering, but only for a second. It might be important. He heaved himself out of his seat, noting the twinge in his knee and went to see who it was. It would be good if it was Mark – there was more to be said on the tale of his father – but through the stained glass he saw the outline of a woman. He opened the door.

'Alex!' It was Alice from downstairs. 'Oh you have a cat.' As she spoke the cat wound its way past her and darted into the flat.

'I don't. It's been hanging about here for the past couple of days. How can I help you, Alice?' He didn't invite her in. Alex valued his privacy, and although he was on good terms with all of his neighbours, he rarely socialised with any of them. A drink at New Year was the most socialising he'd done.

She held up a bottle of champagne. 'I thought we could celebrate the fact you're finally safe.'

A myriad of excuses went through his head: it was late; he was tired; he already had company; he was in the middle of doing paperwork; he was a curmudgeonly old sod. One by one, he dismissed them.

'Come in,' he said. 'But we'll have none of those French soft drinks, thank you. I've got a good bottle of malt.'

She followed him into the living room and sat down in his favourite seat. Anyone who knew him would never dare do that but there wasn't much he could say. This was why he only invited people he knew well to his flat. He lifted his glass off the coffee table that was right in front of her.

'Oh, sorry. Have I taken your seat?' She half rose from the sofa.

Alex was at a loss what to say. She had already moved to the other sofa.

'I am a numpty. I can't stand it either when someone takes my chair and yet here I am, waltzing in and snatching yours from under your nose.'

'I'll get you a drink. You don't have to drink malt if you don't want to.'

'Thank goodness.' She settled herself down on the sofa and held out the champagne to him. 'I'll have a glass of this.'

She was good company, he'd give her that. They discovered they shared a love of classical music.

'Favourite composer?' she asked.

'Beethoven,' he replied without hesitating.

She wrinkled her nose. 'Good one, anyone else?'

'Mahler, especially the Kindertoten Lieder.' His face darkened when he remembered the awful days following his daughter's disappearance. The song cycle about dead children had given him comfort, if only that he was not the only parent to have undergone such a loss. Alice must have picked up on his change of mood and she was tactful enough to make no comment. Thank goodness.

'What about you?'

'Opera,' she said. 'Verdi but especially Mozart. My favourite is *Cosi Fan Tutte*. The sublime beauty of *Soave sia il vento*, those harmonies.'

'Mm,' said Alex. It was not his favourite. Its theme of infidelity didn't sit well with him.

'You don't like it.' She sounded disappointed.

'Oh, I do. But there are others I prefer.' He sensed a drop in the energy in the room and hurried to change the subject. 'Have you ever been to the cinema to watch a live performance from Covent Garden?'

'No, I haven't. I prefer being in the theatre. Have you?'

'No. I thought about it, but like you, I prefer live music. Although I suppose in a way it is live.'

Alice swirled what remained of her drink in her glass. Alex took the hint. 'Top-up?'

'Thought you'd never ask.' She had a mischievous smile. Attractive. No, this wouldn't do. She was his neighbour. They had to remain on friendly terms, that was all. He rushed off to get her champagne out of the fridge, aware he was enjoying her company far too much. When he got back, she was studying his sound system closely.

'I assume you stream your music. I see no tapes or CDs.'

Alex smiled, remembering how he had offloaded his vast CD collection to a local charity shop after paying a company to download them to his new sound system. 'Yes, streaming mainly, but I have over a thousand CDs loaded onto the system,' he said. 'I got rid of them a while ago.'

'You prefer the minimalist look.' It wasn't a question.

'I suppose.' He wasn't sure he did like it better. Recently, he found himself regretting his rash decision to get rid of his music and book collection. He'd kept only a few well-loved books that were on bookshelves out in the hall and told himself the rest had only been gathering dust and he was well rid of them. But he'd gone too far, he saw that now. There wasn't even a painting on any of the walls. Kate often told him he should buy a piece of art. She was always dragging him into fine art galleries to look at landscapes. Come to think of it, there was one nearby he could have a look in at the weekend. He'd treat himself. An abstract, perhaps. Alice's voice interrupted his ruminations.

'What this place needs is a woman's touch.' She drained her glass.

Before he could stop himself, Alex said, 'Are you offering?'

What the fuck. He blushed as he realised what he'd said. Alice laughed and held out her glass for more champagne.

'We'll see,' she said.

The Fallen

Alex woke the next morning with the worse hangover he'd had in years. His mouth was as rough as a badger's arse and his head, sweet Jesus, his head was full of tiny hammers, picking away at his brain. He lay in bed frightened to look in case Alice was beside him. Tentatively he placed a hand on the sheet next to him. Nothing. Relief overwhelmed him that the evening hadn't ended in drunken sex they would both regret. Underlying the relief, though, was a touch of what? Sadness, regret? He wasn't sure, and he didn't have time to examine his feelings now. He had to get ready for work.

Half an hour later, a shower followed by a bacon roll and a coffee made from grounds Mark had left behind and he was ready for the day. As he left, he bumped into the plumber coming up the stairs.

'Kris, please make sure that damn cat doesn't get into the flat again. It's doing my head in. There was another gift left in the shower for me.'

Kris apologised and Alex waved it away. It wasn't his fault. They had a short discussion about how much longer the job would take. There wasn't much left to do now, only painting and a few snagging points.

'I finish tomorrow,' he said. 'Painter come today, and I let him in, then tomorrow I check everything OK.'

Alex ran down the steps, his heart light. It was looking good. As he was passing Alice's door, she came out, a wide smile on her face.

'Someone's cheerful.'

'Yes, my bathroom will be finished soon. At last.'

'And there was me thinking it was my company last night that put that smile on your face.'

His smile wavered as he tried to digest what she was

saying. He was hopeless at flirting. Was she being serious or joking? When it came to reading people he was clueless.

With a muttered, 'Sorry, I'm late for work, must dash,' he was outside running to his car as though his life depended on it.

Chapter Eighteen

IT WAS two days before Hayley contacted Kate. Although she was desperate to know what Hayley was hiding, she had resigned herself to never hearing from her again. Lewis had been so adamant that whatever it was Hayley was going to say, she should keep it to herself, and Hayley was very much under his influence. So when Kate's mobile rang with an unknown number as she was going to bed, she picked it up reluctantly thinking it wasn't important. She was exhausted and looking forward to a good night's sleep but woke up from her dazed state when she recognised Hayley's voice.

'Kate? S'me, Hayley.'

Kate didn't want to scare her off by sounding too keen. She took a deep breath before she spoke. 'Hello, Hayley. You alright?'

'We need to meet. Now. I have to tell you about that guy Callum. S'urgent.'

'What? You want to meet now?'

'Aye, Lewis is away on a job for the gang. He doesn't

want me to speak to you, and he's aye hanging about. Come to my house. I'll give you my address.'

Shit. This didn't sound like a good idea.

'What about your mother?' Kate was desperately trying to think of reasons why she shouldn't go out late at night to meet an unstable teenager in a house with a drug addict. For all she knew, it was a trap.

'Her? She won't be conscious until tomorrow.'

Conor came into the bedroom and made a quizzical face. She shooed him away. She needed all her wits about her.

'It's late, Hayley. Can't you tell me on the phone?'

'No! I need to see you.'

'Tell you what. I'll drive over and meet you outside the café we were in last time, and then we can go for a drive.'

There was a pause. 'Ach, forget it.'

Kate was worried Hayley was about to put down the phone.

'No, wait. Give me your address and I'll come round.'

Conor's mouth tightened, 'No way,' he hissed. She turned her back on him, holding her phone tight in case he tried to take it from her. Hayley gave her the address, which she repeated.

'Right Hayley, I'll see you in about half an hour.' She cut off the call and waited for the storm to come from Conor. It wasn't long in coming.

'What was all that about? You're not serious about going out at this time?'

While she was getting dressed, she told him as quickly as she could.

'Are you mad? You don't know this girl. She's involved in a drugs gang, her mother's a drug addict and her brother, what the hell is he up to? You're not going, Kate.'

Kate looked up at him. 'This story could make a real difference to me. I'm going.'

'You're pregnant.'

Surely he wasn't going to emotionally blackmail her into not going? If she didn't meet Hayley now, she'd never hear from her again. She'd bet her life on it. But before she said anything, Conor said, 'I'm coming with you.'

'I'm sure that's not necessary.'

'It is.'

Despite it all, Kate was reassured. She wasn't keen on going alone. For one thing, she didn't know how to get there. The sat nav in their car was unreliable and had a tendency to lead them down dead ends. Fine when it was daylight, but on her own in the dark? She didn't fancy her chances. It would be good to have Conor there as back up.

Ten minutes later, they were on their way. It was after eleven and the roads were quiet, so they made good time. When they drew up in front of the block of flats where Hayley lived, Kate was more thankful than ever to have Conor with her. The street was dark; one of the streetlights was out, and there was a group of youths hanging around the corner, about a hundred metres away. Fortunately, they didn't appear to have spotted their car.

'I'm coming in with you,' said Conor.

'She might not talk if you're there.'

'This is non-negotiable, Kate. I have to make sure you're safe.'

There was no doorbell to ring, so Kate knocked on the door. After a short pause, Hayley opened it, but only a sliver, using it as a shield. She glared out at them.

'Who's this?' she glared at Conor.

'This is my partner, Conor. Can we come in?'

Hayley opened the door a smidgeon wider, and they went inside. The air was heavy with the stink of weed, but Kate didn't think Hayley had been smoking. She looked far too much on edge. They followed her into the living room, which smelled worse. Here there was an underlying smell of damp. On the wall there were patches of black mould near the ceiling and underneath her feet the carpet was sticky. Hayley had made an effort to clear up – papers and clothes were piled up on the sofa – but the overall effect was chaotic. Kate waited to be told what to do. She didn't want to presume and move the mess. Fortunately, Hayley cleared a space for her and Conor on the larger of the two sofas.

'Do youse want a drink?'

'No, thanks. We're fine. You said you had something to tell me. About Callum Peterson.'

Hayley picked at her fingernails, peeling off the black polish she'd painted them with.

'Look, I might have it all wrong, but...'

'But what?' Kate kept her voice soft and low. Hayley was agitated and looked as though she might take flight at any moment.

'It's not only about Callum. It's about them all or some of them anyway.'

'Go on.'

'I think they were murdered. In fact I'm sure Callum was.'

Kate's mouth dried up. Her palms were sweaty. This was much darker than she'd imagined. On the way here she'd assumed she was going to hear more about the gang's activities, details about the catfishing and how it had been done. She reminded herself of the meeting with Callum's parents and his mother's hesitant voicing of her fear that Callum had

The Fallen

been murdered. One of his friends had also put forward the same idea. Kate hadn't given their suspicions too much consideration. A possibility, she thought, but all the evidence pointed to it being suicide and the revelations about catfishing lent weight to that. But now one of the actual gang was stating that at least one, if not more, of the teenagers had definitely been murdered.

'Why do you think that?' she asked.

Hayley looked around the room as if someone might be listening.

'It was what I overheard one of the Dunmores say. He was raging, kept going on about it.'

'What was he angry about?'

'The plan wasn't working, he said. Callum's name came up.' Hayley stood up and paced round the room like a demented chicken. She rubbed her arms with her hands in a self-comforting gesture.

'Are you OK?' Conor asked.

'Aye, it's...'

They waited for her to speak and when she said nothing, Kate went over to her.

'Is there anything we can do? I can see you're upset.'

The words burst out in a torrent. 'I want out of this fucking dump. I fucking hate it here. There's all sorts coming to the door, anytime day or night and what I have to do to survive. It's... nobody should have to live this way. Nobody. I fucking hate it.'

What did you say to a young person with no hope? Things will get better? Don't worry, you'll get through this? All the while knowing it was unlikely to be true? Kate had no idea, so she said nothing. Fortunately Conor intervened before her silence became damning.

'What age are you, Hayley?'

'Fourteen,' she muttered, looking down at her shoes.

A child. Jesus. Kate wanted to weep. She'd assumed Hayley was at least sixteen. Or older. There was an air of world weariness about her.

'Do you have a social worker? Or a teacher at school you can talk to?'

'I don't go to school and my social worker's off on the sick.'

Conor went over and knelt down beside her. 'Look Hayley, we'll do our best to help you, but you have to tell us what you know.'

'I don't know nothing. That's the problem. How do I prove it? I don't have evidence.'

'Except what you heard. Tell us what you heard.'

Hayley sniffed. 'He was boasting about what he'd do to Callum. Callum had said he wouldn't deal drugs. He didn't care about the photos. Said his parents would support him and go to the police.'

'Did they send Callum the photos?'

'I'm not sure. But they told him they had them and they were going to send them to all his contacts, but he didn't care, or so he said.'

'Wait, how do you know this?'

'Jake Dunmore was bragging about it. Said he was going to make sure Callum had a nasty accident and soon. "He's no use to us alive so we might as well get rid of him."'

'When was this?' said Conor.

'The night before he died. I saw it in the paper a couple of days later and recognised the name. There's more as well. There was another article, and it said his parents and friends were claiming it wasn't suicide, saying that Callum wouldn't do such a thing. They'd asked for an inquiry. I think that panicked the gang, and I was told to contact the papers and say I was a friend he'd confided in. They believed it worked because the inquiry thing said it was suicide. Then there was another suicide. Maybe the same thing happened again. Maybe not. But contact the newspapers with a shit story? Why would they do that if it was a suicide? And now there's this latest one, and I was asked to do the same again. That's all I've got.' Her voice was pleading. 'Is it enough to get me out of here?'

'Let me get this clear. You heard Callum being threatened and then you were told to get in touch with the papers and tell them it was suicide, that Callum had confided in you?'

'No. I didn't hear him actually being threatened. I heard Dunmore say he'd make sure Callum would meet with an accident. "Nobody says no to me," he said.'

Kate and Conor looked at each other. 'You need to go to the police with this,' said Kate.

Hayley started to hyperventilate. 'No, I can't. They'll kill me. You seen what they done to Kai.'

'Kai?'

'He's the boy who was supposed to kill that polis and he fucked it up, so they killed him.'

Christ, could it get any worse? Kate made a decision.

'OK, now listen. Stay calm, deep breaths. You leave this with us. I'll see what I can do to help. Do you have a mobile number you can give me?'

Miserable, Hayley shook her head.

'No, I only have a burner. They change it every couple of nights.'

Kate had only the vaguest idea what a burner was. 'But

you've got my number, haven't you?'

'Aye. I memorised it. Had to get rid of your wee card. If they found that on me, I'd be dead.'

Kate tried not to show her shock. 'We're going now. But like I said, keep in touch.'

'And the money?'

'Once I've got the story published. I promise you. Forty/sixty share, like we said. But it will take time, Hayley.'

Hayley scowled at this. Kate stood up and made her way to the door with Conor behind her.

Once they were in the car, Conor spoke. 'Do you believe her?'

Kate yawned. She was drained by Hayley's revelations and melodrama.

'Yes, I do. She was terrified when she was telling us. Did you see how she kept glancing towards the door even though her brother and mother were safely out of the picture?'

'Yes, I did. Poor kid.'

'It's awful, isn't it? I think she's sound. From what his friends and parents told me Callum wasn't at all like the sort of person who'd kill himself. I don't see him as a boy who'd give into blackmail.'

'Really? What they did to him is pretty humiliating. I'd maybe have done the same in his shoes.'

'You'd seriously think about killing yourself because of something like that? I don't believe you.'

'Not now obviously, but when I was younger. Maybe?'

God, what a waste of young lives.

'I'm going to speak to Dad about it, see what he advises. But let's get to bed, it's after midnight and I'm exhausted.'

The next day, Alex listened carefully to what she had to say. When she finished, he said, 'It's not much to go on, what the girl said. Is she reliable?'

Kate thought back to the chaotic house, to the girl's fear. She had to convince him but at the same time she wasn't going to lie.

'I couldn't swear to it.'

'She's not spinning you a line, is she? In the hope of getting the money you promised her.'

'She might be,' she admitted. 'What would happen if she spoke to the police?'

'Look, I'll speak again to the person who was in charge initially. See what she thinks. When I spoke to her, I got the impression she believed it was all kosher. That all of them killed themselves.'

'Hayley isn't claiming they've all been murdered,' said Kate. 'Only Callum, and maybe Bilal and Alfie, the latest boy. They're the only ones she was asked to contact a reporter about. If she was lying, wouldn't she claim all of them were killed?'

'Does she have any solid evidence? A text message, email, anything. The problem is, she'd be seen as an unreliable witness.' Kate opened her mouth to object, and he held up his hands in surrender.

'I know it's unfair, but we work on evidence.'

'I didn't ask but the only phone she has is a burner, so I doubt it.'

'If there was anything, anything at all to latch on to...'

'There's a photo of Callum on her brother's phone. You know, a compromising one.'

'Well that's something. If we can get hold of it.'

'She'll phone again, I know she will. I'll ask her then if

there's anything else and if she can get a copy of the photo.'

The conversation was left like that. Nothing for it but to wait.

Alex was staggered by what Kate had told him. It had been an open and shut case as far as he was concerned when he read about it, both in the newspapers and then when he read Janey's notes. The obvious conclusion was the teenagers had killed themselves. It happened every day. Or so he had believed until Kate had bamboozled him with figures. It turned out it wasn't as common as he thought, and it looked highly improbable that four, no, five teenagers would have killed themselves in the same city over the course of two months. What was stranger was the fact they'd all effectively used the same method. No, everything about this made him deeply uncomfortable. Although he had piles of work to do, he decided his first priority was to speak properly to the police officer Janey, who had led the initial enquiries.

He popped his head round the door of the open-plan office where she was based.

'Janey, could I have a word please?'

A minute later they were ensconced in his room.

'About these teenage suicides, are you one hundred percent happy they killed themselves?'

If he'd shocked her, she didn't show it.

'Now? Now there's five of them, and with what you said? No, I'm not happy. All schoolchildren. Most from stable backgrounds. It stinks, but bugger me if I know what's going on.'

'We'll have to take another look at them,' said Alex.

'You'll remember I told you my daughter, a journalist, is interested in these? Well, she's spoken to a young girl who passed on interesting information.'

'Oh, yes?'

Alex noted she wasn't at all fazed by what he said. Good. There were many officers who would take umbrage at anything that could be criticism. Janey was more interested in getting at the truth. He outlined what Kate had told him.

'So, what do you think?'

'I think we've fucked up. I've fucked up. Badly. We missed out on checking their phones and computers thoroughly. They weren't sent for further analysis. We had a brief look at what was in them, websites they'd visited, checked their emails et cetera, but there was no deep dive into what else might be on them. I'll get on to it right away, call in a computer forensic analyst.'

'Three of the deaths are especially suspicious, Janey, Callum Peterson's, Bilal Assam's and this latest death. Callum's in particular is worth concentrating on because he's the one who was definitely catfished in order to get photos worth blackmailing him over and the girl heard Jake Dunmore threatening him. Not directly but saying he was going to meet with an accident. Kate's seen a copy of the photo they were going to use to blackmail Callum so that's tangible evidence. We need more though.'

'You're right. We'll concentrate on him first and if I get anything from that, I'll let you know immediately.'

It didn't take long for the message to come through. Janey was breathless as she recounted what the computer forensic analyst had found.

'It was exactly as your daughter was told. He'd deleted the website from his computer and any trace of it from his search history, but it didn't take long to find. It was a games website where you chat privately to other players. A young woman popped up in there and messaged him with a few jokes about the game. He found her funny, and she asked if he wanted to see her photo. He said no, that he'd prefer to meet up IRL—'

'IRL? What's that?'

'Acronym for In Real Life.' She carried on. 'The girl said she lived in London so it wouldn't be possible, but she liked him and was going to send a photo, which she did. All very innocent, a respectable picture of a stunning young girl. The analyst did a reverse picture search on Google and found it was from a Facebook profile, l bet the names didn't match up. It's common in catfishing for the perpetrator to steal images from social media sites like Facebook. There are lots of people out there who don't use their privacy settings.' She sighed. 'Anyway, to cut a long story short, he sent a similar innocent one back. Before long, it had escalated, always with the catfish taking the lead. The pictures from that side got sexier and sexier, pouts and boobs, that sort of thing, until one evening they sent a video of her masturbating. The analyst said the video had been taken from a porn site and PhotoShopped to make it look like the girl.'

Alex blew out his cheeks. 'Hell's teeth. It sounds horrific. I'm glad I'm not a teenager.'

'You and me, both. After that there were constant messages from the catfish, emotional blackmail: "I've exposed myself to you and now I feel like a slut. Please send me one back, to show you care." He held out for a few days and then gave in. Poor sod. The blackmail email came by return.' Janey's face showed her concern. 'I've got two teenagers and we'll be having an explicit and embarrassing conversation tonight. I'm horrified by all this.'

'Do you have copies of the emails?'

'Callum had deleted them of course, which is why they didn't come up in the first trawl, but, yes, we now have copies. Now I have to visit his parents and tell them we're re-opening his case and why. I'm not looking forward to that, I can tell you.'

'How are we getting on with the others?'

'I haven't heard, sorry. No doubt they'll be moving on to them now. I'll let you know.' With that, Janey rang off.

Alex had no sooner put down his phone than it rang again. It was Kate.

'Dad, Callum Peterson's parents phoned me five minutes ago.'

'Oh?'

'Do you know anything about this new search of Callum's computer?'

'Kate, I can't say anything.'

'Of course, I understand. It's... well, they're upset. They want to know what's going on.'

'I'm sure. But it makes no difference. I'm not able to discuss this any further, I'm sorry, Kate. But an officer will be going out to talk to them soon to tell them what they've found out. For now you have to stay out of it.'

Her reply was subdued. 'Yes, you're right. And I shouldn't have phoned you. I'm sorry.'

Alex put his phone down. It was time to get ready for his prison visit.

Chapter Nineteen

ALEX HADN'T SET foot in Barlinnie for, oh, what? Twenty years at least, and in all that time, it hadn't changed. An imposing building, it had opened in late Victorian times and now housed over eleven hundred prisoners, though its capacity was less than a thousand. On a sunny day, it looked bleak. On a dreich day like this, it was beyond awful. The stonework was dark grey. Many other sandstone buildings in the city had been cleaned of the smoke that stained them, but not this one. It was dire on the outside and worse inside. There were rumours of a new prison in the offing, but until it was built, which could be years away, they were stuck with this. At least they'd stopped the slopping out. For years, prisoners had to get rid of their overnight urine and faeces in the common toilets. The stench had been horrific, and once experienced, it was not easily forgotten. There were those who claimed the smell lingered. Alex breathed cautiously as he entered but there was only a faint whiff of bleach in the air.

Alex had been granted use of an interview room where he would be able to talk to Stuart Nicholson in private. Pamela had filled him in on the evidence that he was behind the attacks on his son. It wasn't only Liam Brown's word they had to go on. There were phone calls, overheard conversations and more. As yet Alex hadn't made up his mind exactly what he was going to say but he'd have to keep his cool no matter how hard it might be. It wasn't long before Nicholson was in front of him. He was in handcuffs, but it didn't make him any less menacing.

Mark had told him he was fifty eight. Not much older than Alex was. It seemed too young to be the father of Mark, who wasn't yet forty. He'd been a teenager when Mark was born; ruining his life as he'd told Mark over and over. Trapped with a wife and weans when he should be out enjoying himself. Alex thought of that now as he faced the cunt. He was a vicious-looking bastard.

Nicholson was tall, taller than Mark, but he wasn't slim like him. He was built like the side of a bus. It wasn't fat, though. Muscles bulged under his t-shirt. This was a man who worked out. His face had a bashed-in look. A broken nose helped to exaggerate this effect. Earned in here, no doubt. If Pamela was right, his reputation as a hard man was second to none.

He scowled at Alex as he sat down.

'Who the fuck are you?' he snarled. 'Polis, they said. And I said to them, "What the fuck does a pig want with me?"'

There were many reasons why the police might be interested in him, but Alex was here for one purpose only.

'I want to talk to you about your son,' he said.

Nicholson leaned forward. 'I don't have a fucking son.'

Alex didn't move though Nicholson's face was too close.

The prison guard intervened.

'Nicholson, move back now.'

With a sneer he complied. Thank fuck.

Alex leaned back in his chair and stared at the man.

'You do have a son and you've been calling in favours in order to try to get him killed.'

'Prove it,' he sneered.

'We have one witness who has told us you were behind an attempt to set your son's flat on fire. He heard you boasting about it to another prisoner. We also have another witness who overheard your conversation with a would-be arsonist, which corroborates his account. The phone call was made on the eleventh of last month at four forty-five p.m. We've checked. There's a search of your cell going on at this moment, which will no doubt show up the mobile phone that's illegally in your possession.'

'What the fuck are you're talking about?'

'Come off it. You're done. This'll add a few more years to your sentence.'

'No son of mine would ever be a polis. If I had a son.'

Alex wanted to smash his face in, but he forced himself to remain polite, thinking this would annoy the bastard more.

'Mr Nicholson, you do have a son. We have the records to prove it, and he is a police officer. Is that why you're trying to get him killed? Bet it wouldn't go down well in here if anyone found out. A hard man like you connected to the police. You'd be a laughing stock. Is that why you're trying to get him killed?'

Nicholson didn't reply. He turned to the guard and said, 'I'm finished here.'

The guard looked at Alex.

'You sure?'

'Aye, take him away. I'm sick of the smell of shite.'

Alex had hoped for an adverse reaction, perhaps a punch but Nicholson ignored him. Fuck, it. Alex wouldn't have minded taking a swing at him. It was not to be. Rage built up in him as he imagined Mark and his wee boy being trapped in that flat. He'd have loved to have had a go at the bastard. The guard came back into the interview room as he was getting ready to go.

'That you now?'

'Aye, I suppose so.'

'Waste of time, was it? Sounded like it.'

Alex didn't reply. He had no wish to go into the whole story with the prison guard.

His lack of response didn't deter the guard.

'Is this about the visitor he got a few weeks ago? The guy told him the son who had dobbed him in all those years ago was now a police officer. Bastard didn't take it well. Broke up his cell, so he did. Smashed it. Earned him a week in solitary. Can't say I was sorry, gave us peace for a while.'

'Are you sure about this? He didn't know until then that his son was in the police?'

'Nope. Never talked about him. Somehow, he managed to keep it quiet what he did to his daughter. And of course he's been in and out a couple of times, so his original sin so to speak was all but forgotten. Just as well for him. The other prisoners don't like that sort of thing. Other men have been half killed for less but that cunt never gets touched.'

'That's hard to believe. I mean, that others don't know.'

The guard thought for a second before replying. 'You're right. It's brute force and being in with the right people that does it. Occasionally, there's a rumour, but once they find out who's behind it, they never repeat it.'

This was an interesting development. A visit followed by attempts on Mark's life. It had to be linked to the drugs case.

'Don't suppose you have any idea when the visit was?' Alex had visions of leafing through a grubby visitor's book with hundreds of illegible signatures and getting nowhere.

'I know exactly when it was. It was my daughter's birthday. Her first.' His cheeks were pink.

Alex grinned.

'No, you don't forget things like that. Is she your only child?'

'Yes, but we're trying for another. I want at least three.' He beamed at Alex. 'No luck yet but we have fun trying, as they say.'

Fuck's sake, what was this? Too much information. Alex changed the subject before the man went into detail.

'Can I see the visitor's book?'

'No problem. I'll get it now.'

He was back within five minutes and handed the book over to Alex, open at the relevant page. Alex scanned the prisoners' names looking for whoever visited Stuart Nicholson that day. After a few seconds, he found it. He stared at the familiar name scrawled beside Nicholson's in disbelief. It couldn't be... and yet, he recognised the handwriting. What in God's name was going on? He left the prison and got into his car. For several seconds, he sat there trying to control his emotions. When he thought of all the time and worry he'd spent on this case, only to find that all along Mark had been the one behind it. Why the fuck would he do such a thing? He'd better have a good explanation.

'What are you talking about?' Mark's voice was high with indignation. A pulse ticked under his left eye. 'I have never visited my father in prison. I told you. I assumed he was dead, and even now, now I know he's alive, I won't be going to see him. Why the fuck would I when he put us all through such misery? What's all this about?'

Alex's pulse was racing. 'Do you swear it?'

'What? Am I in court now? I'm fucking telling you, I haven't been near him.'

Alex studied Mark's face for a few seconds, looking for a tell that he was lying, but he had to hand it to him, he was doing a convincing job of telling the truth. However, there was the small matter of the signature in the visitor's book. He didn't want to believe it, but it was there in black and white.

'Mark, it'll be best if you come clean now, son.'

Christ, Mark was going to hit him. Alex knew he had a temper. Fuck it, hadn't he had to stop him from beating up a man early on in his career? Mark had been new to the job, and it was a bad, bad case. A man who had killed his own child. Alex thought he understood why Mark did it at the time, but he'd only had half the story. But nothing excused his temper now. He'd been caught out in a lie. A big, fat lie. Worthy of that bastard who was their current prime minister.

'Think about what you're doing, Mark,' he warned as Mark loomed over him. 'I won't protect you this time.' He was more relieved than he could say to see Mark return to his seat.

Mark had his head in his hands.

'At least tell me what this is about. You can't come in here and call me a liar without good reason.' His voice was shaky.

Alex told him what had happened.

'Your signature was there, Mark, in the visitor's book at Barlinnie. I recognised it at once, the funny squiggle at the end of your first name. It's distinctive, Mark. Immediately recognisable.'

Mark's eyes narrowed.

'I don't believe this,' he said. 'That you of all people would think this of me. That I would lie like this. Why? Why would I do it?'

'You tell me,' said Alex. 'Look, I'm sure you didn't mean to start all this vendetta. Maybe you didn't realise what sort of power your father had over other criminals. And once all the attacks were underway, then obviously you didn't want to say anything about it. But—'

'But nothing, Alex. I did not visit my father in prison. I repeat, I thought he was dead. Whatever you think you saw, it wasn't my signature. So, if you're done, I'll get back to work now.'

Time to play his ace.

'There's CCTV footage as well, which I've requested. It'll come through shortly.'

'Maybe it will but it won't show me on it. Not a chance.'

Alex felt the stirrings of doubt. Mark was convincing, nobody would argue with that. And he hadn't seen the CCTV footage yet. Who knew what it would show? Was it possible for someone to have impersonated Mark? But who would do that? And why? Alex made a decision. This was a man he'd shared a home with for over a year. A friend who had entrusted his child to him, a man he liked and respected. Despite the evidence, there must be more to it than this.

'Right, enough said. I believe you. Get back to work now.

The Fallen

I have to chase this up further. Try to find out what's going on.'

If he expected Mark to be grateful, he was out of luck. Mark left the room without a word, drawing him a look that would fell trees. Alex hoped this little contretemps wouldn't affect their relationship, but he doubted it. He'd offended Mark, that much was clear. Shit.

Alex was in his room trying to get through to Barlinnie when Mark stormed in.

'Has the CCTV footage come through? I want to see it.'

'Sit down, Mark, and calm down. I've already said I believe you.'

'You didn't at first, though did you?'

Alex wasn't going to waste time arguing. He held a hand up as Mark opened his mouth to speak. He'd finally got through to the right department.

'Yes, that's right. Footage from the eighth of February this year. I'd have thought it would be through to me by now. I need from two thirty to two forty-five. Entrance hall. And the visitors' room too, please.' He listened before saying, 'OK. Nothing from there. What about the corridor on the way to the visitors' room?' He paused. 'Right, good. Send it through, please. Yes, as soon as possible.' He gave his email address and then turned to Mark. 'They're sending it through now.'

'You should have looked at it first before accusing me.' grumped Mark.

Alex slammed his fist down on the table.

'Drop it, will you, Mark. This is the first chance I've had to see it. Stay here and have a look if you want, and while

261

you're at it, cast an eye over this.' He opened up his phone to a photo he'd taken of the visitors' book page and handed it to Mark.

That shut him up all right. Mark paled as he looked at it, studied it for a full minute before saying, 'Shit. It looks exactly like my signature.'

'You get my point now?'

'I suppose so.' Mark ran his fingers through his hair. 'But who did this? And why? Don't visitors have to get a pass in advance? How would he get one in my name?'

'He could have used his own name and then signed yours when he got there. It's easily done. There's more than one Donald Duck in the visitors' book.'

A ping from the computer signalled an incoming email. Alex looked at it.

'Right, we have two lots of CCTV footage. Let's have a look.' He downloaded the first file. It was typical grainy CCTV footage. It always surprised him that with all the advances there had been in technology, that it stayed as bad as it was. Together, they watched as a man the same build and height as Mark, approached the reception and signed in.

'You have to admit. It does look like you.'

Mark was laughing. Alex glared at him.

'What's the joke, mate? This is serious. I'm going to have to report back to her upstairs about my visit to the jail today and you laughing isn't helping.'

Mark only laughed harder.

'I'm sorry but it's so fucking obvious it's not me.'

'Is it? Well, let's take a look at what we have here. Height – tick. Build – tick. Hair – tick. Even the clothes are identical to what you wear.'

The Fallen

'Aye, me and a hundred other polis. The fucker's wearing a baseball cap. When did you ever see me in one of those?'

'You bought one last week. In Edinburgh. Don't you remember?'

'Oh, aye, right enough. But look at this. Wind the video back. Now stop. Here. Look at him signing in. What hand is he using?'

It was beginning to click with Alex. He smacked his forehead.

'Of course. He's using his right hand. And you're left-handed.'

'I am that,' agreed Mark. 'I am that.' He leant back in his seat, fingertips pressed together. 'But it doesn't tell us who this is and why they would set me up in this way.'

'Let's have a look at the other file. See if we can get anything from that.'

They watched in silence. It showed a man walking along a corridor. At one point he stopped and scratched his head. But like the other footage it was unclear.

'Anything?' said Alex.

'Let's have another look.' Mark pressed the rewind key. 'There's something here. Damn, I wish we could home in on it, but look, when he scratches his head. On his right hand, is that a ring?'

Alex squinted at the screen.

'I think it is but better than that, look at his middle finger. The tip is missing, and I know exactly who it is.'

'The wee shit,' said Mark. 'What do we do now?'

'Take it to her upstairs,' said Alex. 'She needs to see this.'

Pamela was on her way out of the office when he caught up with her.

'Sorry Pamela, but you're going to want to hear this.'

She raised an eyebrow. 'Can it wait?'

His answer was blunt. 'No.' She stared at him waiting for more. 'There's CCTV footage of one of our officers signing into Barlinnie and pretending to be Mark.'

He had her attention.

'What? Come through and tell me what you know.'

It didn't take him long to fill her in on what had happened.

'Are you sure it's him?'

'Completely. You can see it quite clearly on the footage. He adjusts his baseball cap, and you can see his left hand clearly. The tip of his finger is missing and he's wearing a distinctive signet ring. It's definitely McGowan.'

'Shit.' She put her head in her hands and was silent for a few seconds. 'I thought it was going to come to this. I checked up on his so-called visit to Barlinnie. He didn't go. There was no record of him having visited, and the two guys he supposedly interviewed? No such people. I was just about to start disciplinary procedures, but this is much more serious. He's one of the officers you suspected, isn't he? Was this a long-standing suspicion or more recent? Tell me again why. This needs to be watertight. We've got to get enough evidence for a conviction.'

'Don't we have enough?'

'Yes, I think so, but I want to be sure. A corrupt police officer is like a cancer in the force. It grows and grows. This needs to be shut down once and for all.'

'What are we going to do?'

'I'll need to speak to the chief constable. He has to be

kept informed, and he might want to do the honours, though, frankly I think it ought to be you. Hang on, I'll give him a call.'

Two hours later, after a long discussion with the chief constable to fill him in on the evidence, Alex had the go ahead to arrest and question McGowan. He and Pamela were going to do the interview together. He was out on a job, but Alex was going to arrest him immediately on his return. He didn't have long to wait. At three o'clock, McGowan strutted into the station with his usual wide-legged swagger. It was going to be fun taking him down. Alex might have read him his rights in a more private space, but when he saw him laughing and joking with other officers, it enraged him, and he decided there was no place better suited. It was hard not to smirk when he saw the man's reaction. His face lost all colour, and his usual arrogant expression was replaced with one of fear.

'If you'll come with me, please.' Alex held out an arm to usher him through.

For a moment Alex thought he might make a run for it, but then his body sagged as if there was no fight left in him.

'Do you want a lawyer?' asked Pamela, once they were seated and ready to begin.

'Yes.'

'Do you have one you can call, or shall we ask for the duty lawyer?'

There was no answer for at least ten seconds. Was he contemplating phoning the drugs gang? No doubt they had their own corrupt lawyer. Alex hoped not. But evidently, he decided against that because he asked to see the duty lawyer who was duly brought in.

Once everyone was settled, the questioning began. But before Pamela had got to the end of the first question, he raised a hand. 'I'd like to speak to my lawyer now in private please.'

'Of course. We'll be back when you finish.'

Alex followed Pamela back up to her room.

'I hope you have nothing on tonight.'

'No, you're fine. I can stay all night if need be.'

'Good, now let's take the opportunity to go over everything we have.'

Twenty minutes later, Alex looked at her in despair. 'We don't have enough to charge him, do we?'

Pamela inhaled deeply. 'Honestly, it could go either way. It will depend on the procurator fiscal. There will be more to come from his phone I suspect and there's a search going on in his flat as we speak. Who knows what will turn up?'

Alex had a bad feeling about this. He felt ill-prepared and wrong-footed. A PC came to tell him the lawyer and his client were ready now, and he got up from his seat with the air of a man going to his execution. They were about to go into the interview room when a voice came from behind.

'DI Scrimgeour, can I have a word, please?'

He turned round. It was Chloe Gray, looking dourer than ever.

'Can't it wait?'

Alex feared she was about to come out with a defence of the accused and he wasn't in the mood.

'No, sir and if the DCI could come, too. Please,' she added.

Alex exchanged a glance with Pamela who gave a shrug so slight he might have imagined it.

'This sounds serious,' said Pamela.

'It is.'

'We can use my room,' said Pamela.

Once they were seated, they waited for Chloe to speak, but she looked as though she'd lost her nerve.

'You asked to speak to us,' Alex reminded her.

'Is it true Shane McGowan has been arrested, and you think he's impersonated Mark Nicholson?' She spewed out the words as if they were making her ill.

'It is. Now, what do you have to say? We need to get on with interviewing him.'

'I think I've got relevant evidence. I'd have told you before, but I didn't know what it meant, but it's making sense now.'

Interesting. 'Go on.'

'It was back in February. I heard him making a call. To the Bar-L.'

This was interesting. Alex waited for her to continue.

'He was asking for a visitor's pass. To see Stuart Nicholson.'

Brilliant! Corroboration that he had gone to see Nicholson. Not that they needed it. The CCTV footage would be enough. But there was more to come.

'He didn't give his own name. He gave Mark's name. I was in the room, and he didn't see me when he was on the phone, but when he came off it, he noticed me and made a comment about Mark being busy and having asked him to arrange it. I didn't think anything of it. But then last night he asked me to phone the hotel Mark's staying at.'

They already knew this of course, and perhaps she was trying to cover her own back but still...

'And did you?'

She looked down at her feet.

'Yes.'

'What happened then?'

'I phoned and the woman on reception said he wasn't in, but Shane had already said to me all he wanted was to find out if Mark was there and to hang up if he was.'

'Didn't you think that was strange?' asked Pamela.

'Yes, but when I asked, he said he wanted to check Mark was OK.'

A plausible excuse, but on top of everything else, this was beginning to look bad for Shane McGowan.

'Is there anything else?' said Alex.

'When I told him Mark wasn't there, he swore. We were in a squad car, and he stopped it and jumped out to use his phone.'

'Do you know who he phoned?'

'No, but whoever it was, Shane was placating him. He kept saying, "It's not my fault, Jake." I heard him say it three times.'

With difficulty Alex refrained from jumping up and punching the air. This was brilliant. They'd got him for sure with this corroborative evidence. With any luck, they'd be able to charge him later today.

'Chloe we'll need to take a statement from you. What you've said helps us a great deal,' said Pamela. 'But I feel you're not telling us everything.'

Chloe turned bright red. 'I don't understand.'

'Have you noticed other odd behaviour from PC McGowan?'

'Not odd, no.' Her voice was so quiet they it was barely audible.

'But?'

'He said horrible things to me. That I had a face only a mother could love, that I was a rank lesbo, that the roughest of dykes wouldn't look at me.' Her voice was thick with tears. 'I could go on, but you get the picture.'

'Did you tell anyone about this?'

Miserable, she shook her head. Alex was ashamed of how he'd suspected her. She was an unhappy young woman who was being bullied, and he should have realised there was more behind her apparent dourness and unwillingness to join in with the rest of the team than he realised.

'Right,' said Pamela. 'There's two things here. The first is your statement about the visit to Barlinnie. We'll take that down now. But this other business is also completely unacceptable, and I'll phone HR about it as soon as I'm able. I don't suppose you have any witnesses to what he said?'

Chloe gave them the names of two other young police officers who were being bullied by McGowan.

'Now he's been arrested, they're more likely to speak up,'

Statement in hand, Alex went through to the interview room much happier than he'd been half an hour ago. He was looking forward to this.

The interrogation went much better than he'd hoped. McGowan, like all bullies, was a coward at heart and he buckled as soon as he heard the evidence they had. There was no trace of the swagger now. In less than an hour, they had the full picture. In vain, his lawyer tried to silence him, but he'd started his story, and he was going to finish it. McGowan had been working for organised crime since he got a job in the police service three years ago. At first, they'd asked little of him, like dropping information on the where and when of drug raids, but recently, they'd demanded more.

'They wanted to know about Mark Nicholson. It pissed them off that their plan to take over distribution on the southside was thwarted by him.'

'It wasn't only Mark, though,' Alex reminded him. 'The drugs squad were much more involved in their comedown than Mark ever was.'

McGowan massaged his forehead.

'Any chance of a paracetamol? My head's killing me.' Once he'd been supplied with two tablets he carried on. 'I don't know how, but they found out Mark was Stuart Nicholson's son. Stuart was heavily involved in the gang. He ought to have been out of the game by now, an old guy like him, but he clung on. I was told to go and see him and pass on the information his son was in the police and had been involved in taking down so many of the gang. He was due to get out of prison later this year, and his retirement fund had gone.'

'What happened when you told him?'

'He got up and left the room. Didn't say a word. Next thing I heard he'd ordered a hit on Mark.'

'And you didn't think to warn him?'

McGowan wouldn't look either of them in the eye. Alex waited but he said nothing. What could he say? In Alex's eyes he was the worst kind of scum. A total traitor. Perhaps he thought he'd get more favourable treatment if he came clean now, but Alex doubted it.

Another two hours of questions and they had all they

needed to convict the man. He deserved every minute of any sentence he'd get.

The next thing he had to do was update his team on what had happened. His first task was to tell them about McGowan.

'Some of you may have heard that Shane McGowan was arrested earlier this afternoon.' He took their silence as assent and carried on. Shane is suspected of being involved with the criminal gang, some of whose members were put away last month. He has been passing information to them since he joined the police service.'

Their shocked faces showed him they had no knowledge of this.

'I won't say any more about this at present. Obviously, we will not be investigating this case. It has already been passed to organised crime. There was more to say, and he held a hand up as they started to gather their things together. He had to tell them about Mark's father before the gossip mill started grinding. However, it seemed it had already got out.

'Is it true that Mark Nicholson's father is in jail?' asked Ryan McDonald.

'Where did you hear that?' snapped Alex. There were only a select few in the service who knew. He had agreed with Pamela to keep it quiet and tell everyone in his team at the same time.

Ryan was startled to be spoken to so abruptly, though he ought to be used to it by now.

'I...I don't know. Everyone was talking about it when I came in this morning.'

Alex looked round his team.

'Well?' he demanded.

No-one was willing to meet his eye, too interested in their feet, it seemed. His voice was cold.

'Let me make this clear. This is a personal tragedy affecting Mark's family. I will outline the facts, and I expect that to be an end to it. I don't want to hear of anyone gossiping about it. That is an order, are we clear?' He waited until he saw nods from everyone before continuing. 'When Mark was a child, his father attacked Mark's sister. She was left in a vegetative state as a result and died some years later.' There was an intake of breath from someone near the back. Alex ignored it and carried on. 'Unsurprisingly, Mark is estranged from his father and was not aware he was still alive. The last he'd heard, he'd been released after serving twenty years. However, after his release, Stuart Nicholson became involved with the drugs gang who we managed to make a dent in earlier this year, thanks to Mark and to others of you both in this team and in organised crime. He's been back in prison a couple of times since, caught with enough drugs to warrant a charge of possession with intent to supply. Straight back to jail with him.' Alex looked around the room. They were absorbed in his words. If only they all showed that level of attention on a daily basis.

He continued. 'The last time, he got a five year sentence. It appears that Nicholson was very involved in the drugs scene in Barlinnie. During his time there, he had palled up with a lot of bad bastards. I won't say any more other than this. He ordered Mark's death.'

A loud 'Fuck's sake' came from the back of the room, which Alex ignored.

'The case has been handed to Organised Crime as we as

a team are thought to be too close to it. Mark will return to work tomorrow. That's it. Back to work all of you.' There was absolute silence in the room as the officers digested this information. There was little hope of them not gossiping, but he had to make the point.

Alex made his way back to his office and prepared to hand the case over. Time to see what was to be done about the teenage deaths.

Chapter Twenty

IT HAD BEEN a bit of luck, McGowan confessing like that. And a relief to know Mark was safe again. But the whole episode had shaken Alex. It stung that one of their own had been involved in the attacks against Mark. But there was no time to reflect on it. He had a funeral to get through.

To be honest, Alex was thankful to be so involved in a case. It saved him thinking about what was to come. Kate had invited him to stay for the night before the funeral, but he declined. He wanted to be on his own with his memories. After a late dinner of chicken salad – he was, once again, trying to keep the weight off after his recent relapses into cheeseburgers and fish suppers – he poured himself a dram from a bottle of fifteen-year-old Bowmore and fetched the box of photographs his mother had had for as long as he remembered. It was part of his childhood. His parents brought it out regularly to show to him and his brother when they were children desperate for a game of footie, and worse, when they were teenagers aching to go out and get a lumber.

He looked at the box now. Would it be too maudlin to open it? Yes. Then again, if you weren't allowed to be sad and sentimental on the eve of your mother's funeral, then when?

He held the box in his hand. It was battered and didn't shut properly. A biscuit tin, he'd guess. Turquoise, decorated with silver fleur de Lys and with the name of a long-gone firm embossed on it. Once upon a time it must have been new and shiny, but not in his lifetime. Perhaps not in his mother's. He remembered her saying once that it had been handed down to her from her own mother. He saw her now, taking the photos out, one at a time. Each with its own story.

'This is your grandfather, My dad. He was a hard man, a miner. His name was Billy, too. He was harder than the coal he used to dig, but he had a right soft spot when it came to you two.'

Alex hadn't believed her. His memory of his maternal grandfather was of a grumpy old git, always telling him and Billy to be quiet and skelping them if they didn't comply. If that was him showing his soft side, hell knows what his hard side was like. Right enough, he'd been seven when the old man died so he might be remembering wrong.

There were countless photos. Wee Auntie Aggie.

'She had a hump back, poor soul.' His mother said the same thing every time.

He didn't remember how she was related to them. Was she his aunt? No, the photo must be from the thirties. She'd have been his great-aunt, a sister of the grumpy grandfather, perhaps. The tin was full of photos of long dead relatives, Edwardians and Victorians, dressed up in their Sunday best in stiff formal poses. He barely glanced at them. The only ones of interest were the few there were of his parents and those of him and Billy. There were two years between them: Billy, proud to be the big brother; Alex, the adoring wee brother who saw no wrong in him. He picked up a photo of them dressed in their primary school uniforms, aged nine and seven, cheeky grins on their faces, no knowledge of what life had in store for them.

He missed Billy, especially now when there was no one left to share memories with, unless you counted Gillian, and he was sure he didn't want to share anything with her. It was bad enough they had DNA in common. More than ever, he wished Kate had known her grandmother properly. He'd never allowed himself to fantasise what life might have been like if Sandra had been faithful and Mairi never taken from them. It was always too painful to imagine.

He put the photos back thinking as he did, that he was the only one left now who remembered who was who. All that effort his grandparents and great-grandparents had put in to get photographed for austerity and in thirty or so years – if he was lucky and survived that long – he'd be dead and there would be no one left who cared who they were. Fuck, he was getting mawkish. If he wasn't careful, he'd end up snivelling into his drink. Best go to bed.

Alex woke early the next day. Rain pummelled the windows in a way that suggested the wind was high. He glanced at his watch: five thirteen. Too early to get up but too late to go back to sleep. Nonetheless, he didn't make a move. The last three weeks had been exhausting: being shot at, flu, his mother dying, the stress of arranging a funeral, dealing with his niece, not to forget the attacks on Mark and the day-to-day stress of police work. He was knackered.

Three hours later, he woke with a start, bewildered. He'd

been dreaming of a holiday in Arran with his parents when he was a child. It lingered on, and he couldn't shake it off. It was several moments before he realised the calls of the seagulls he could hear were from outside his window and not part of a dream. They'd been a pest in the area for years now. Noisy when they were mating, noisy when they were hungry and noisy for the sake of it. Dog walkers had to be careful when the fledglings were born as each brood had a cabal of seagull aunts and uncles ready to dive bomb any dog they saw as a threat. Rooftops were their favoured places for nesting, high enough to kid themselves they were on a clifftop.

The funeral was at two o'clock, so he had plenty of time to get ready. He would have preferred to have had the service in the morning, but Gillian had continued to try to control the arrangements. When she expressed a preference for an afternoon service, he conceded at once. His mother hadn't specified a time, and Alex thought, wrongly as it turned out, that Gillian would be mollified to get her way. The fact that his mother had detailed her wishes, foiled the more outrageous plans that Gillian came up with. A lilac coffin? A horse drawn carriage? Thank goodness his mother had specified the cheapest coffin available and forbidden limousines or anything else she deemed to be 'showy'.

'I want a plain funeral. Cheapest coffin there is. I'd say cardboard, but Bobby next door says they're dearer. You'll need a hearse of course, but the mourners can make their own way there, and that includes you and Billy. They're a waste of money.'

Her voice was as clear in his head as if she was standing beside him. So clear that before he knew what he was doing he had looked round to reassure her it was all going her way.

Kate and Conor came for lunch, bringing a quiche and a salad, as promised. More salad! Just as well, given his recent lapses back into junk food. At one o'clock, they got themselves ready. It was a fifteen minute drive to the crematorium, but Alex wanted to be there to greet people as they arrived. They got to the entrance as the skies opened: a downpour that soaked the people walking up the path to the ceremonial chambers. He only recognised a few of them. They were mostly elderly ladies, ex-colleagues of his mother. It was good to see she was remembered.

He intended to remain outside with Kate until the hearse arrived. Gillian arrived a few minutes before the service was due to start. He muttered a curse under his breath when he saw her mother was with her. Kate looked at him in horror.

'Dad, language.'

'Sorry, sorry. My brother's ex-wife has turned up. Gillian's mother. God help us if the second one turns up, too. They'll be at each other's throats. There's something to be said for keeping funerals private. Damn, they're coming over.'

He could feel Kate willing him to behave as the two women approached him and he forced a smile.

'Gillian, how are you? And Jacqui, you, too.'

For the life of him, he couldn't bring himself to say the usual pleasantries of 'good to see you' or even, 'thank you for coming'. Gillian had a right to be here – she was a blood relative after all –- but Jacqui, not a chance. Not after how she had treated Billy. Jacqui looked as mean as ever. Age had done her no favours. She'd been pretty when she was younger, but now, years of bitterness had taken root in her face, so it was criss-crossed with lines, although she was

The Fallen

only in her fifties. She ignored him and turned to her daughter.

'Come on, Gillian. We'd better get in and get a seat.' She made it sound as though Alex was holding them back. 'I'll see you later,' this to Alex who nodded in return.

How long was it since he'd seen her? Not long enough. He'd be happy never to set eyes on her again. The last time was at Billy's funeral when she had wept so many crocodile tears that Alex feared that she'd become dehydrated. His second wife hadn't turned up to the funeral but had gone off on a cruise instead, so Alex was hopeful she wouldn't come today. At that moment, he was diverted by the arrival of the hearse.

He, Kate and Conor had decided to follow the coffin in rather than go in before it. Too late he realised he should have given Gillian the option, too. Damn. He didn't look at her as they made their way to their seats at the front. She was already sitting there with her mother. The cheek of Jacqui, taking the role of one of the principal mourners.

The service passed quickly. His mother had specified a humanist service, and Alex and Kate had met with the woman celebrant beforehand to pass on their memories. Gillian had refused to meet her despite Alex's pleas.

'At least tell me what to say to her,' he'd said.

But she refused, stern in her rigid belief that her grandmother would have wanted a Christian burial.

'She must have been out of her mind to agree to those wishy washy pagans.'

It felt wrong to exclude Gillian but what choice did he have? He watched her out of the corner of his eye, sitting straight backed, not an emotion showing on her face. It was a moving service, ending as it did with Raymond Carver's poem about what you want from life 'To be loved'. As he listened to the words, he thought he'd never heard anything more true and how lucky he was to have found his daughter.

The reception was at the House for an Art Lover as his mother had requested. When it had opened over twenty five years ago, Janet had liked to go to the café there for lunch with her ex-colleagues and other friends. Even once she had been diagnosed with Alzheimer's, she'd respond well to a trip there, occasionally surprising Alex with a reference to her funeral purvey being held there.

'Better than a church hall, don't you think?' He'd never found the right words to reply.

A good number of the people from the service came along. Alex was surprised to see his boss among them. He hadn't thought she would come to the funeral service, let alone the wake. He walked over to her now.

'Pamela, I'm so pleased you're here.'

As he said the words, he realised it was true. He was touched she'd taken the trouble. Pamela smiled at him, and it transformed her face.

'I'm here as a friend, Alex. Not as a representative of Police Scotland.'

He half-smiled in response, not knowing what to make of her statement. They chatted for a few minutes before he moved on, leaving her to chat with Mark and Megan who were also there.

'If you'll excuse me, I have to go and mingle.' He went over to where Gillian and Jacqui were sitting, catching Kate on the way. 'Come and meet Jacqui. My brother's first wife.'

Neither Gillian nor her mother looked up as they approached. They were speaking to no one, sitting nursing their drinks along with their sense of outrage. Alex pulled over two chairs and they sat down beside them.

Gillian sniffed. Was she a user of coke? It would explain a lot. The last few times he'd seen her, she had a runny nose, and she was habitually irritable and restless. Or perhaps he was misjudging her, and she had hay fever. No, she'd been fine as a child.

'I thought you were ignoring us, leaving us alone like that,' she said.

Like what? They'd been in the place for ten minutes. Alex didn't rise to the comment.

'Jacqui, I don't believe you've met my daughter, Kate, not since she was a baby at any rate.'

Jacqui looked Kate up and down.

'Doesn't look much like you, does she?'

'Don't you think so?' Alex was taken by surprise as people regularly commented on their likeness, especially round the mouth and nose. Eyes, no. They definitely came from Sandra. Same shade of blue, same shape. Jacqui muttered beneath her breath, but Alex didn't hear it.

'Sorry, I didn't catch that.'

'Nothing,' said Jacqui.

But Kate had heard. Her face was pink.

'She said it wouldn't surprise her if I was an imposter.'

'What?' Alex gaped at Jacqui.

She tossed her hair back, Miss Piggy style.

'Well, you have to admit, it's convenient her turning up like that. She looks like Sandra, I'll give her that, but you, no chance. Wasn't Sandra having an affair?' She smirked. 'Odds on she's your old pal's daughter and not yours at all. In which case, she'd be entitled to nothing from your mother's will.'

There was a gasp from Kate. Alex turned to her. 'Can you leave us please, Kate. I'll deal with this.' His temper was rising. Rarely had he been so angry. When Kate was safely out of earshot he let loose. 'You are, and always have been, a vicious cow, Jacqui. Thank God Billy got shot of you all those years ago. It must have killed you when you saw how much he left, and you got none of it. Money grabbing doesn't begin to describe you.'

'Huh, you can talk. You've had control of your mother's finances for years. No doubt, you've squirrelled away plenty for yourself. That's my daughter's inheritance we're talking about.'

She really was ugly. It was true that as you grew older your face showed your character, and years of bitterness and bile had turned hers sour. Alex took a deep breath before he spoke.

'Three things. Firstly, every penny of my mother's money is accounted for. Secondly, it's not your daughter's inheritance, it is for all my mother's direct descendants. To be clear, her descendants are me, Gillian, Kate and any child of theirs that might be *in utero* at the time of Mum's death. Finally, Kate is undoubtedly my daughter. Perhaps Gillian didn't tell you but a DNA test at the time proved conclusive. Gillian, I'll leave you to fill in the details. I'm not wasting any more time here. If I hear any repetition of these outrageous claims, you'll be hearing from my lawyer.' He was pleased to see both Jacqui's and Gillian's faces pale.

Kate was waiting for him a short way off.

'Wow, she's a piece of work.'

The Fallen

Alex was shaken, but he took a deep breath determined not to let the scene get to him.

'Don't waste time on either of them. Once the will is dealt with, I'm never having anything to do with them again. Come on, let's get a drink.'

The rest of the afternoon passed in a blur. Funerals were never exactly pleasant for those left behind, but when a person had lived a long life like Janet and was well regarded, it didn't get much better. There were a few nurses there who had been friendly with his mother at the best time in her life and he enjoyed listening to their stories of how strict she'd been on the ward and how patients and staff had loved her. One woman who was in her nineties and very genteel spoke about the time they worked in accident and emergency together.

'This young man came in,' she said. 'He was complaining about stomach cramps. The doctor examined him and discovered a large carrot in his back passage. Once it had been removed, one of the student nurses who'd been observing said to your mum, "Sister, how did that man manage to swallow a carrot without choking?" Your mum didn't blink an eye but said, "I think you'll find that people are like houses and have both a front door and a back door. In this case, the carrot definitely went in the back door." The poor student looked totally bewildered until one of her peers whispered in her ear. Her bewilderment didn't lessen, and she said, "I don't get it. Why would you try to eat a carrot that way." Your mother looked at her in disbelief and added, "Someone, please tell Student Nurse Mitchell the facts of life."'

The little group of elderly women dissolved into hysterics and Alex joined in. It felt both wrong and good to be laughing.

Later, back at his flat with Conor, Kate and Conor's parents, Margaret and Aodhan, he made tea for them all.

'It all went well, I think. Apart from the intervention from my ex sister-in-law.'

'Has she always been so nasty?' asked Margaret. Her face showed her concern for him. Over the past year, Alex had grown fond of both her and her husband.

Alex closed his eyes. Thinking about Jacqui made him tired.

'She's never been on my list of best friends, but I have to say that today was a new low.'

'To question Kate's parentage like that, I, I'm speechless...' said Aodhan. 'It's... why would you do that?'

Alex finished his drink and took a moment before speaking. 'She's insecure and lonely. She ditched my brother in favour of another man who left her not long after. Now she's bitter and twisted as a result. The man she left Billy for swindled her out of her money. She lost out on inheriting any of Billy's money and she's never managed to get another man.' He stood up, anxious to change the subject in case he or anyone else started to feel sorry for Jacqui. 'Anyone want a proper drink?'

Kate came through to the kitchen to help him with the drinks.

'Listen, Dad, I don't need the money. What if I give my share of the inheritance to Gillian? Maybe it would help ease things between you.'

'Don't you dare. That woman cares only for herself. If you don't need the money, then give it to charity or save it for any children you might have. Gillian has hardly been to see

The Fallen

her grandmother in the past few years, and she missed years altogether when she was younger.' He caught himself. 'Though, to be fair, that was more her mother's fault than hers. However, she's had years to catch up and you've seen more of your grandmother since moving up here than Gillian did in twenty years.'

Kate looked embarrassed. 'Listen, Dad. If I tell you something, do you promise not to say anything? Especially now, when Conor's parents are here?'

God, what was coming? Alex hoped she and Conor weren't about to split up. 'Of course I won't say anything. What is it?'

She went over to the freezer and took out a tray of ice cubes. 'It's a clause in the will that's bothering me. The one about descendants *in utero* at the time of Gran's death.'

'Yes?' Alex's heart beat a little faster. Where was this going?

'It's... I'm pregnant, Dad. But I don't want the money. It will only cause more bad feeling.'

Alex crossed the room and took Kate's hands in his. 'I'm thrilled beyond words for you. I assume you're not too far on? That's why you haven't told Conor's parents.'

'I'm twelve weeks, so it should be OK, but I thought that the last time and look what happened then. I'm waiting until the scan to say anything.'

'When's that?'

'I haven't heard from them yet, soon I hope.'

'You have to take the money.'

'But—'

'But nothing. I'm the executor of the will. By law, I have to see that Mum's wishes are carried out. So your child will have the money. And we'll say no more about it for now.

Apart from this.' He drew her into his arms and hugged her tight. 'Congratulations,' he whispered. They stayed like that for a moment or two. It was a long time since Alex had been this happy. But it was tainted with apprehension, which he shoved aside. This time, he prayed, make it all right.

Chapter Twenty-One

WHEN ALEX LEFT his flat the next morning, the last thing he expected to see was the remains of a dead mouse, its guts spilled all over his doormat. He managed to avoid stepping on it. But it was a near thing. Muttering curses under his breath, he went back inside to find kitchen paper to clean up the mess. Too busy trying to stop himself from gagging, he didn't notice the cat slipping in through the open door.

Later when he phoned Kate to tell her, she was surprisingly unsympathetic.

'It's a cat, Dad. It's trying to show you that it likes you. You should be flattered.'

'Don't talk rubbish,' he said. 'Cats don't have feelings.'

'All right, then, it's trying to show you how to kill things and bring them home.'

'It's trying my bloody patience that's what it's doing. I'll wring its neck next time.'

'Poor thing,' said Kate. 'It chose the wrong door, didn't it?'

After she'd hung up Alex reflected on her words. Despite

his scepticism, he was quietly chuffed that the cat kept coming back. There were eight flats up his close and the cat had chosen his. Perhaps... No, definitely not. He was not going to adopt it.

Two days later and with four more cat visits under his belt, Alex googled what to do. The best advice was to take it to a vet to see if it had been microchipped. So he looked up the nearest vet, hunted through his cupboards until he found an old shoe box to put her in and set off on his quest.

It took only a few minutes for the vet to check her over. 'No, she's not microchipped though she has been neutered so someone looked after her.'

'Should I post on a local Facebook group then?'

'Oh goodness me, no. I wouldn't do that. Take her to the SSPCA shelter if you don't want her but first check the lampposts in your area. In my experience, people who lose pets are desperate to get them back. Check out whether anyone has lost a cat, but don't for goodness' sake ask if anyone has lost one. The danger of opening it up to social media in that way is you might get someone who either wants to sell it on or worse.'

Alex didn't bother asking what the worse was – he could imagine.

'What are my options, then?'

'After you've checked out the SSPCA shelter and the lampposts?' The vet shrugged. 'You could look after her yourself or do you have a friend or relative who would?'

There was always Kate, he supposed, or Mark.

The Fallen

Kate was firm in her refusal. 'I like cats, Dad, but I'm not going to have one in the same house as my baby.' Alex was pleased to see she was speaking more positively about the baby.

Mark was equally brief with him.

'Nope, not a chance. It's hard enough looking after Gus and the idea of having to clean out a litter tray gives me the boke.'

It was going to be up to him. Now he'd accepted that fact, he found the thought wasn't too unpleasant. Kilmausky, as he'd taken to calling her, was cute in her own way, though he could live without her offerings. He shuddered remembering the dead mouse.

But over the past couple of days he'd found himself looking out for her as he came up the stairs and was surprisingly disappointed when she didn't appear. He made up his mind. He'd walked around the local area and the vet was right, there were posters of a couple of missing cats, but none of them was Kilmausky. He made a decision. He'd keep her. It was the weekend, so the first thing to do was to buy in supplies. There was a pet shop in Shawlands, so he walked down to see what he needed. An hour later, having parted with the best part of a hundred quid for the basic necessities of a litter tray and litter, cat carrier, scratching post, food bowls and food, he realised he wasn't going to be able to carry it back up the road.

'Can I leave this here? I'll need to go and get my car. I'll be about half an hour.'

'No problem,' said the sales assistant. 'I'll put your stuff aside.'

Forty-five minutes later, he was hauling the second load upstairs when he bumped into Alice coming out of her flat.

'What's this?' she said. 'Oh, you're not taking on that wee cat, are you? How adorable. He's a real beauty.'

'She,' said Alex.

'Oh, so I have a rival for your affections,' she tapped him on the arm and when she saw him blush, said, 'Don't mind me, Alex. My first husband always said I'd flirt with anything with a pulse. I don't mean anything by it.'

The words were out of his mouth before he could stop them.

'That's a shame. I was about to ask you out for dinner.'

Fuck, what was happening to him? Had someone tampered with his prefrontal cortex? He waited for the inevitable rebuff.

'I'd be delighted. Where and when?'

Alex went out to restaurants so rarely now he was stumped for an answer.

'You decide,' he said. 'I'm free next Friday.'

'Good, let's go to a local place so we don't have to bother with taxis, or why don't you come to me.'

Alex wished he'd never said anything. Dinner in her flat was altogether too cosy. The last time, the only time they'd had a night in together, had ended with him being extremely drunk. The restaurant in Battlefield, which was once a tram terminus, came to mind.

'What about Battlefield Rest?'

'Lovely.'

'I'll book it for eight p.m. and call in for you about ten to eight.'

'Come in for a drink first. Seven o'clock. We can make a night of it.'

The Fallen

His arms were almost out of his sockets with the weight of the various accoutrements he was carrying so he quickly agreed and rushed upstairs. What on earth was he doing?

Chapter Twenty-Two

KATE FOUND it hard to shake off her apathy. She was too tired to do anything. She tried writing up what Hayley had told her, but it wasn't coming together in the way she hoped. Conor suggested they tell their parents about the pregnancy – she hadn't told him that Alex knew – and she agreed, telling herself it would make it seem more real. Yet the feeling of underlying dread gripping her stomach lingered, making it hard to eat anything. Fuck, she had to shake it off. Wearily, she went about her daily tasks with little energy, hoping the lethargy would lift.

Her mobile rang and she picked it up without looking at it.

'Kate, is that you?' It was Hayley. Her voice was shaky.

'Hayley, yes. Are you OK? You sound—'

'We need to meet. I have more to tell you.'

Kate wasn't sure but she thought she heard voices in the background.'

'What's wrong, Hayley? You sound upset.'

'You have to come and meet me, Bridge Street subway

station at the popup coffee spot in the car park there. One hour. Be there.' The line went dead.

Bit presumptuous, thought Kate who hadn't liked the peremptory way Hayley had spoken to her, but she got herself together and made her way to the bus stop. For once, the bus came right away but when she got to the subway, there was no sign of Hayley. It was a sunny day, so she decided to get herself a tea and find somewhere to enjoy the sun while she was waiting. She'd no sooner paid for it, though, when she noticed a homeless guy sitting at the entrance to the station, the same one she'd given coffee to the last time she'd been here. Her interest was piqued. What was his story? A few of the homeless people she'd seen in the city centre were ex-servicemen, some of them clearly traumatised by their experiences, but this guy was older, in his fifties. Didn't mean he hadn't been a soldier. But she had a feeling his story might be worth hearing. On impulse, she went over to speak to him.

'How are you today?' she said as she handed the tea over to him. He stood up to take it from her and smiled.

'Thank you,' he said. He was well spoken, she noted. 'Cheers,' he said, taking a gulp. 'Still no bacon roll?'

He'd remembered her. 'They don't sell them there. It's a bit too pretentious for bacon rolls.'

'I was only kidding. This is exactly what I needed. How are you?'

'Oh, I'm fine,' she lied, trying to smile.

'Now that's not true, is it? You can tell me. I'm hardly going to pass it round your social circle now, am I?'

Kate laughed. 'No, I don't suppose you are. Tell you what, you tell me your story, and I'll tell you mine. But first, what's your name? I'm Kate.' She held out her hand and he took it in a firm grasp.

'Jim. Are you sure you want to hear this? You might want your tea back once you know what I did.'

'No judgement, Jim. I promise.' What was she saying? He might be a serial rapist for all she knew, or a child abuser. But whatever it was, there was a sadness in his eyes suggesting he wasn't proud of what he did.

'If you're sure.' He took another sip of tea and began his tale.

It was devastating. This was no tale of woe from someone who blamed all around him for his misfortune. He knew he was to blame for the car crash that had killed his wife and child over twenty years ago. He'd been drinking, his wife had begged him to let her drive, he had ignored her. He didn't go into details about the crash and Kate didn't ask for them. He lost his licence of course and spent half of his fourteen year sentence in prison.

'I deserved every minute of that sentence and more,' he said.

By the time he came out, his parents were dead, and his in-laws would have nothing to do with him.

'I don't blame them.' he said. 'I killed their daughter and their grandson. I tried to see them to tell them how sorry I was, but they sent me away. I would have done the same. I was fifty by the time I left prison, and I couldn't get a job. It wasn't long before the drink called to me again. It's a jealous mistress, won't let you go, never gives you any peace. Before long, I was homeless.' He took another gulp of tea, leaving an inch in the bottom. 'That was good, I needed that. Now what's your story, Kate?'

Kate blinked away her tears. 'I'm sorry for your losses, Jim. You've been through so much.'

'And all of it self-inflicted. But the deal was you'd tell me what's up with you.'

Kate didn't want to bother him with her problem. It was so small compared to what he'd gone through, but a deal was a deal.

'I'm pregnant.'

'I see, and your boyfriend isn't happy about it.'

'No, no. I mean yes. He's ecstatic about it. We both are.'

'What's the problem, then?'

'I've had three miscarriages. I'm so scared I'll lose this one, too.' She looked at Jim. He wasn't listening to her. Drink calling to him perhaps? But no, without warning, he sat down looking ill.

'What's wrong, Jim? Are you OK?'

'Dunno, wanna sleep,' he slurred.

Kate's phone rang. She looked at the screen. Hayley. She was torn. Jim didn't look well, but she'd promised Hayley she'd be there for her.

'Hayley? This isn't a good time.' She kept one eye on Jim as she spoke.

'Thank fuck I caught you. I managed to get away from them. They made me phone you. Listen, I know how these deaths happened. There's pop up coffee stalls at a couple of the subway stations and they're run by the gang. Those kids were given Rohypnol and Ketamine in their coffee. That accounts for people saying they were drunk. They weren't. They were drugged. But they've found out you've been nosing around, and they know what you look like. Don't whatever you do, buy coffee from them.'

Kate's mouth dried up. She'd poisoned a homeless man.

295

'I've got to go, Hayley. Sorry.' She closed down the call. Jim was up on his feet now, stumbling across the car park to the station entrance. Kate dialled 999 and asked for police and ambulance. She had the foresight to lift the cardboard cup up from where Jim had left it. It was hard evidence. Moving as fast as she could she reached him as his legs buckled, and he sank into oblivion.

It felt like hours before the ambulance arrived. Kate stuttered out her story, realising as she did so that she had a lot of explaining to do. She tried her best, but it was clear they were sceptical.

'Are you sure it's not a reaction to heroin?'

'I was talking to him, and he was totally lucid. Anyway he's an alcoholic not a drug addict.'

'But you said he's taken Rohypnol?'

'Not deliberately. I told you already. It was in a cup of tea I bought from a vendor. Over there, look.'

They followed her pointing finger.

One of them said, 'There's no-one there now.'

It was true; the booth had closed. Shit, what could she do now? The male paramedic was tending to Jim.

'I've kept the remains of his tea. Can it be tested?'

'Best give that to the police. Here they are now.'

Two police officers were rushing towards them. When they were satisfied there was no immediate danger to anyone in the vicinity, they turned their attention to Kate who told them as succinctly as possible what had happened.

'Please, you have to ensure he gets tested for Rohypnol. My source told me that there's a gang using it to drug noncompliant youngsters, and I'm sure it's been implicated in these teenage deaths.'

'What teenage deaths?'

'Five teenagers have allegedly killed themselves by jumping. Four in front of either a bus or subway train. The other jumped from Jamaica Bridge. Over a very short time period, one of them, only a few days ago. You must have heard about them? Some of the parents have been very vocal about it not being suicide.'

'The younger officer gave a brief nod.

'Yes, I've read about them. What more can you tell us?'

Kate detailed what Hayley had told her, careful to keep Hayley's name out of it. Out of the corner of her eye she'd noticed Hayley come up the stairs from the underground at the same time the police arrived. She'd immediately turned and left. Kate hoped she wasn't in danger.

The paramedics came over to tell her that they were taking Jim to hospital, and the police officers took their chance to leave saying they'd be in touch later. Kate turned to the paramedics.

'Will you let me know how he is?'

They made non-committal sounds until one of them muttered something about patient confidentiality. Kate left it. She'd find out from her father what was going on. Once they'd gone, she set off to look for Hayley in the hope she hadn't gone far. She found her inside the station, shivering with fear.

'You fucking bitch,' spat Hayley. 'Why did you do it?'

Kate recoiled from her.

'What are you talking about?'

'You called the polis.'

'I had to. That man had been drugged. I bought a tea

from the pop-up stall and gave it to him. He collapsed when he was talking to me.'

'Shit, fuck.' Hayley looked wild. 'That's why they've fucked off. Oh fuck. I've had it, so I have. They're going to kill me for this.'

'Did you tell them who I am? How did they know to give me the drugged tea?'

'No! They found the card you gave me.' Hayley launched into a story that was garbled and rushed as well as impossible to follow. She was crying.

'Why did you go to the polis? If they're watching...'

'I had no choice! What was I going to do? Let a man die in front of me?'

'He wouldn't have died. It was you Jake was after. Oh fuck, what am I going to do?'

'You're going to speak to the police, that's what.'

Hayley stared at her for a full five seconds.

'You have no idea, do you?' Then, before Kate could stop her, she'd run off back down the stairs to the platform. Kate ran after her, but as she didn't have a ticket, she was stopped at the barrier. Frantically, she ran back to the ticket office, almost crying at the length of time the man took to process the ticket. She grabbed it from him earning a snarky, 'In a hurry, are we?'

Kate ignored him and rushed down the stairs. The platform was more crowded than she'd seen before and there was a commotion going on at the far end. She was sure she could see Hayley's red jacket in the midst of it and started to make her way towards her. She was almost there when a scream rang out. The crowd seemed to surge as one towards the noise. Why was the platform so crowded? It wasn't usually like this. Another scream and yelling followed by a collective

The Fallen

gasp. Someone was on the rails. She could see something red lying there.

Kate swallowed the bile that rose in her throat. This was her fault. Hayley was there, dead because of her. That child, what chance did she have? With a deadbeat mother who hadn't been there to look out for her. She didn't blame Lewis for what he had done, introducing her into his life of drug dealing. From what he'd said, he'd been a child at the time and with little choice. Someone touched her arm.

'Are you all right, dear?'

Kate's face was wet with tears. She brushed them away.

'I, it's just, I think I know the victim.'

'The victim?' The woman's voice changed from gentle to disapproving. 'He was no victim. He was trying to push that wee lassie over when he fell himself. I saw it all.'

'It's a man?'

'Yes.'

'But, I saw her jacket. I can see it now.'

'Right enough. She wriggled out of it, but he had it in his hands when he fell. Are you sure you're alright?'

Kate thought she might faint, but she swallowed hard and said, 'Where did the girl go, did you see?'

The woman shook her head.

'Ah, there's the emergency services now. I'll need to get ready to give my statement. You should give one, too, if you knew the girl.' She marched off to speak to the nearest police officer.

It took some time to take everyone's statements. No one was allowed to leave until they had spoken to a police officer.

Kate had found Hayley in the midst of a group of people who were trying to comfort her. She'd grabbed Kate when she saw her.

'It's Jake. I've killed Jake. I'm dead.'

'No, you haven't killed anyone. Somehow, he missed the live rail and he's being taken to hospital now. In any case, he was trying to push you on to the line. We all saw it, didn't we?'

The elderly man who'd spoken looked round at his companions who nodded and murmured their agreement.

'I'll tell the police what happened. Officer, over here, please.' His voice had the sort of authoritarian confidence that isn't easily ignored, and sure enough, a police officer came to take their statements. But when he heard there had been an altercation, he immediately cautioned Hayley. Kate was about to tell her to say nothing when the elderly man stepped in.

'Utter nonsense. Now, listen young lady. I'm a lawyer, and I recommend you say nothing. In fact, I'll stay with you until a lawyer is appointed for you.'

'And I'll be your responsible adult,' said Kate. The thought of Hayley being alone in a police station filled her with horror.

As it turned out, though, they weren't there for long. There was CCTV footage at the station that showed exactly what happened. Hayley, on the platform, was approached by Jake Dunmore, who tried to push her on to the line while others looked on in horror. Hayley managed to wriggle out of her jacket and that movement was enough for Jake to topple over the edge. Two people had filmed it on their phone, and while Kate didn't approve of this practice in general, it served to corroborate the CCTV and what everyone was saying.

But the interview wasn't the end of it for Hayley.

'What will happen now?' Kate asked the detective who had spoken to Hayley.

'First things first. We'll contact social work for an emergency placement for Hayley and her brother. It isn't safe for them to stay in the family home given what we know about the Dunmore triplets. We'll take statements from Hayley and her brother about what they know about the gang. We've been waiting for a break like this for a long time.'

Kate looked round to see where Hayley was. She was talking to her lawyer who she'd taken a liking to.

'They won't be charged, will they? I mean, Hayley and Lewis.'

'We've already spoken to the PF, and there's no way they'll be charged. They're victims. There's a long road ahead of us collecting more evidence, but today we have enough to charge Jake Dunmore with attempted murder. This ensures he'll be inside until his trial. We'll just have to wait and see what else comes up but between Hayley's statement and, hopefully, her brother's, as well as the evidence we're gathering from the phones and computers of the so-called suicides, I'm optimistic.'

Kate waited with Hayley until she was safely in the care of social work.

'You'll remember your promise, won't you? About the share of the money if you sell the story?'

'Of course. But I won't be able to sell it until after the trial.'

'I know, but just don't forget us, will you?'

Kate smiled.

'There's no chance of that, Hayley. You have my number, keep in touch.'

It was late before she got home. She phoned Conor and he came to pick her up. She was ravenous and demanded to stop at a local takeaway for a curry. Once home, she devoured her meal. Conor watched her, amused.

'Your adventure hasn't affected your appetite then?'

'It's ten hours since I last ate.' She grabbed the last piece of naan bread before he could.

'I'd say you're feeling a bit happier, am I right?'

'Nothing like a brush with death, even if it wasn't mine, to make you appreciate what you've got.'

He was right. She was feeling more optimistic. Perhaps all would go well with this pregnancy after all.

Chapter Twenty-Three

THE INITIAL EUPHORIA from her escape was gone, and two weeks later, Kate was still shaken from the attempt on her life. Conor had suggested postponing the scan, but she wanted to get it over. It all felt unreal to her. Over and over again, the face of the coffee vendor as he passed over the tea to her would come to her. His smile had seemed so sincere as he told her to enjoy it. Or had there been a look of disdain in his eyes? She tried and tried, but nothing came to her. And then there was the homeless man she'd passed the tea to. She felt ill when she thought about what might have happened. Thank goodness she had noticed the slurring of his speech that showed the drugs were having an effect. If not, would he have become another victim, either staggering down to the subway platform and falling or stumbling out into traffic only a few yards away? It would have been her fault. She tried to shake away the feeling of doom that had enveloped her ever since. Jim *hadn't* died, and she'd heard he was in rehab. His brush with death had made him determined to have another go at life. She was going to see him next week. Better still, the vendor had been arrested, his links to the drug gang established, and best of all, he was talking, giving up names to the police. It was over, she was safe, Mark was safe. She needed now to concentrate on her baby.

Conor chatted on their way to the hospital, updating her on family news. His sister-in-law, Isabelle, had announced last week she was pregnant again. Conor was thrilled.

'The baby will be the same age as ours. Maybe they'll go to school together, be best friends.'

'Mm,' said Kate. 'It's great news.' How she envied Izzy who had sailed through two pregnancies producing babies as if it were no harder than going out to pick up a litre of milk. No doubt this third pregnancy would be just as easy for her. She hated herself for the envy she felt.

'We're here,' announced Conor. 'Now let's find a parking place.'

It was hard to think of it as anything other than a blob – a formless outline on the screen. Try as she might, Kate was finding it hard to see it as a baby. Perhaps this was a way of protecting herself. If she refused to see it for what it was, then perhaps it wouldn't hurt so much when she lost it.

Conor squeezed her hand. 'Isn't it fantastic?'

'Yes.'

She smiled, but Conor's frown showed he wasn't fooled. The nurse didn't notice their brief exchange and chattered on. 'It's all good. This here,' she pointed to a blob within the blob, 'is baby's heart. Beating nice and strong.'

Kate blinked back tears. She was not going to get attached.

'Well, everything is tickety boo,' said the nurse. 'All as it should be. 'We'll have you back in a few weeks, and by then, we'll be able to tell whether you're going to have a little boy or girl.'

'I can't wait to find out,' grinned Conor. Kate readjusted her clothing and got up from the trolley.

'And you, Mum? Are you keen to know?'

She was taken aback to be referred to as Mum and it was all she could do not to snap at the woman, but her manners prevailed as she said politely that she hadn't decided.

Back in the car, Conor turned to her. 'You're not OK, are you?'

'No.'

He took her hand. 'Kate, it's going to be fine. Believe me.'

'I wish I could.'

'Kate, you're fourteen weeks now, the scan showed everything is going well. Please, try. But remember, no matter what happens, I love you and you love me and nothing will change that.'

She grabbed his hand. 'I'll hold you to that. We'll tell them tomorrow, OK?'

Alex was pleased with the way things had turned out. The gang had been broken up. They were all safely in jail awaiting trial. Mark was fine, for the moment at least, although it had shaken him badly to discover how much his father hated him.

'I always knew he was a bastard,' he said to Alex. 'But not how deeply ingrained it was.'

Alex gave a half smile in sympathy. Stuart Nicholson was

evil in his eyes. A wife beater who had killed his daughter, a little girl of only four years old. And who had carried on his vicious behaviour while in prison building up a crime syndicate while inside and using it to terrorise a community. Recent events should ensure he died in prison. Shane McGowan was going to plead guilty, but nonetheless he was looking at a nice long term inside. God help him, ex-cops had a rough time in jail. He didn't waste any time feeling sorry for Shane though. Those who abused their positions of power deserved all they got. He poured Mark and himself another Bowmore, an eighteen year old. They both took an appreciative sip.

'Heaven,' said Mark. 'I was happy with blended brands until you corrupted me with these nectars. And this ups the game. Just when I was able to afford a twelve year old for the first time, you go and tempt me with this. How much is a bottle?'

'I don't know,' said Alex. 'Kate gave it to me.' He changed the subject.

'How's the wee man?'

'Good. No word from Suzanne for a while though. I'm beginning to worry about her. She contacts me every two months or so, but I haven't heard from her for ages.'

'Have you been round to the flat? See if there's a message there.'

'Not with all that's been going on. I haven't had time. But that's a good point. I'll go round at the weekend. She might have left more money.'

'Are you short?'

'No, not at all. But it all comes in handy. He's growing so fast.' The pride was evident in Mark's voice.

Alex was desperate to pass on the news that he was to

be a grandfather, but Kate hadn't given him the go ahead yet. To tell the truth, he was a little worried about her. Her first scan was earlier today, but instead of being upbeat at being told all was well, she seemed depressed. But he wasn't going to say anything. Instead, he made approving sounds about Gus's progress and reconciled himself to keeping schtum for the time being. There would be plenty of time to brag later on when the baby was born. He ignored the little voice saying, *If the baby is born.* It would be fine. It had to be.

'How are you, anyway. Everything good?'

Mark swirled his whisky round in his glass.

'I need your advice.'

'Sounds serious.'

'It is. I'm at a loss as to what to do.'

'Go on.'

'You remember that case the year before last, the bodies in the bungalow?'

Where was this going? That case was done and dusted.

'I won't forget it in a hurry. What about it?'

'That woman, Edith Drummond. She wrote to me.'

'She wrote to you? When?'

'That's it, you see. The problem. It was well over a year ago.'

'Why haven't you said anything before now? Whatever she said, it's clearly bothering you.'

Mark finished his drink before going on. 'The letter was in my dookit at work. I picked it up on my way out of the office and shoved it in my inside pocket and forgot all about it.'

'For what? Nearly a year and a half?'

'I haven't worn the jacket since then. I was going through

the pockets because I was intending to give it to a charity shop, and I found Edith's letter.'

'Was it important? Sorry, that's a stupid question. It must have been, otherwise you wouldn't be telling me about this now.'

'I'm in a right fix.'

'Come on, man. Spit it out.'

Mark swallowed. Jeez, the man was nervous. What the fuck had been in the letter?

'Mark, you're pissing me off. Either tell me or don't. I don't care. But stop this fucking fannying about.'

'She told me that she'd killed her parents.'

The words hit him like a blow. 'You're fucking kidding me.'

'I wish I was. It's all in there, a full confession.' He held the letter out to Alex. 'Go on, read it.'

Alex took the letter from him. He wasn't sure he should. Quickly he read it through. It didn't take long.

October 2020

Dear Mark,

I hope you don't mind me calling you Mark. I wanted to thank you for being so open with me the other day. You don't know what it means to speak to someone who understands the horror of living in an abusive household, and I was so sorry to hear about what your father did and what happened to your sister. I think you of all people will understand what I am about to tell you. You must do as you think fit with this information. Perhaps you will stick to the law, perhaps you will take pity on a fellow survivor, I don't know. But it is time I confessed to what I did, and it feels like you'll understand. You see, I killed my parents. A long time ago when I was young, before they could steal what remained of my youth.

I thought about it for a long time. How to do it and when. It was only after I experienced a week at on Open University summer school and the sense of freedom I gained then, that I had the courage to do what I did. They were going away for the weekend. I stuck a knife in one of the tyres of their car as they were about to drive away. The tyre blew out when they were on the motorway and they crashed into the central reservation. There was a fire and little remained of either them or their car. I hadn't envisioned there being a fire, and to be completely honest, I hoped but didn't expect my plan to work. But it did and I was free.

By the time you read this, I will be on my way to Devon to meet the aunt and the family I didn't know I had. I have a chance to be part of a proper family for the first time, and I feel at peace. I feel no remorse for what I did. They were not good people. Look at what they did to their own mother and to their children. They murdered their mother, abused me and killed another child, a newborn baby. They were monsters and deserved to die.

What will you do with this letter? Destroy it? Hand it on to your colleagues so they can build a case against me? Ignore it? You must do what you think best but I thank you again for sharing your story with me. It helped me enormously to learn I am not alone.

With fondest regards,

Edith

When he finished, he put it down on the table beside him and then put his head in his hands.

'What the actual fuck, Mark? She's saying she let down the tyres of her parents' car and it crashed.'

Mark gave a miserable nod. 'Yep. It burst into flames and there was virtually nothing left of either the car or their bodies. What should I do?'

Jesus. Five minutes previously he'd been thinking about his grandchild, wishing he could share the news, tell Mark, celebrate with him. And now? This. He closed his eyes. This wasn't his problem. Hadn't he done enough for Mark over the years? Getting him out of a sackable offence when he had attacked that man guilty of killing his child. Chasing after a madwoman who'd kidnapped Mark's youngest child. Taking in him and his son when another woman deserted him. Jesus, not six weeks ago he'd almost taken a bullet for him. Fuck. Surely it was time for Mark to do him a favour? And the biggest favour Mark could do him now would be to walk out of here and forget he'd ever told him about this. Nobody would believe he'd not read the letter before now. Mark's question intruded into his thoughts.

'What am I going to do, Alex? How do I explain this away?'

Alex waved the question away resisting the response that came to mind. He wanted to rail at him, tell him he was an idiot. For fuck's sake, he'd told Edith Drummond about his own murderous father! The woman had the cheek to tell him she thought he'd understand. Well, maybe Mark did. How would he know?

'Well?'

The Fallen

'Shit, Mark. Why on earth has she confessed to you?'

'Because she sensed something in me,' said Mark. 'She had an abusive childhood and so did I. She saw us as equals. It would be a betrayal of her trust if I take it anywhere, don't you think.'

'You don't believe that, not really. You wouldn't have shown it to me if you had any doubts. You have to hand it in. It's our job to collect evidence and pass it on to the Procurator Fiscal for them to decide whether there's enough there to secure a conviction.'

'She'll be in her seventies by now, what good would it serve for her to go to prison.'

It was late and Alex was tired. He did not want to spend hours debating the rights and wrongs of this.

'You asked me what you should do. Well, I've told you. Hand it in.'

'But what good will it do? It was over thirty years ago, and they deserved it.'

'No, Mark. You don't go down that road. That's why we have a justice system. Do the right thing. For your own sake. She might tell someone else and then where would you be? Up in front of a judge for withholding evidence, that's where.'

Mark was slumped down in his seat.

'You're right. OK, I'll hand it in tomorrow. But shit, Alex, what if they don't believe me that I forgot about it? What then?'

'Look, you had a lot going on at the time. Suzanne had dumped her baby on you, you'd separated from Karen. It'll be fine. Tell her what you told me.'

'Her? You mean DCI Ferguson?'

'Yes, it'll have to go up the ranks from me. I don't have the authority to deal with this. Best not mention you told me about it first. She wouldn't like that. But if you're honest with her, tell her when you found it, then it'll be fine, you'll see.'

In truth, Alex had no idea whether it would be fine or not. Pamela Ferguson was fickle, and if she happened to be in a bad mood, this might well go pear shaped but Mark would have to take his chances with her.

It was the middle of the next morning when Alex was called up to her office. She was sitting upright behind her desk, the picture of officialdom.

'Did you know about this?' she barked.

'Sorry?'

'The letter Nicholson got from that woman. Did you know about it?'

Alex wanted to avoid telling a direct lie, so he prevaricated.

'What woman? Has Suzanne been in touch?'

'Who's Suzanne? Oh never mind, it's obvious you're not in the loop. You remember the bodies in the bungalow?'

He tried to hide his relief. The ruse had worked.

'Won't forget it in a hurry. What about it?'

Pamela kneaded her forehead.

'The woman, Edith Drummond, has written to Mark claiming she killed her parents thirty years ago. Actually, more than thirty years ago. She interfered with their car or some such nonsense. And,' her face turned puce, 'he's sat on it for nigh on eighteen months.'

Shit, she hadn't believed his story of forgetting about it. He frowned and put on his gravest voice.

The Fallen

'Doesn't sound like Nicholson. He wouldn't withhold information like that. Wait!' he made a show of remembering. 'When was it written did you say?'

'Over a year ago. Seventeen or eighteen months.'

'Mark's gone through a lot in his personal life and eighteen months ago would be the peak time. You remember the affair he had with the sister of Julie Campbell?'

Pamela frowned. 'Remind me.'

'She dumped their baby on him then. The split with his partner Karen was finalised when she found out about that. Up until then, Mark had been hopeful of getting back together with Karen.' He emphasised his next point. 'No, it's far more likely he forgot than that he withheld evidence.'

Pamela narrowed her eyes.

'Mm,' she said. 'Perhaps you're right. Anyway it's out of our hands. I'm going to pass it back to Edinburgh.'

'Why would you do that?'

'Drummond lives there, doesn't she?'

'Well, yes. But you said it happened thirty years ago. So, when the crime was committed, she lived in Glasgow.'

'Oh fuck,' said Pamela. 'Oh fuck. Well, we'll ask them to take a statement from her and take it from there.'

'Is Mark in trouble.'

'Honestly?' said Pamela. 'I hope not. It'll depend on what the PF says. It's a shame he ever told us about it.'

'He had to though, surely?' said Alex, surprised. 'What if she'd contacted the police again to ask why no one interviewed her?'

'I suppose. Well, let's not worry too much about it. Fifty to one the PF takes it no further.'

It was all very well her saying not to worry but Alex knew how stressed Mark was by it. It would take time for the investigation to be done, and no one could second guess its conclusion.

It was a shock to get the email later that day. It was brief and to the point. Mark was to be suspended pending an investigation into the letter from Edith Drummond. Alex looked up from his computer to see Mark in front of him.

'You've heard the news?'

'I'm sorry, Mark. I didn't think for a minute they'd suspend you. What did they say?'

'Well, I'm suspended on full pay, so that's a relief anyway. They're taking no chances of corruption—'

'But it doesn't make sense. There's no way this is linked in any way to corruption. I mean, it was an honest mistake. That's rubbish.'

Mark shrugged. 'After our recent foray with corruption, they're being extra cautious. They said the investigation wouldn't take long. A detective is being sent to interview Ms Drummond, to make sure there's no connection between us. It doesn't help, of course, that my father is a violent criminal.' His voice was tinged with bitterness.

'Nobody will hold that against you, Mark. They all know how you've suffered at his hands.'

Mark's silence said he wasn't convinced. Well, why should he be? Alex chose his next words carefully.

'This is perhaps a chance to sort yourself out. Get the flat painted, do that DIY you're always talking about. Perhaps speak to Karen.'

Mark's jaw was clenched. 'You think she'll speak to me

The Fallen

now? I'm a right fuck-up. She won't have anything to do with me. And who can fucking blame her?'

'You have to try.' Alex was desperate for Mark to have a project to focus on over the suspension period. He'd had anger issues in the past and this could set him back. With nothing to focus on, he might internalise the anger and end up depressed, or worse.

Mark stood up. 'I'll get out of your hair, now. Drink tonight?'

'Not tonight, sorry.' Alex hesitated. There was no harm in telling him for he planned to announce it at work tomorrow anyway. 'Kate's coming round tonight with Conor and his parents. They've got some good news.'

'Have they set the date at last? That's great.' Mark tried to inject enthusiasm into his voice but to Alex it sounded more like despair.

'No. Well, not a word to anyone, I mean it. Kate would kill me if she knew I was telling you before Conor's parents. She's pregnant.'

This time Mark's reply was more animated. 'Congratulations. You'll be a great granddad, I mean you'll be very good at it,' he stuttered after realising what he'd said.

'Yeah, yeah. You don't have to labour the point. Now go, and I'll come round tomorrow night, and we'll talk more. But think carefully about what you'll do during this time off. Don't sit around and brood.'

'I'll drop into B&Q now and get a few tins of paint. Or some paint samples at least so I can think about colours.'

'Why not ask Karen's advice? Or not,' as he saw Mark's face.

'I'll see you tomorrow.'

When Mark had gone, he put his head in his hands. Fuck, what a time of it Mark was having. Alex had no idea how long the suspension would last. He had no doubt that Mark would be reinstated, but it wouldn't stop him worrying. All it needed to tip him over the edge was for Suzanne to make a reappearance. Alex wasn't a believer, but he sent out a prayer, in case anyone was listening. A beeping sound from his watch reminded him he needed to get home in good time. He'd brought in a whole load of canapes from Marks & Spencer and there was champagne in the fridge. For the time being Mark would have to take a back seat. Things were going his way for once. Both at work and at home. He had a third date with Alice later this week. He liked her, more than anyone he'd met for a long time. And then there was the baby to look forward to. This was a joyful time for him and his family, and nothing was going to spoil it. He shut down his computer, put on his jacket and set off home.

THE END

Acknowledgments

Four years ago, I was scrolling through Twitter when I spotted a tweet inviting submissions to a relatively new publishers. I was in a particularly low spot at that point. I'd parted with my agent not long before, and attempts to get another one were not going well. Nobody, it seemed, wanted my work. So, I sent off yet another submission with no great hopes. I certainly did not expect to be sitting here four years later writing the acknowledgements to my fifth book with that publisher, who is of course, Hobeck Books. I'm so thankful I saw that tweet and very grateful to Rebecca and Adrian for believing in me.

Thanks are due to Alex Shaw who did an excellent job with copyediting *The Fallen*. The striking cover was designed by Jayne Mapp. I love it and hope you do, too.

I'd also like to thank the HART team who read and report back on the proofs.

Every book I've had published by Hobeck Books has been supported by a blog tour so a big shout out to the bloggers who have been so kind about my previous books. You are all an inspiration. I don't know where you get the time to read and review so many books. Do you have extra hours in your day? If so, can I get some?

I am so lucky to have many wonderful writing friends: Ailsa Crum, Alison Irvine, Alison Miller, Ann Mackinnon, Bert Thomson, Clare Morrison, Emily Munro, Emma

Lennox Miller, Griz Gordon, Heather Mackay, Les Wood and Natalie Whittle. More recently I have joined the Battlefield Collective and although they haven't read any of *The Fallen*, I look forward to sharing my work with them. Their website is https://battlefieldwriters.com and you can find a couple of my short stories and some blog posts from me there.

The Fallen introduces a new character in the shape of Kilmausky, a cat who adopts DI Alex Scrimgeour. Lynsey Linn won a competition to name the tabby cat who wanders in to Alex's flat and leaves him unexpected and unwanted gifts. Thanks for the great name, Lynsey.

Geraldine Smyth, who has been my friend since we met in first year at Glasgow University over fifty years ago, is a great advocate for my work.

My family continue to be a huge support to me. I'd be lost without them.

Finally, I want to thank my readers. Writers without readers are nothing and I am grateful to every one of you for taking the time to read my books. If you have the time, please do post a review. It means so much.

MAUREEN MYANT

About the Author

Maureen worked for over 25 years as an educational psychologist but has also worked as a teacher and an Open University Associate Lecturer. She is a graduate of the prestigious University of Glasgow MLitt in Creative Writing course where she was taught by Janice Galloway, Liz Lochhead, James Kelman, Alasdair Gray and Tom Leonard among others. She also has a PhD in Creative Writing. Her first novel *The Search* was published by Alma Books and was translated into Spanish, Dutch and Turkish. It was longlisted for the Waverton Good Read Award and was one of the books chosen to be read for the Festival du premier roman de Chambéry. Her second novel, *The Confession*, was published by Hobeck Books in 2022 and introduces DI Alex Scrimgeour and DS Mark Nicholson. In an earlier incarnation it was shortlisted for a Crime Writers' Association Debut Dagger. There have been more novels since, including this one.

Maureen has been a voracious reader since the age of six when, fed up with her mum reading Noddy stories to her, she picked up her older brother's copy of Enid Blyton's *The Valley of Adventure* and devoured it in an evening. She hasn't stopped reading since and loves literary fiction, historical fiction, crime fiction, psychological thrillers and contemporary fiction but not necessarily in that order. Her favourite book is *The Secret History* by Donna Tartt and go-to comfort read is *Anne of Green Gables*.

Maureen lives in Glasgow with her husband. She has three grownup children and six grandchildren who love to beat her at Bananagrams.

Hobeck Books - the home of great stories

We hope you've enjoyed reading this novel by Maureen Myant. To keep up to date on Maureen's fiction writing please do follow her on Twitter.

Hobeck Books offers a number of short stories and novellas, including *You Can't Trust Anyone These Days* by Maureen Myant, free for subscribers in the compilation *Crime Bites*.

- *Echo Rock* by Robert Daws
- *Old Dogs, Old Tricks* by AB Morgan
- *The Silence of the Rabbit* by Wendy Turbin
- *Never Mind the Baubles: An Anthology of Twisted Winter Tales* by the Hobeck Team (including many of the Hobeck authors and Hobeck's two publishers)
- *The Clarice Cliff Vase* by Linda Huber
- *Here She Lies* by Kerena Swan
- *Fatal Beginnings* by Brian Price
- *A Defining Moment* by Lin Le Versha

- *Saviour* by Jennie Ensor
- *You Can't Trust Anyone These Days* by Maureen Myant

Also please visit the Hobeck Books website for details of our other superb authors and their books, and if you would like to get in touch, we would love to hear from you.

Hobeck Books also presents a weekly podcast, the Hobcast, where founders Adrian Hobart and Rebecca Collins discuss all things book related, key issues from each week, including the ups and downs of running a creative business. Each episode includes an interview with one of the people who make Hobeck possible: the editors, the authors, the cover designers. These are the people who help Hobeck bring great stories to life. Without them, Hobeck wouldn't exist. The Hobcast can be listened to from all the usual platforms but it can also be found on the Hobeck website: **www.hobeck.net/hobcast**.

The Glasgow Southside Crime Series

The Confession

2001 SHORTLISTED FOR A DEBUT DAGGER
'Superb. Fast-paced and intense. A truly original premise and an addictively intense plot.' Linda Huber

The Deception

'Wow, what a gripping book – I couldn't put it down yet didn't want it to end.' Gillian Jackson

The Shame

'An addictive, gripping crime novel with real psychological depth.' Stacey Murray

The Glasgow Southside Crime Series

The Fallen

'From hired killers to family feuds, *The Fallen* is a fluently written crime story with depth and intrigue. Maureen Myant goes from strength to strength with her Glasgow Southside Crime Series.' Rachel Sargeant

All four books available from Amazon or Hobeck Books.

The Search

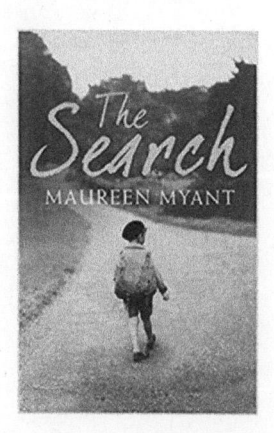

In Czechoslovakia, 1942, Jan's father has been summarily executed by the Nazis. His mother and his older sister Maria have disappeared, and his younger sister Lena has been removed to a remote farm in the German countryside. With Europe in the throes of war, the ten-year-old boy embarks on a personal journey to reunite the family he has been violently torn from. The experiences he goes through and the horror he faces during this desperate quest will change his life for ever. While examining the devastating effects of war on ordinary families, *The Search* provides an exploration of fear and loss, and of the bond between parents and children. Riveting, moving, at times disturbing, Maureen Myant's debut novel will haunt its readers for a long time after they have put it down.

Available from Amazon.

www.ingramcontent.com/pod-product-compliance
Ingram Content Group UK Ltd.
Pitfield, Milton Keynes, MK11 3LW, UK
UKHW021830040925
462609UK00003B/74